08/08 JBD

D1444609

The
Amnesia
Clinic

James Scudamore

Harcourt, Inc.
Orlando Austin New York San Diego Toronto London

Requests for permission to make copies of any part of the work
should be submitted online at www.harcourt.com/contact or mailed
to the following address: Permissions Department, Harcourt, Inc.,
6277 Sea Harbor Drive, Orlando, Florida 32887-6777.

www.HarcourtBooks.com

First published in the UK by Harvill Secker.

Library of Congress Cataloging-in-Publication Data
Scudamore, James, 1976–
The amnesia clinic/James Scudamore.—1st ed.
p. cm.
1. Best friends—Fiction. 2. Teenage boys—Fiction.
3. Storytelling—Fiction. I. Title.
PR6119.C39A46 2007
823'.92—dc22 2006012293
ISBN-13: 978-0-15-101265-7 ISBN-10: 0-15-101265-2

Text set in Minion
Designed by Cathy Riggs

Printed in the United States of America
First edition

A C E G I K J H F D B

To my parents

The first thing she felt was a sinking in her stomach and a trembling in her knees; then, a sense of blind guilt, of unreality, of cold, of fear; then a desire for this day to be past. Then immediately she realized that such a wish was pointless, for her father's death was the only thing that had happened in the world, and it would go on happening, endlessly, forever after.

—JORGE LUIS BORGES, *EMMA ZUNZ*

Grown-ups are always thinking of uninteresting explanations.

—C. S. LEWIS, *THE MAGICIAN'S NEPHEW*

one

Sometimes great storytellers die before their time. It's only right that great stories should be told about them in return. I will do my best.

On the 8th of September 1995, less than a year before the death of my friend Fabián, an anthropologist named Johan Reinhard and a mountain guide named Miguel Zárate discovered the frozen body of an Inca princess near the summit of a Peruvian volcano. Aware of the importance of what they had found, Reinhard brought the corpse down from the mountain, wrapping it for insulation inside his foam sleeping mat.

The find was not universally welcomed: the mule driver who met the climbers at the foot of the mountain blindfolded his animal to stop it bolting at the prospect of carrying a dead body, and the proprietor of the hostel where they'd been staying sent them away, fearing bad luck. Eventually, however, Reinhard and Zárate made it to the town of Arequipa, storing the body there in Zárate's freezer until the proper authorities could be alerted.

The likelihood was that Juanita, or the "Ice Princess," as she was dubbed on subsequent international tours, had been clubbed to death in a ceremony of sacrifice for the god of the mountain. She had been preserved in the ice for five hundred years and was in near perfect condition, apart from a pretty severe head wound.

Six months later, a feature on the Ice Princess appeared in an Ecuadorian national newspaper, and my friend Fabián Morales marched into our classroom at the Quito International School waving a copy of it in front of him.

"Anti! You have to see this," he said. "They found some five-hundred-year-old Inca girl up a volcano in Peru."

My name is Anthony but, as a child, I could never pronounce it. I called myself Anti, and so Anti is what I became. Just one example of how a perfectly innocent mistake can stay with you for ever.

"Listen to this," said Fabián. "*Before being sacrificed, it is likely that the Ice Maiden was made to fast, and to participate in rituals involving the consumption of hallucinogenic drugs and strong drink.* Sex, too, I bet—and it says here she was only fifteen. Verena, you'll do. What do you say we take you up a mountain, get you high and show you a good time? We may have to kill you, but you'll be immortal, baby!"

"You wouldn't get me alone up a mountain, you disgusting pervert."

"No problem. How about just getting to it right here? *Mamacita!* Just give me your hand, baby. I'll be as quick as I can."

"You'll go to hell for saying that, Fabián."

Verena Hermes wore three earrings in her left ear, tinted

her hair and doused herself daily in cheap perfume. She was one of our most treasured wet dreams, but Verena's taste was for older men—or so she boasted—and contrary to what we told each other, neither Fabián nor I had ever elicited more from her than crushing words. Unchecked, the discussion might have carried on degenerating for some time. But for now it would have to wait. Our teacher, draped in the regulation corduroy of the British expat, ambled through the doorway, came to rest behind his desk, and exhaled just vocally enough to communicate his wish to bring us to order.

Juanita the Ice Princess was, for the moment, forgotten.

Later that day, as we sat by a basketball court waiting to be fetched from school, Fabián and I considered the discovery more seriously. A pair of snow-capped volcanoes—our own local mountain gods—loomed behind the boxy constructions of the New Town: Cotopaxi, peaking coyly over a scarf of cloud and pollution, and Cayambe, tonight refracting a violet splinter of sunset.

"We've got to get out there," said Fabián. He practiced a few listless conjuring moves, palming a Zippo in his left hand whilst misdirecting with his right, before pocketing the lighter tersely and sighing. "Everything's being discovered too quickly. If we wait any longer, there'll be nothing left to find."

"We can't go to Peru," I said. "Weren't we at war with Peru only a few months ago?"

We—by which I meant Ecuador—had been. Although the border dispute had been effectively deadlocked since 1942, tensions between the two countries periodically rose. According to my father, who was cynical in such matters, this tended to happen around election time as a way to score political points, but a series of border skirmishes the previous year had proved more serious than usual, eventually claiming over one hundred lives. At fifteen, we were not yet of an age to take the deaths seriously, but had both enjoyed the melodrama that went with being A Country At War: electricity rationing, anti-Peruvian sloganeering and even the possibility (however far-fetched) of an actual invasion.

"Stop pricking around," said Fabián. His English was perfect, but he had a distinctive habit of swearing by improvising on half-remembered expressions that he'd picked up from cable TV, which sometimes resulted in bizarre, untried constructions. It was something of a trademark for him. "I'm not saying we should go to Peru. The Ice Princess has already been found. That's what I mean: *everything* will have been done soon if we're not careful. At the very least, I want to discover a new species before this year is out. Or something."

"We went to the Galápagos last year," I said. "That was pretty cool. That's probably where you should start looking."

"I know that. Don't fuck me around with your holiday snaps. We need to make our name. All the magic's going out of this place, and being put in museums. I want a piece of it before it's all gone."

"Something will come up. Here's Byron—let's go."

Byron was the man who chauffeured Fabián's uncle, although he had, in a former career, been a policeman. Fabián told me that his uncle hadn't known this until they arrived back at the house one day to find a burglary in progress. Byron told Uncle Suarez to remain in the car, retrieved from the glove compartment a gun that Suarez didn't even know he owned, and shot both the burglars in the back as they ran away. That's what Fabián told me, anyway. There had been no opportunity for independent verification, as he said his uncle didn't like to talk about it, and I certainly wouldn't have asked Byron, who, though jocular enough, terrified me. My parents had told me horror stories about kidnappings taking place at gunpoint in the backs of cars. I became secretly uneasy whenever Byron's hand strayed too far from the gear stick, and I never held his gaze when his bloodshot eyes swiveled towards us in the rear-view mirror.

In spite of this, I loved going to stay with Fabián and his uncle. Even the journey was fun, and not just because we were picked up by an armed chauffeur in a black Mercedes. Byron's wife Eulalia would leave us sandwiches on the back seat for the ride back, and there was a particular set of traffic lights on the journey where a mestizo on crutches sold packets of multi-colored chewing gum that were a perfect antidote to the cloying effects of peanut-butter mouth. On one celebrated occasion, following a poorly-supervised school excursion to the Equator during which Fabián and I had managed to consume half a liter of filthy *aguardiente* between us, we'd initiated a game on the journey home, the object of which was to chew a packet of gum and consume an entire sandwich simultaneously. Reeking of booze, and feeling very clever, we sat in the back of the car tipping handfuls of lurid pellets into faces already crammed with sandwich, allowing the artificial fruit flavors to detonate inside wedges of white bread and peanut butter and then munching away, digesting the sandwiches piece by piece until only the wad of gum remained. Swallowing one thing and retaining another would have been difficult enough had we been sober, and it wasn't long before things backfired. Having accidentally bolted everything in his mouth, Fabián screamed at Byron to pull over and vomited a flamboyant mixture of cane alcohol, peanut butter and fruit gum into the gutter. Byron found the episode hilarious and, even now, continued to glance hopefully over his shoulder whenever he picked us up for evidence of more drinking on the sly.

Quito is not one city but two: the New Town and the Old Town lie at opposite ends of a long, thin valley running from the north to the south. At the northern end is a bland sprawl of glass and concrete boxes: apartment blocks, shopping centers and offices. The business district. A city of tethered Alsatians, lawn sprinklers and air-con. It was here in New Quito that I lived with my family, in a block of flats devised for the purpose of formal entertainment. Arranged on strata of open-plan, polished surfaces, the place was a veritable gallery of picture windows, each one of which provided spectacular views over the city and the volcanoes beyond. The vantage point allowed you to watch incoming airplanes as they hurled themselves down between buildings and on to the floor of the valley, where the airport was situated. It also meant that if you took a pair of binoculars and followed the city as it curved away to the southwest, you could make out, buried away at the opposite end like a dirty secret, the whitewashed walls, crumbling churches and narrow streets of the Old Town.

The story went something like this: once upon a time, high in the Andes, among the volcanoes, the Incas built a city in the clouds. But when word came of the approach of the conquistadores from the south, General Rumiñahui, whom the great

Atahualpa had left in charge of the city, destroyed the place himself rather than let it fall to the enemy. Not one stone of the great Inca city remained. What we referred to as the Old Town was the colonial city that had been built on top of the Inca one, whose arched balconies and terracotta roofs were now in disarray themselves, repossessed in some cases by *indígenas*, but rotting all the same. And so, while the New Town continued to unpack itself to the north, like prefabricated furniture, the Old Town sat still, slowly settling on top of its predecessor, like compost. Like geology.

Today, thanks to various international protection orders and heritage schemes, I read that this process of decay has been arrested, that the Old Town has been sanitized, and that all those derelict whitewashed buildings, reclaimed by the rich, gleam once more. That collapsed mouth full of bad teeth is now, apparently, capped and sparkling. I find this impossible to imagine. Perhaps it was the manifest poverty of the place, or perhaps it was the thrill I associated with any forbidden location, but to me Old Quito, or El Centro as it was widely known, always stood for life in its most concentrated form. It crawled with the stuff. You couldn't set foot there, it seemed, without having to fight your way through the billow of steam from a mobile soup stall, fend off a market trader trying to press you into a hat or a frilly blouse, or intercept some urchin trying to tickle your wallet. Then there was the intoxicating, head-spinning cocktail of smells, exacerbated by the high altitude: diesel fumes, rotting fruit, stale urine. And, during festivals, cane alcohol, and the charred flesh of guinea pigs grilled over coals.

Only once had I been let loose in the Old Town alone, and the experience had merely served to whet my appetite. Due to its proximity to the Equator, the weather in Quito is schizophrenic at the best of times—at any time, the most tedious cloud formation might suddenly admit an impossible rainbow or dump a preposterous hailstorm—but, being in the Old Town, this particular episode stuck in my mind. I was out with my father and, to save time, he had sent me to get a key cut while he bought something at a market stall. I was thirteen at the time, and welcomed this opportunity for solo exploration. Hearing the ripple of thunder in the distance, I stopped in the street beneath a terracotta awning and looked behind me towards the peak of Cotopaxi to see the flash of a jaundiced, smoky fissure in the sky. The Indian ahead of me geed up his mule by tapping its back with his stick. Stallholders stowed their wares beneath plastic sheeting. Then, with only a couple of warning droplets beforehand, the rain arrived. Walls became vertical rivers. Brown torrents foamed down the streets and frothed into holes in the ground. The pavements felt greasy underfoot with drenched pollution. Dogs gazed out from under tables, waiting for it to pass, and for about ten minutes, I watched as the storm drains choked, gulping down the weather as best they could. Afterwards, it was as if nothing had happened: the blue canvas of the market stalls quietly dripped dry, and their proprietors tapped out their pipes to do business once again.

Perhaps the storm would have been equally impressive had I been on a playing field at school, or sitting on the balcony of our apartment in the New Town, but at the time I believed that it was the fact of where I was that had made it so striking, that such freak weather was particular to Old Quito, and that everything, rain included, was more interesting there.

As someone who had spent all of his life nearby, Fabián's attitude to the Old Town when we talked about it was one of complacency, as if he knew it well and could no longer be surprised by it. In spite of this, I knew that he too had never spent much time exploring it on his own and longed to do so almost as much as I did.

Fabián lived full-time with his uncle on the very southern outskirts of the city, beyond both New Town and Old, and even though he was my best friend, at no point over the previous two years had I asked him what had happened to his parents. At the back of my mind I was always conscious of their absence, but Fabián never mentioned it, so I kept a respectful distance from the subject, wanting to show that I could manage the concept of bereavement as tactfully as anyone else, however alien it was to me. I wasn't actually *trying* to be sympathetic; I just thought that not mentioning it was the adult thing to do. Besides, a setup as brilliant as living with Fabián's Uncle Suarez wasn't the sort of thing I wanted to question.

The house they lived in was built in the style of the colonial buildings in the Old Town—white walls, red tiled roofs, Moorish balconies—but it was a modern construction, and the area where it was situated was not fashionable either among the professional class or the expatriate community. I had stayed there countless times over the previous couple of years, and not once had I left its gates without having been infected by some new and captivating idea or story. As a result, the place had attained a magical status for me, and whenever the electronic security gates parted to admit us in the back of Byron's Mercedes, my imagination would start working overtime in anticipation.

In stark contrast to the New Town apartment where I lived with my family, Suarez's house was a place where nothing was static or out of bounds, where dogs cascaded downstairs to greet you on arrival, and where anything queried—a dusty old accordion, the sea-bitten figurehead of a sunken boat, a case of Mayan arrowheads—yielded a story of one kind or another, bearing testament in turn to the curiosity and learning of Suarez himself. So although it wasn't my home, and although it was the largest house for miles around, it felt welcoming and comfortable to me. Not that just anyone would have felt at home there. I am quite sure that uninvited guests would have got pretty short shrift from Byron.

Byron and his wife Eulalia, who kept house and cooked for Suarez, lived in their own apartment within the house. Byron doubled up as the gardener and prided himself on the range of flora he cultivated—giant prickly pear cacti, acacia trees, exotic roses—all carefully tended in the deep-red earth, which would bleed from the garden on to the driveway in rusty streams during heavy rain.

Ecuadorians from the south have a theory that Quiteños are uptight. Something to do with living at high altitude, it is said, deprives their brains of the oxygen necessary to live the laid-back, party-going lifestyle of their southern or coastal counterparts. Even if that were true, Suarez was definitely an exception to the rule. He wore his respectability very casually, or at least he did when Fabián and I were around. Moreover, anyone who takes the trouble to build a miniature nightclub in his house can't be all that strait-laced. The room was known as "the library," but in addition to ceiling-high bookshelves, a serious-looking desk and a fireplace it contained a checkerboard dance floor, a bar with proper red leather stools and an antique jukebox stocked with 1950s singles.

Suarez, a surgeon of some repute, did have a first name. According to Fabián it was Edison, though nobody had ever used it or even heard Suarez using it. He was known simply as Suarez, even to his nephew, and even to his nephew's friends. Suarez. He squats in my memory to this day, stinking of acrid bachelordom marked with cologne and tobacco. I see him now: smoke rings evaporating into the air before him along with the stories that emerged constantly from his wet, red lips; his salt and pepper moustache; his incongruous fondness for tweed; his short-sleeved shirts and spanking, tasseled loafers, which he referred to as "beetle-crushers." He sits there, tapping his foot to Bill Haley and pouring himself another *cuba libre* or lighting a long Dunhill International as he embarks on the answer to yet another of our inane questions—which would invariably spring open such a mess of tangents and shaggy-dog stories that what we had originally wanted to know could rarely be remembered. More than anything, though, I hear him: his measured, mid-Atlantic accent (he'd lived in both the US and Europe), always sounding slightly amused, was to us spellbindingly authoritative. He could tell us anything and send us into a sideways world which we never failed to believe in, even though we knew that what he said couldn't possibly be true. I still hear that voice, chuckling away at our expense, and I expect I always will.

That evening, over dinner, the conversation turned to Juanita the Ice Princess. Fabián and I were speculating on the state of decay she must have been found in after five hundred years in the ice, and Fabián was talking again about his own aspirations of exploration and discovery. Suarez was unimpressed.

"This Ice Maiden is all very well," he said. "You want to see something really special? I'll show you. Come into the library. Bring that bottle with you."

When we were in the room, Suarez put down his drink and went over to the safe by his desk. He opened it with a couple of deft twirls of the dial and withdrew a small package wrapped loosely in green tissue-paper. Keeping his back to us, he unwrapped the contents tenderly and then turned and held up the object with all the berserking triumph of a medieval executioner.

"Mother of God," said Fabián.

I fought an urge to step backwards.

"*Impresionante, no?*" said Suarez.

"Jesus Christ," said Fabián.

The thing itself was the size of a large orange, but its hair, shiny and black, was easily two feet long and had vitality better suited to a shampoo model than a battle trophy. When we'd taken it in enough to approach, slowly, I studied the features. A concentrated reduction of nose and chin that resulted in a grotesque, implacable caricature, with thick, rubbery lips and eyes that had been sewn shut with clumsy black twine. The skin was dark and burnished, like a piece of rainforest mahogany.

"That's right," said Suarez. "It's a *tsantza*. A shrunken head."

"Where'd you get it?" said Fabián, trying to stay casual. But he couldn't keep up the pretense for long, and his excitement came spilling out as he talked. "Is it yours? Is it *real*? How long have you had it? Why have I never seen it before? Christ, Uncle."

"There are only a few of these left in the world, you know," said Suarez, cupping the monstrosity in one hand as he reached for another swig of rum.

"How do they get them like that? How do you do it?" said Fabián.

"First, you just have to win your battle," said Suarez. "That's the easy part. Then you have to make sure that your defeated foe's face is spotless, so that you can preserve the victory." He carefully laid it face down on the desk before continuing.

"You sever the enemy's head and then you make an incision, here, following the line of the skull." He grasped my head methodically and ran a surgeon's finger down from the crown of my head to the top of my spine. I shuddered.

"Then you remove the entire face, hair included, from the skull, and find a stone that's almost but not quite as big. You wrap the skin around the stone, leave it in the sun to shrink, and then you find a slightly smaller stone. And so on, with smaller and smaller stones, until you have this—essence of enemy. And now we could have a good game of cricket with it, right, Anti?" he said, looking at me and laughing.

"Just laugh, Fabián," I said, backing off. "Keep him happy. We don't know what he might do. Sleep well tonight, my friend," I said, pretending to leave. "Your uncle is a madman. He keeps heads in a safe in his library."

Although he smiled at this, Fabián was mesmerized. But Suarez wasn't finished. "Now sit down, and I'll tell you the really good part. Have a *roncito*. You may need it."

He passed the bottle of rum over and Fabián poured us a glass each. Suarez settled himself, knowing he had us hooked. Fabián and I fought for the chair facing the desk.

"It's got a curse on it," said Suarez, quietly.

"Of course it has," said Fabián. We were beginning to recover now, and were both anxious to make up for our feeble initial reactions.

"Yeah," I said, "of course it has. What self-respecting shrunken head wouldn't have a curse on it?"

"Yeah," said Fabián. "Yeah, right."

"You don't believe in curses, boys?"

"No," I said, too quickly.

"I do," said Fabián, trying to stay ahead of the game.

"Well, I do a bit," I said.

"Either way, listen to this," said Suarez. "The *tsantza* you see on that table once belonged to a friend of mine. Now, because the majority of such artifacts are held in museums, to find one under private ownership represents a rare opportunity for collectors. Private collectors, you understand. People who will stop at nothing to own something—not so they can put it in a museum, or study it for everyone's benefit, but so they can put it in a glass case, tick it off in a catalogue, or show it to their dinner guests over expensive cognac. There's a nasty little international community of them—the same group of people who will, I'm sure, soon be at each other's throats over who will end up with the body of your Ice Princess.

"A wealthy American collector approached my friend in an attempt to purchase this piece. My friend said that it wasn't for sale, but the collector insisted. He offered large sums of money. My friend had vowed never to part with the head, which his grandfather had bequeathed to him, and he said so to the collector. He added, furthermore, that it wasn't necessarily in the American's interests to acquire it, since legend had it that totems such as this could bring very bad luck to those who did not inherit them."

Fabián and I exchanged brief looks to gauge how seriously the other was taking the story, then turned back to Suarez.

"The collector laughed at this and told my friend that he believed firmly in the persuasive powers both of science and of money, but not in shrunken heads that brought bad luck. It was a museum piece, he said, nothing more. He offered a final, incredible sum, which my friend declined, and then he left."

"So who was he? Who was the friend? Had his ancestors killed this person? The friend's not Byron, is he?"

"Slow down, Fabián. The story isn't finished. I dare say you are implicating poor Byron in this due to what you have heard about his illustrious namesake and Anti's fellow countryman. As you are doubtless aware, *that* Byron was fond of drinking from skulls plated with silver and fashioned into cups. It is a perceptive link, but you are wrong in this instance."

"I don't know what you're talking about," said Fabián.

"Never mind. That's another story. No, our own Byron may have once been a fierce upholder of the law, but I doubt he ever decapitated anyone—this was not standard police procedure, even in 1960s Ecuador. And if you took some time to think about it, my unobservant nephew, you would see that Byron's ancestors are more likely to have been African tribesmen than Shuar warriors from the rainforest. Don't you want to hear the rest?"

"Of course. Sorry, Uncle Suarez."

"My friend—whose name, since you ask, was Miguel de Torre—was a wealthy and powerful man. He had no need for the American's money, and he wanted to keep the head for himself. It was a part of his past. To sell it would not have been right. But not long after he had sent the collector on his way,

Miguel found himself in a situation where money had suddenly become paramount. More important than his ancestry—which, as you should both know by now, is one of the most important things there is. His wife was diagnosed with leukemia.

"Miguel, who had come close to discarding the business card left for him by the American collector, now found himself thinking differently. His love and his desperation were so acute that he was adamant his wife should be treated by the best bone-marrow man in America, at the kind of prices that even his considerable personal fortune could not possibly accommodate. And so he found himself telephoning the office of the collector and explaining the change in his circumstances. He made it clear that he was parting with the piece against his will, but he offered to sell it.

"Miguel's wife received the best treatment that the money could buy. Sadly, she did not live long—her disease was too far advanced even for the best—but it is nice to think that that poor little warrior over there went some way towards keeping two lovers together for a few precious years, don't you think? Even in death, he has done some good—not that this will help him now. Let us rescue him from his undignified position on that desk. His hair is still growing, after all. It's just possible he may be thinking ill of us inside that little stone that now passes for his skull."

"It's still *growing*?" said Fabián.

"Of course. Look at how long it is. I must check with the relevant people, actually. It may be up to me, as its current guardian, to groom the thing."

As Suarez pondered this responsibility out loud for our benefit, we looked at the head with renewed interest.

"Pass it over, will you, Anti?" he said casually. "I'll check it for split ends."

"Listen, Uncle Suarez, stop trying to scare us. We know its hair isn't still growing. Where's the rest of this story?" Fabián was bouncing back, but then he wasn't the one who'd been asked to pass it over. Even during this tough talk, he was glancing in my direction to see how I was rising to the task.

I got up, went over to the desk and picked up the head. It was disarmingly light. I cradled it in the palm of my hand as Suarez had done, but although I had resolved to try and avoid touching the features at all costs, my fingertips brushed its withered little nose as I moved it and I leapt quickly in Suarez's direction to get the transportation over with. The locks of hair swung beneath my outstretched hand, bearing a preservative smell, of pickles and hospitals.

"Thank you, Anti. You have earned yourself a refill," said Suarez, gesturing at the rum bottle. "Now, where had I got to? Ah yes, the American. Needless to say, Miguel de Torre was an honorable man. Having sold the piece in good faith, he wouldn't have dreamed of trying to reclaim it. Besides, who would have contemplated a change of heart on the part of the rapacious collector? He thought he had seen the back of this head, if you'll forgive the expression, for ever.

"Miguel was distraught at the loss of his wife. He resolved to go on a long voyage around Europe to cope with his loss. And he took with him a keepsake, which you may find curious. He took with him his poor dead wife's wedding finger.

"Without leaving any forwarding address, he set out on a voyage of no fixed duration. It would take as long as it took. He was in no hurry at all. He took his loved one in his mind—and her finger in his pocket—to see again some of the places where they had spent time together, and to discover some new ones as well. They went to the opera in Verona, just as they had on their honeymoon, dined at fine restaurants in Chartres and Barcelona, and walked for long hours together through the Scottish Highlands. I think they even completed a portion of the pilgrims' trail to Santiago.

"Throughout the trip, Miguel kept his dead wife's finger in his pocket, occasionally touching it as he went and enjoying conversations with her as he had throughout their happy life together. Eventually, when he had said all he needed to say, he found a beautiful place near a river—where, he did not tell me—and buried the finger in the ground. Then he returned home to resume his life, his mourning at an end. Isn't that a beautiful story?"

"Suarez," said Fabián. "What has any of this got to do with the curse?"

"Be patient," said Suarez. "When Miguel returned home, he found evidence of desperate attempts to contact him: a mountain of letters and messages, many of them delivered by hand. His relatives had also been contacted several times. It seemed that the American had regretted his purchase after all.

"Since acquiring the head, his life had taken several wrong turnings. He had been implicated in a financial scandal and had lost his job at the merchant bank where he worked. Many of his friends had disowned him in his disgrace. To make matters worse, as he was on his way to the courtroom to plead his case, he was knocked down by a speeding taxi. His injuries were so terrible that the ambulance crew were forced to amputate both of his legs there and then on the court steps. As if this weren't bad enough, when he woke up in the hospital, he found out that the reason the taxi had been in such a hurry was that his wife was inside it, encouraging the driver to get to the court as quickly as he could in order that she could file for divorce.

"Nor was this the end. Just as the collector was beginning to cope with his new life, as a disgraced, divorced, convicted criminal in a wheelchair, he began to suffer from a strange muscle-wasting disease which could not be explained by any of the specialists he consulted. Eventually, it dawned on him that he must return the head to its rightful owner. Which he did.

"And when, years later, Miguel died, having reclaimed his property, he left it to me in his will. I have inherited it rightfully, you understand, which means it should bring me good luck— and may you too one day, Fabián, if you believe in that sort of thing."

Fabián was thinking.

"I don't believe the bit about the finger," he said. "That's the only bit I don't believe."

"That, my boy, is the truest part of the whole story. The loss of a loved one can make people do very strange things. You know, several friends of mine asked Miguel at the time why he had chosen to react to the death of his wife in such an . . . unorthodox way. Miguel would simply smile and say, very quietly, 'Grief asks different questions of us all.' And he was right. I have seen some highly eccentric responses to death over the years. There was an old lady when I was working over in Andalusia whose child had died before she could get it baptized. Rather than allow it to be buried in unconsecrated ground, she kept the child preserved in a pickle jar in her kitchen for the rest of her life."

"I hope she didn't get drunk and accidentally use it as an ingredient," said Fabián.

"I hope so too," said Suarez. "I enjoyed her cooking on several occasions."

"What do you think, Anti? Shall we ask Suarez if we can take his cursed head into school to scare the girls?" said Fabián.

"It would certainly be a good conversation piece," I said.

"Forget it," said Suarez. "You two might decide to give it to someone you don't like as a present, and I suspect that being indicted for witchcraft would not do my medical career much good. Having said that, given the superstitious nature of some of my patients . . . No. I'm afraid it stays here. But you see that your Ice Princess isn't the only exciting relic around here, in spite of all this anxiety of yours to get out and discover things. You need look no further than your own family, Fabián."

He smiled as he said this, and then stood up to give his nephew an affectionate kiss on the forehead. He shook hands with me, as was customary, and then said, "Goodnight boys. All this weaving of yarns has tired me out. Sleep well. Don't drink all my rum."

It was a calculated display of tolerance. There was only enough left in the bottle for a tiny slug each, but the idea that we might stay up all night putting the world to rights over Suarez's rum was a fiction in which we were both willing participants.

Later, Fabián and I said goodnight, and I went upstairs to Suarez's spare room expecting my head to spin, not only with the rum but with frozen princesses and battle trophies, with severed fingers and pickled babies. My mind *was* on fire—not, as I'd expected, with all the peculiar objects of the day, but with

visions of Miguel de Torre, striding through the heather, checking into hotels and enjoying candlelit meals, all the while in
conversation with his dead loved one, moving continuously
until he could find the right place to leave her behind.

As a result, I was still awake when I heard the sound, echoing round the dark house like a cry from the bottom of a well:
Fabián was calling out in his sleep for his mother.

two

Two years and three months previously, my family had moved to Ecuador. In that time, Fabián and I had become close friends, but I'm pretty sure that wouldn't have happened were it not for the trajectory of a water balloon at the end of my second week in the country. Without that thin membrane of latex, topped up and bulging with cholera-tainted water, tied in a knot and taken forth into the street for battle, we might not have got beyond the first month.

For a start, we were very different. Fabián was tall and dark, with eyes like a pair of flawed emeralds: a languid panther to my wheezing albino pig. He looked older than he was, while I was consistently mistaken for somebody's kid brother. What's more, he enjoyed a kind of universal adulation that hardly cried out for a new friend.

He had a range of essentially pointless but impressive physical tricks at his disposal, which he would deploy at key moments to impress the younger kids (and also, he hoped, the girls): double-jointed fingers, disappearing matchsticks, back-flip dives, smoke-rings. You name it: anything that required a bit of showing off, he was good at. He could pick locks. He could tie knots in a *capulí* stalk with his tongue. There was a patch of skin on his hand which he claimed didn't have any nerve endings and was therefore immune to pain. Occasionally, but not so often that it became common knowledge, he muttered darkly about being descended from a shaman. He would do anything, in fact, to stop you from jumping to the easy conclusion that he was a standard-issue human being, somehow making the posture look effortless at the same time. He was the most charming liar I have ever known, and, on the surface at least, he had no need in his life for an asthmatic English kid who didn't even speak the language. And yet, with the magnanimity of the omnipotent, he chose to become a public friend to me right away, shouting the other kids down when they spoke too much Spanish in my company and inviting me back to Suarez's after school on the Friday of my very first week. He was also witness to many of the asthma attacks and nosebleeds I suffered early on in the thin Quito air, and took it upon himself subsequently to become the default carer whenever my sickly system let me down. But it was the water balloon that fixed it.

My family arrived in Quito during the carnival season, just before Lent, when the water fights in the streets were in full swing. It's a tradition: at that time of year, anybody is fair game, and it's very important that you take your drenching in good humor. If you're lucky it's just some five-year-old with a water-pistol, but some of the young citizens really go to town, cruising around in cars with whole arsenals of ready-prepared weaponry. It's just what happens. And I suppose Suarez must have said to Fabián that it might be nice to take the new boy out to witness some of this colorful local madness.

We were wandering around the cobbled streets of the Old Town when some older kids ambushed us. One of them chucked a water balloon straight at Suarez's head. It didn't explode—just bounced off his shoulder—but for some reason, and unusually for Suarez, he didn't see the funny side. He walked towards the kids, muttering threateningly, but the way they stood their ground and began squaring off meant this probably wasn't such a good idea, and Fabián said so to his uncle. Suarez turned around, said that we were leaving and stormed off. I would never have done it even a few months later, but as a thirteen-year-old innocent in a new country I didn't appreciate the danger of the situation. Without really thinking about it, I picked up the unexploded water balloon and hurled it back at the bunch of kids as hard as I could. To their amazement, and mine, it burst all over them. The three of us then ran off through the streets, Fabián and me laughing and Suarez trying to be furious but finding it too funny, until a cataclysmic wheezing fit destroyed my bravado a few blocks from the scene.

Fabián was impressed. He reckoned that the older kids would have had knives, or worse. They almost certainly didn't. All that water-fighting is nothing more than a bit of fun—the only crime is taking it too seriously, as Suarez did—but that wasn't how Fabián saw it. He talked me up at school for weeks before he realized that the story made him look a bit spineless by comparison. Naturally, in his version, the street kids had their knives out already and had slashed at the arm of Suarez's jacket by the time the balloon was thrown, so we knew they were serious.

From that point on, I suppose I had proved my credentials, and we found more and more common ground as we got to know each other. When I first arrived I had a way of staring at perfectly normal things as if I had landed on an alien planet, and Fabián liked provoking it. He said that sometimes, when he had to explain them to me, things he had previously taken for granted became more interesting to him. He took these tour-guide responsibilities too far on occasion, diligently pointing out pigs, shopping centers and airplanes before being told, with tact, that these also existed where I came from. Later, he went on holiday to England with Suarez, telling me jokingly on his return that he was surprised to find that the country wasn't made up entirely of thatched cottages, and that the Queen didn't execute people in person. He brought me back some shortbread.

And here we were, over two years on. *Carnaval* had happened again only a month or so before, but this year we had stayed in. We were far too occupied, shooting the breeze with Suarez and his shrunken head, to be bothered with jeopardizing ourselves out there in the real world.

However much I might have wanted to seem tactful and empathetic on the subject, it seems incredible to me now that for over two years I had a friend who had lost his parents, but that we had never once touched on the subject in conversation. And yet I know this to be true because I can remember thinking to myself that the cry in the night at Suarez's house was the first time I'd ever heard Fabián even mention his mother. Until that point, all I knew for sure was the stuff I'd heard at school: that his father was quite definitely dead, and that his mother was . . . absent.

There were rumors, of course.

"That guy's mother was kidnapped by guerrillas," said a red-haired kid I spent my first day with then hardly spoke to again.

"Huge ransom," confirmed the daughter of one of my mother's friends, as we queued up for a fire drill.

"Cut his daddy up like a hog roast," asserted a boy with a bandanna and serious personal problems of his own.

"I heard there was a botched rescue attempt," said one.

"Yeah, and his uncle got sent a human ear in the post," said another.

The stories didn't stack up, to say the least, but they were ubiquitous, and everybody seemed to have a different one. By the time I got to know Fabián properly, they seemed so absurd that I never gave them a thought—and then we went beyond the point at which it would have seemed reasonable to ask. Besides, the closer we became, the more I realized how unlikely it was that anything that was said about him at school bore any resemblance to fact. He was the king of the doctored story, the gingered-up version of events, and nothing he said could be taken at face value.

When I became established as a friend of his, I was asked more than once to confirm or deny some unsavory detail dreamed up by the latest fabulist eager to contribute to Fabián's legend. I remained silent, which appeared dignified on the outside but, in reality, served to cover up the embarrassing fact that I was no wiser to the truth than anybody else. This had the effect of making people believe that what I supposedly knew was far more shocking than anything they had imagined for themselves, and the rumors evolved even further. Fabián, by making it clear that the subject of his parents was the one thing he would never talk about, allowed an aura of mystery to develop around him without ever having to endorse or reject any of the stories that were told or risk trampling on whatever sad, prosaic truth lurked behind them. In the end, the only fact that really seemed to matter was that his parents just weren't there.

But all of this was about to change. Hearing him call out in the night was perhaps a warning sign that his outer carapace of cool was under strain, but it was when Fabián told me that he had seen a vision of his mother in the glass case of the Virgin Mary during the annual *Semana Santa* parade that I knew we had a serious problem.

The parade took place fourteen days after our shrunken-head evening, in defiance of an official earthquake warning. The seismologists weren't predicting a big one, and besides, it would have taken more than a little quivering of tectonic plates to threaten a tradition as sacrosanct as Easter in Quito.

The cobbled streets seethed with people. Grand gilded floats and groups of wailing penitents processed through an atmosphere of bunting, open-air cooking and music. A high-altitude mist dappled the air, in spite of strong, warming sunshine.

On this occasion, I was not there.

Fabián and I had planned to spend the day together, but I had been collared by my parents at the last minute and forced to duck out. As a result, our mornings were very different, and while Fabián had his religious experience down in the Old Town, I stood in an awkward suit between fragrant rosebushes, looking down towards the parade through a telescope and wishing I was watching it with him instead of drinking warm Buck's Fizz while my parents worked the British Ambassador's garden party.

The following has been pieced together from my own memories of the garden party, and the detailed account of the parade that I heard from Fabián the following Friday, as the two of us sat drinking beer in Suarez's library. Well . . . that, and a negligible amount of poetic license. Let's just say that it went something like this:

Fabián ambled through the crowds alone. He'd arrived at the parade with Suarez and some of Suarez's less interesting friends, but ditched them as quickly as possible. He and Suarez had agreed to meet near the main entrance to the Monastery of San Francisco at 3 p.m. if they should happen to separate, and Fabián peeled off into the crowd as soon as he could. Perhaps he enjoyed the parade more now that it was a world to be explored instead of an imposed family chore. Perhaps the rituals felt more significant to him. I don't know. There's no easy way of explaining what followed.

Market stalls still traded in spite of the crushing crowds, but with more of a party theme to them than usual. The practical items—batteries, cleaning utensils and electrical goods—had been cleared away in favor of more frivolous wares: panpipes and ocarinas, CDs and cassettes of indigenous music, and, for the coke fiend in your life, tiny silver nose spoons (whose use Fabián had only just begun to suspect). Clothing stalls sold colorful local gear and mountains of fake foreign sportswear. An old woman charged customers for the use of an illegal tap into the phone system. Trilby-topped Indian families held up exquisite children to watch the parade. The children's eyes, pairs of bright, black beads, darted around, absorbing it all, just as Fabián's had at their age. The parents looked weather-beaten and impoverished but still beamed in spite of it all, as if they were extras hired in specially to act out a cliché about emotional riches. The floats passing through the streets carried the usual religious icons, intended originally to terrify the *indígenas* into worship through the depiction of pain and violence—attributes which went on to become an unquestioned, traditional part of the pageantry. Processions of barefoot penitents followed the floats, some of them wearing sinister Ku Klux Klan-style hoods, others happier to bear their shame in public. Many dragged eight-foot-long wooden crosses and wore crowns of thorns—even of barbed wire in one case. Nor was penitence limited to the able-bodied: one man edged past Fabián at waist height, his right arm propelling his wheelchair while the left remained fastened to the cross he bore on his shoulder, its tail catching on the cobblestones as he went.

Fabián remembered coming to the parade with his father when he was four or five years old, being hoisted on to his shoulders to get a better view of things, and imagining the pain. He couldn't understand why they did it, and leaned forward to whisper into his father's ear: "Why do they do it, Papi?"

"They feel bad because of things they have done," his father said. "They're here to show God they are sorry."

Fabián couldn't imagine feeling bad enough about anything to want to drag a tree through the streets. With one hand he had tightly gripped the red and white neckerchief that his father always wore, and with the other he'd gathered a soothing fistful of his father's hair, so as not to pitch forwards into the crowd.

The memory made him hungry for comfort food. He stopped at a stall selling empanadas and *cuy*, bought a cheese empanada and strolled with it. The smell of *cuy* grilled over charcoal reminded him of an incident that took place shortly after my arrival from England. I had been both thrilled and disgusted to learn that guinea pigs were a national dish: I had kept one as a pet back home. Fabián had fed me one of its scrawny legs before revealing what the flesh was, testing to see the expression on my face when the information registered and claiming to be impressed by my acting abilities when I tried not to look surprised.

He finished eating his empanada and licked his fingers clean. This made him think back to Miguel de Torre, and his lover's keepsake. He wouldn't actually want his mother's finger, or anything sick like that. But he wouldn't have minded a lock of her hair, like you saw in films. Or he could have, say, half a gold doubloon on a chain round his neck until the day when the two of them were gloriously reunited. His half would fit with his mother's half, and she would turn towards him with disbelieving tears in her eyes. He felt embarrassed for thinking like this, and found himself looking around to see if anyone caught sight of his mooning expression. Fabián never cried, either at his father's funeral or his mother's memorial service.

He'd seen me crying. I was homesick early on, and some of the other kids thought I was a bit pathetic—notwithstanding the odd psychotic episode with a water balloon—but for some reason, crying in public didn't seem to embarrass me. It wasn't as if Fabián couldn't get away with crying if he wanted to. His circumstances meant he could behave pretty much how he liked and be forgiven. His orphanhood had set in motion a machinery of sympathy that worked beneath the surface at all times, allowing him to get away with anything, but still he didn't cry.

Another wheelchair penitent edged past. It reminded Fabián of the unfortunate American *tsantza* collector in Suarez's story. It also reminded him that he wasn't too badly off, all things considered—at least he wasn't voluntarily dragging a cross around in a wheelchair. A strip of tripe stuck in its spokes impeded this one's progress. Discarded by some market seller, the tripe was caught up in the wheel and now attracted interest from a stray dog. Helping these people was supposed to be bad form, but Fabián stepped forward from behind, so the penitent didn't see, and whipped the obstacle away. He dropped the tripe into the gutter for the dog before wiping his hand on his trouser leg and walking on.

He wondered how the Ambassador's party was going.

The answer to that question is that it was ludicrous—a party in a style so Grand Old English that it would never have happened any more in England. The Old Town teemed and crumbled away just down the hill, but up there in the garden the atmosphere couldn't have been more different. Stilton had been flown out especially in a diplomatic bag, and the guests strutted about sporting medals and feathered pith helmets—even spurs in a few cases. If these had been gauchos, fresh in from barbecuing cattle and killing each other with knives out in the pampas, then okay, I could live with that; but they were former public schoolboys in pressed white linen, who'd hardly been outside an embassy in their lives. Their spurs were buffed to a high shine and had probably never seen anything resembling a horse's flank, unless you counted some of the imperial-sized wives on display.

My mother, a conversational up-swell, surged around from group to group keeping people on their toes. My father bobbed about somewhere in her wake, browsing the canapés and trying to sniff out interesting political gossip from local officials.

I looked towards the Old Town, wondering if Fabián would stick to our agreement to aim a salutary firework at the statue of the winged virgin on the Panecillo. I didn't hold out too much hope for this—of all the plans Fabián and I made, hardly any ever came off—and I was far more preoccupied with trying to talk to the daughter of a French flower exporter. A ripe seventeen, with freckles and dark hair wet from the shower, she wore the most ruthless white dress I'd ever seen, and I had spent much of the party discreetly falling in love with her. She'd been fighting off a lecherous old moustache with a ceremonial sword for half an hour, but had now managed to break away, and I was trying to get drunk enough on weak Buck's Fizz to go over and goose her in the bushes.

I picked my moment and began to advance down the stone steps, rehearsing my speech for the wedding a few years hence ("we met under the shadow of Pichincha at a garden party") and wishing I had some spurs with which to pique her interest, when my mother materialized and handed me some cherub of thirteen who had only just arrived in the country and didn't know anybody.

"This is Eugène," she said. "He's French. I said you would show him around, darling. Enjoy the party—are you eating? There are some compelling miniature shepherd's pies."

"Salut, Eugène," I said. "My French isn't very good, but I know someone we can go and talk to."

"I am bilingual," said Eugène, with an angelic smile.

"Good. You can translate."

Fabián watched the approach of the float carrying the Virgin Mary. It reminded him of his mother, which in turn made his head ache. His memories of his father were concrete, which matched the certainty of his demise: statements, opinions and actions. Those of his mother were more elusive, tallying with her fate of disappearance over death. This made it more diffi-cult for him to mourn his mother, which in turn made him feel guilty. In fact, even the realization that he *wasn't* thinking about her made him feel guilty.

Fabián watched the float as it drew near and tried to posi-tion himself where he could only hear music from *one* of the tourist stalls. Wherever he stood, it seemed, he heard different pan-pipe songs in mid-collision, often with a manic voodoo counterpoint of salsa music. The aroma of guinea pigs on the grill was no longer evocative; it had blended with sour body odors to produce a musky and unpleasant scent. The edges of things began to blur together, like soft pencil-markings under a thumb. A group of policemen pushed the crowd back from the side of the road, and Fabián was caught off balance in the surge. He lost his footing and landed half on the pavement, half in the cobbled gutter, looking stupidly up at the colored bunt-ing across the street. The crowds, in agitated protest at this heavy-handed approach, were still being pushed backwards over him. He'd hit his head on the pavement, and it began to throb. The Virgin loomed over him, bobbing on the surface of the crowd, clasping her hands before her and gazing into the distance from within her glass case. Fabián noticed that her complexion seemed faded next to all the gold of the parade, but he knew he should be concentrating more on getting to his feet.

At this point, the nearest policeman got impatient and a bit panicky. He gave the crowd a bigger shove with his baton, and a tightly packed bunch of people fell backwards as one over the supine Fabián, trampling him beneath them.

A blade of vivid light tore through his vision, and the last thing he saw before the crowd cut off his line of sight was a new face looking down at him from within the glass box of the Virgin. The waxy lady with her enigmatic smile had disappeared, replaced by his mother, in flesh and warm blood. Joy blazed in her eyes, and the tear on her cheek no longer sat in a dummy's artificial furrow, but slid tenderly down real skin.

The astonishment and pleasure he experienced both overrode his panic at being crushed under such a large crowd of people, and distracted him from the fact that his arm was broken in two places. Covered by the third and final backward surge, the vision of his mother disappeared, and information from his arm and head began going off around his body like one controlled explosion after another.

Consequently, he failed to notice the dust clouds puffing off the building behind him as the earthquake started.

Having got well into my wooing routine with the French flower dealer's daughter, and congratulating myself on the idea of bringing Eugène along to translate for me, I was put out when it emerged that the girl was his older sister, that she spoke perfect

English herself and that the pair of them had been taking the piss out of me from the beginning. I wasn't, therefore, in mid-seduction, but sulking furiously behind a statue of Columbus and wondering if I could risk a cigarette when the tremor started.

Whereas down in the Old Town an earthquake would manifest itself as something serious, like rotting whitewash tumbling off the masonry, or the collapse of an entire stall full of rain sticks and hash pipes, up there in the garden the event was infuriatingly incidental. The only real physical manifestation of it seemed to be the faint clinking of glassware on the Ambassador's trestle tables, which meant that the earthquake operated more as a humorous addendum to the party than anything serious. The sort of thing that ladies in lilac might compliment their host on: "An earthquake! But how *charming*, David." People instinctively moved away from the house, but a lackey came on a loudspeaker and said that no one needed to worry about that because this was one of Quito's most earthquake-proof buildings. Everyone relaxed and laughed. Someone said, that's the advantage of living in a modern house, isn't it? A butler theatrically opened fresh champagne with a saber.

I thought of Fabián down in the Old Town. He would have remembered the earthquake drills we did at school, and would be fine, so there was nothing to worry about. But it annoyed me that I wasn't there. I was, it seemed, destined to live a boring life, never around when the good stuff happened. Fabián had it all, right down to the uncle with the shrunken head, while I was that pale English kid who couldn't even get it on with some florist's daughter without being made a fool of by her baby brother. Nothing ever happened to some people unless they went out looking for it, I thought. So I resolved there and then to go out looking at the next opportunity, and turned away from the view to see where the booze had got to.

The tremor had passed. It only measured 2.1 on the Richter scale but many people were shaken up by it, not least the float-bearers carrying the Virgin Mary. She must have weighed almost a ton and a half, and had nearly toppled into the crowd during the confusion. People began to pick themselves up off the ground. The policeman admonished them for their unruly behavior and said, look how easily accidents happen. A penitent had dropped his own cross on his head, and now his wailing was genuine. Panic ensued as families realized they had been separated.

Fabián lay crumpled in a wet gutter with his arm bent at a crazy angle, and miraculously Suarez found him after only a few minutes. He stooped to have a look at his nephew's injury, assuming it to have happened during the earthquake. The arm had sustained a nasty couple of breaks, but it would heal. What worried Suarez far more was his nephew's behavior. He hoped Fabián wasn't suffering from concussion. He didn't seem to have registered that Suarez was beside him, and he was staring up at the sky with a broad, foolish grin, the like of which Suarez had never seen before.

As far as Fabián was concerned, everything was fine. He was waving at his mother with his floppy, broken arm, and at that point, nothing else mattered.

As I said, it went something like that.

At the time, I had no idea of the full drama of what had happened, and it wasn't until we returned to school the week after Easter that the story began to emerge and develop, when Fabián turned up with a dramatic plaster cast encasing his right arm. The celebrity conferred by a glamorous injury can, in the right circumstances, be considerable, and Fabián milked the situation for all it was worth.

My mother had just dropped me off and I was walking towards the classroom, preparing a daring adaptation of my encounter with the French flower dealer's daughter for the benefit of Fabián—and of anyone else who would listen—when I was out-trumped before I'd even had the opportunity to begin. Verena Hermes collared me in the corridor and gave me the news.

"Have you seen Fabián yet?" she demanded.

"Not yet."

She seemed pleased to hear this. Her multiple earrings jangled, and a wave of her scent engulfed me as she leaned forward conspiratorially. "He's had a terrible accident. Fabián was right in the middle of that earthquake, and he broke his arm saving a little girl who was about to get crushed to death in the crowd."

"Sounds very heroic," I said.

"He's so cool," said Verena. "But he doesn't like to talk about it too much. So you go easy on him, okay?"

"I'll try," I said to a swaying, tinted bob of hair as she turned her back on me and flounced into the classroom.

Fabián sat at the center of an admiring throng, gesticulating wildly with the plaster cast even as some members of his audience tried to sign it. I noticed as I drew nearer that Verena had already scrawled her own name in thick red marker pen on the most prominent location.

"I hear you don't like to talk about it," I said.

"I don't," said Fabián. "It brings back too many memories. Now shut up and listen. Andrea, thank you, what a lovely signature. So, if you guys would care to make your way over here to the model skeleton, I will show you where the breakage occurred. These are called the radius and the ulna, and my ulna is broken both here, and here. A small portion of this bone will always be adrift inside my arm—a reminder of the cost of being a hero. Please don't weep, ladies. You know I would have done the same for many of you. I guess some people are just in the right place at the right time . . ."

three

Unlike Suarez, my parents weren't equipped with an adventure playground of a house, so when Fabián came to stay with me we would spend most of the weekend at the Sporting Club, a sealed New Town compound where expats could paddle safely up and down the deep blue Olympic rooftop pool towards the volcanoes on the horizon, take an aerobics class or, more likely, enjoy a lightly grilled cheese sandwich with their Campari and soda.

Fabián and I would maraud around, making the place less relaxing for others by openly appraising budding daughters in bikinis, messing around in the bowling alley or attempting elaborate formation dives into the pool. My mother, meanwhile, would rain earnest sweat on to the clay tennis courts as my father made polite conversation with fellow club members in the library—a room which couldn't have been further in spirit from its namesake at Suarez's. This one qualified for the name on the grounds that it had paneling, a couple of yellow paperbacks and the *Herald Tribune* on a table, and I can confidently assert that not a single interesting word was ever uttered within its walls. To me, at that time, my parents seemed so crushingly predictable that I could never understand why Fabián sometimes seemed to covet them: a fine illustration of how the comparative glamor of the world he lived in blinded me to its downside.

We were due to go to the Sporting Club that weekend, but the trip was called off at the last minute because of Fabián's arm and no contingency plan was made in its place. Secretly this was a relief to me, because it prevented Fabián from performing his latest and most embarrassing routine in the pool: using what he called his "negative buoyancy" to sink to the bottom of the deep end with a lungful of air and lie stock still, to the mounting agitation of some poor old lifeguard. Instead I spent a solitary Saturday afternoon bobbing about by the steps at the deep end, trying to discover the elusive secret of negative buoyancy for myself, or at the very least to better my own pitiful, gasping record for staying underwater. Most importantly, though, it meant that we missed a valuable opportunity to discuss what had *really* happened to Fabián on the day he broke his arm.

I saw little of him the following week either. Ours was a friendship that tolerated separation, and I naively assumed that he wasn't around much because he was busy dining out on his new, heroic reputation. It was only later that I found out the truth: he spent most of that week alone, coping with the increasingly disturbing mental adventures his mind was taking him on, and allowing his own personal version of what had happened at the Easter parade to take root.

In my defense, I had distractions of my own at home. A monster threat, which had been lurking in the shadows for months and which I'd been doing my best to ignore, lumbered blinking into the light without warning, and all of my energies had suddenly to be diverted into urgent evasive action.

The crunch came one evening when my mother collected me from school. Regardless of mood, she punished her Japanese jeep like a getaway driver, but as we roared away from the school gates that evening, it felt more than ever as if she were trying to escape the tedious gravity of New Quito once and for all and put us into orbit. I should have noticed straight away that she was tense, and played things safe, but I can be hopelessly unobservant at times.

I'd been telling her at the start of the journey about what we'd covered that day in a history lesson: the famous meeting in 1822 between San Martín and Bolívar at Guayaquil, after which, for no obvious reason, San Martín had agreed to stand down and let Bolívar take his place in history as the Great Liberator of South America. It wasn't customary for me to come fizzing out of school talking about what I'd studied, and I didn't usually have much interest in history, but every so often something caught my attention. Not only was this a continent-shaping event that had happened right here in Ecuador, but it was a captivating story for other reasons. To this day, nobody really knows what went on at that meeting—or why San Martín, who had done more liberating than most, should have meekly stood aside to let Bolívar be remembered as the man responsible for the freedom of the continent. It could have been straight from some *Boy's Own* story about Men of Destiny, and like King Arthur, born so conveniently to take the sword from the stone, Bolívar seemed to me to have had it easy. If people are willing just to step aside for you because of your place in the story, power and responsibility become a lot easier to deal with, in my view. And where does that leave those of us with more mediocre destinies? Where did it leave me, the pale English kid with faulty lungs and no shrunken-head-wielding uncle?

My mother was unmoved by my enthusiasm for the subject. She asked, in a dry tone of voice at odds with the death-wish apparent in her driving, whether I didn't think I ought to be more concerned with what was going on in my *own* country in 1822, and my sarcastic response (something like, "Do *you* know what was happening in England then?") was met with silence and a flooring of the accelerator. Another warning sign. But, fatally, I was feeling bored, and a bit antagonistic.

Knowing what an affront they were to her own intellectual rigor and attention to detail, I would sometimes repeat parrot-fashion to my mother some of the things that Suarez said to Fabián and me at the weekends, to see what sort of a reaction they provoked. Usually this would be indulgent laughter, followed by a jokey admonishment that I was hanging out with the wrong crowd and it was high time I got a decent education. But not today.

I announced that I had been thinking about the war with Peru.

"What about it?" she said, warily.

I launched into one of Suarez's favorite tirades, about how all the petty squabbling between us and the Peruvians was distracting Ecuador from the larger project. How the pre-Colombian civilizations were just as bad. How South Americans had lost their one chance to unite, because they had lost touch with their mystical side thanks to failures of imagination inherited from the conquistadores. That expression. "Failures of imagination." That really got her. The second it was out, she started driving even more recklessly, the bangles round her wrists jangling in time to her increasingly hectic gear changes. The exact ins and outs of the subsequent conversation are irrelevant, but it involved me voicing Suarez's view that believing something because it was a good story was just as worthwhile as believing something that happened to be true, and it ended with her gunning the engine and saying:

"All I can say is that this sounds like a *repellent* attitude to take towards history."

In silence, we sped down one of the highways of New Quito, passing a detailed graffiti copy, on concrete, of Picasso's *Guernica*.

And then she said it.

"I think it's about time we brought forward that plan to send you to school in England."

Looking back, it seems obvious that my semi-digested regurgitation of Suarez's fluid view of history would irritate my mother. The fact that she had pretended to find previous doses of the Suarez medicine amusing was neither here nor there. If I had known her as well then as I did later, I would have been fully aware that my mother's currency in the world was, and always had been, facts. The same cannot necessarily be said of my father.

Among the many dark arts at my mother's disposal was her Ph.D. in psychology, which I am convinced she somehow deployed repeatedly over the years as a tool to get her own way with both me and my father. Before I was born, when my parents decided on the globe-trotting lifestyle that came to define their married life, it was in answer to demands placed on them by my father's job. His precocity as a young reporter boosted him into the position of Reuters' West Africa correspondent at an early age. That he achieved this in spite of the fact that he didn't have a degree was a testament to the esteem in which the agency held him. He was perceived as one of those seat-of-the-pants, university-of-life sort of people, and respected for it.

My mother leapt at the chance to go with him and live in Kinshasa and threw herself zealously into further academic work, writing what is now considered to be a seminal paper on the psychology of displacement, based on a series of recorded interviews with those who were beginning to return from the New World to discover their roots. In so doing, she took the circumstances imposed on her by my father and made them her own, until eventually even my father himself might have wondered whether it was his or her work that had originally brought them there.

Things tipped definitively in my mother's favor following the events that precipitated their departure from Africa. When I was young, this story was shrouded in mystery, but I have since heard it enough times from Dad when he's had a few drinks to know the details. In a nutshell, he was fired from Reuters because he made up a press release on a slow news day. There had been rumblings of a civil war in Angola, and he had spent three months trying in vain to find evidence of interesting atrocities in order to stoke up the atmosphere. Then one of his military contacts muttered something at a drinks party about an impending coup, and the next day, he put the story out on the wire without stopping to think about whether or not it had any factual basis. It caused quite a stir.

Any early promise in the field of serious journalism was not, therefore, fulfilled, and although he was now working for a small news agency in Quito, it was my mother's work on the social status of mestizo and Indian families that was keeping us in South America. There had been what people now refer to as *El Levantamiento*—"The Uprising"—in 1990, and the status of *indígenas* was a hot social topic. My mother loved this, and churned out stuff not only on the Indians who were supposedly reclaiming their birthright and redressing centuries of repression, but also on the hitherto dominant Caucasians and the effects their meteoric descent from favor was having on *their* sense of self-esteem. To me, all this couldn't help but seem painfully earnest, but I would never have said so to her. And of course she, like my father, was writing for markets outside South America—to have presumed to publish comment on such issues as an outsider in Quito at that time would have somewhat defeated the point of the "revolution."

In a smooth see-sawing motion, and with far greater permanence than the supposed overthrow taking place in the country we lived in, my father's career had faded into the background; it was understood that we would leave the country when her work was done, and not the other way round. He no longer had a say in their trajectory. Which isn't to say that there was some sort of power struggle—just that he was perfectly happy to stay in her slipstream and keep his head down.

On serious matters in which I hoped to have any say, it was always more advisable to approach him first, or at least the two of them together. Taking her on alone was suicide. So, as soon as the threat was uttered in the car, I knew enough to clam up and make no further comment on the subject of my education until dinner that evening, when I might hope for some backup.

I stalled my mother as best I could until we were almost home by asking her about her work. The monologue that ensued gave me a much-needed opportunity to collect my thoughts, and start planning how I might respond to the threat she had issued. Finally, the jeep banked into a steep incline, punched through the fug of diesel and aircraft exhaust that clung to the city, and we landed on the well-tended lawns of suburbia.

The neighborhood where we lived was called Quito Tenis, and it was named after a tennis club; not an early hamlet, a river, or an ancient Inca burial ground, but a tennis club. Well-heeled settlers had been drawn as early as the 1970s to the area's abundant tarmac surfaces, agreeable shrubbery and secure, gated developments, and it wasn't long before a select community thrived: lawyers, politicians, doctors, engineers, foreigners. In spite of the fact that Tenis was situated high on the northwestern lip of the valley, its architects elected to build several huge apartment blocks there. The result was a cluster of white earthquake-proofed columns that rose high up out of the smog. Picture a teetering tower of sugar cubes standing in a puddle of gravy.

Our own block stood in a secure compound, with armed guards at the front gates. As our car drew up, they would open the huge metal doors that led down into the basement garage. When we'd first moved in I found it an exciting novelty—a bit like living in the bat-cave—but this had long since worn off.

My mother brought the jeep at speed into its allotted space and turned off the engine with a snap. The radiator fan heaved hot sighs of relief. She had been furniture shopping, and the rear of the car sat low under the weight of a chair carved from highly polished rainforest hardwood, which I was instructed to bring up to the apartment.

"But use the service lift, will you?" she said. "Don't want to get in trouble for scratching the floor of the normal one. And for God's sake, stop *sulking*. Nothing's been decided yet."

With that she was off, clacking away on the concrete floor of the basement towards the non-service lift, my bag dangling from her fingertips at a safe distance. I locked the car, shouldered the chair and struggled over with it to the service lift. Mahogany is heavy.

Watching numbers turn yellow in the gloom as my mother ascended, I pressed the other, dirtier button that hailed the service lift. I'd never been in it before, and was surprised by what I saw when the doors slid open. The interior was padded with thick brown material, put there to absorb the blows of furniture or appliances as they were delivered to the show apartments above. It had absorbed more than that, too—the smells of stale smoke and sweat, of coffee and pollution. The residents' lift, which I was used to, was finished in shiny, faux-industrial metal and contained no such soft furnishings charged with atmosphere. This one had the same dimensions, and led from the same starting point to the same destination, but inside it couldn't have been more different. It was as if I had momentarily slipped into an alternative version of reality. Even the ping as the doors opened came through the same coarsening filter—it was louder, and more ragged, as if some crucial, restraining part of its apparatus had been snapped off. I put down the chair and sat enthroned on it for a moment, taking in these new surroundings. Then I reached up, pressed button number seven and wiped the oily deposit this left from my fingertip on to the brown cladding. The machine jerked into action.

Halfway up to our apartment, the lift stopped with a jolt, the strip light overhead flickered and died, and a wheeze of dying machinery shuddered through the building. Due to the state of emergency over the war with Peru, power cuts were frequent, but they didn't normally spread as high up the food chain as Quito Tenis. In its quest for energy conservation, the Ministry of the Interior preferred to reserve its strictures for those with fewer energy-hungry appliances and less political clout. Nevertheless, they did happen, and I knew I would have to sit this one out in the lift until the power came back on. My mother knew where I was, and would take steps to get me out if necessary.

I inhaled deeply and relaxed into the chair. Now that the lift was in darkness, I was hypersensitive to the smells infused into its fabric sides. It smelled of the outside world; a world about which, in this country at least, I still knew very little. I pictured condors circling above waterfalls, Indians in ponchos trudging through misty mountain villages and olive-skinned kids playing with a battered football on the beach before realizing that what I had in mind were mere holiday-brochure images of my adopted country. I had no more laid eyes on these sights than I had watched fireworks burst over the cathedral in Cuenca, mountain-biked down the slopes of Cotopaxi or "roughed it" in some eco-tourism lodge in the rainforest. I might as well have spent the entirety of the past two years sitting in that darkened, padded cell, straining to imagine what lay outside, and now my chances of ever seeing it for real were dwindling by the hour. When the light stuttered back on and the lift lurched upwards again, I opened my eyes, in which boyish tears had sprung. I wiped them away quickly, and dried my hand on the lift walls just before the doors opened.

The two lift shafts were side by side, but each lift had a corresponding hallway leading to different areas of the apartment: whereas the residents' lift brought you to a reception area with a slate floor, the service lift delivered you before a garishly tiled vestibule leading out to the back—an area that we continued to refer to as the maid's quarters, even though my mother had never bothered hiring a maid. "I don't agree with it for one thing, and for another, I don't see any reason to bring any nubile young girls to your father's attention unnecessarily," she said. The idea that my father might dare to transgress with anyone, particularly under the same roof as my mother, was laughable, but the first reason she gave was deadly serious. So, although the apartment was fully kitted out for domestic servitude, the brass bell-push embedded into the dining-room floor had never been used except in jest, and the tiny maid's bedroom at the back served as a box room for cartons of "essentials" brought over from the UK, which had remained unopened since we arrived. Scowling at these reminders of "home" as I entered, I lugged the chair inside, put it down and went to the kitchen. My father kept a tray of short bottles of beer at the back of the fridge, and I decided I deserved a surreptitious reward for my trouble.

It wasn't so much that my mother always had to have her own way; it was more that if you disagreed with her, the rhetorical power this unleashed would shock you into seeing things from her point of view. The minute she sensed resistance, all of her intellect would be summoned into an irresistible arrowhead of purpose, and the most sensible strategic approach was therefore never to disagree with her too forcefully. My father, like a farmer working the slopes of a much-loved yet active volcano, treated her with respect and knew when to back off, but I didn't yet have the benefit of his years of experience.

All you had to do was to know when to keep your mouth shut. It was elementary. And clumsy as I was, under normal circumstances I would probably have reached this conclusion. Apart from anything else, if I'd had access to Fabián that week, I would have been able to canvass his opinion and work out a more considered strategy. Instead, alone in my room in the hours before dinner, I decided that the best approach to the crisis was to bluster through it, appealing to my mother's heart. If she saw how much I had learned about South America, how much I loved it there, then she might come to see the value in my staying put. It was, after all, a passion of her own. All I had to do was persuade. Not for the first time, I wished I had Fabián's bullshitting prowess. In its absence, I boosted my confidence with several clandestine trips to Dad's cache of beer in the run-up to the meal.

When the three of us were round the table, I hit the ground running, giving my parents one of Suarez's most emotive tirades, on the subject of Machu Picchu. I held forth for a quarter of an hour on how the place had a talismanic power for South America, that it held collective memory and was therefore the key to the eventual realization of the Bolivarian republic.

"If talismanic power is what you want, go to the encyclopedia and look up Stonehenge," my mother said.

Scornfully, I dismissed Stonehenge as a pointless load of old rubble, knowing even as I said it that I was already off target. I was supposed to be demonstrating my love of South America, not my hatred of Europe.

"It sounds to me as if your friend Suarez has been reading too much Neruda and not enough sensible journalism," my mother went on. "And as for you: you should be taking more of an interest in finding things out for yourself instead of blindly believing everything that man says."

It was only a matter of time before the subject of school came back up. When it did, I tried to keep things abstract and hypothetical, asking why we couldn't just cross that bridge when we came to it and slipping in a request for the salt at the end of my sentence in the hope that this would start a new conversational thread. I could almost hear Fabián's laughter at how badly I was performing.

"We can see the bridge from here, Anti," said my mother. "There are big holes in it."

Even at this point, if I had been less hot-headed, or more sober, I might have let the comment pass, nodded quiet agreement and waited for somebody to raise another topic. My mother's mind was capable of jumping about from topic to topic with all the agility of a mountain goat, and it might not take long for a new, mutually agreeable theme to arise, after which the previous assertion, however vehemently declared, would probably be forgotten. In my inflamed state, though, her implication here shocked me. I said that I didn't see anything wrong with the International School, and that furthermore it was inhuman of the two of them to contemplate expelling me from Ecuador when they were planning on staying there themselves.

"Spare me the emotional blackmail," said my mother, smiling. "You'll enjoy it there."

I was fast running out of options. I turned to my father, who had been holding back up to this point, and appealed for assistance.

"Sorry, mate," he said, infuriatingly. "I think I'm going with your mother on this one."

My position was bad enough. But now, as if someone were out to get me, my chest tightened in preparation for an asthma attack, and all my last-ditch appeals were undermined by a crippling wheezing fit.

Rarely for her, my mother lost her temper.

"You can spare us the attack of consumption as well," she snapped. "You know perfectly well that the doctor said your asthma is ninety per cent psychosomatic, so don't think you'll get that much sympathy on that score. Besides, if it's really that bad then getting back to the UK and away from this high altitude can only be a good thing." She took a sip of wine and looked me right in the eye. "Right?"

My father put a hand between my shoulder-blades and told me to take deep breaths. I nodded weakly.

"It's settled then," said my mother. "We'll aim to get you out of here by the end of this summer."

And after that I suspect there was an unedifying spell of shouting and door-slamming that is best forgotten about.

———

There was an old knife-sharpener in Quito who did door-to-door calls in a pre-war pick-up truck. He used to announce his arrival by calling in the street outside, regardless of the neighborhood he was in or the type of building. I had never before thought quite how ridiculous, and how glorious, he was—this relic, calling out to a whole apartment block, as if it were no different to him from a little hut in the mountains—until I watched him later that evening while smoking an angry, furtive cigarette out of my bedroom window.

I had been two years younger when we left the UK. What going back to school there would be like now I had no idea, but I was not optimistic. I had visions of atrocious food and sanctioned violence. There was every chance this initiative might not go anywhere. My mother blustered quite a lot, particularly when contradicted, and often it meant nothing. On the other hand, she seemed quite serious about this, and I couldn't count on my father to help me out. Even if he didn't agree with this outrageous proposal, which I wasn't so sure about anyway, there was every chance that he would roll over and let it pass without a veto.

From our flat on the seventh floor, you could look down straight through the tops of the pine trees on to the street. I watched and listened as the knife-sharpener parked his truck and walked up and down with his canvas tool-bag, calling out lustily to entire blocks full of people who would never respond. In a gesture of solidarity, I shouted down at him and waved, but, as if he had never expected a response in the first place, he loaded his bag back in his truck and drove away without noticing me.

I had a premonition of two traces of future emotion: first, the regret I would feel if I left this country without taking a proper look at it for myself; second, a terror of the sly, creeping approach of a more colorless world. As a result, I felt determined to make the present worthy of nostalgia while it lasted.

four

The following Friday, I went to stay with Fabián and Suarez as per usual. But a shrill note of self-pity was already playing in my head over every custom I took for granted, as I began in earnest to feel as sorry for myself as I could. It's something I have always been pretty good at. In spite of this, I was desperate to keep reality at bay for as long as possible and had resolved to keep quiet about my proposed exile for the moment, however much I was seething within.

The three of us sat around the kitchen table, having dinner. Suarez was on the rum, and Fabián and I were drinking *naranjilla* juice. On any other day, I might have moaned about this, as I had never really got used to it and sometimes wondered why we couldn't just have plain lemonade. But on this day, the juice—the fruit is a bizarre amalgam of orange and tomato—had become another familiar feature of the landscape that I was melodramatically preparing to miss, and I savored every vivid, transient mouthful as a result. Such distinctive physical memories mean that my youth is nicely compartmentalized. I drank a glass of *naranjilla* from some exotic juice bar years after leaving

Ecuador and a whole series of neatly bookmarked memories fell open—although on that occasion, I didn't enjoy the taste at all.

"I hear that Fabián is a hero," I said.

"Is that so?" said Suarez. "I didn't think it was customary for heroes to do their own public relations, but I suppose you may be right. What is he said to have done this time?"

I recounted the story about Fabián saving the girl in the earthquake, which had, over the course of the last few days, acquired several new and thrilling dimensions. One version had Fabián being tear-gassed by a rogue policeman during the rescue. In another, he'd had to hold off a rabid dog that was trying to steal the girl's tripe sandwich.

"Well, if that is what people are saying, then I suppose it must be the truth," said Suarez. "Congratulations, Fabi." He raised his glass in a toast.

"It was nothing, Uncle. Just what any man would have done," said Fabián.

"It was especially self-effacing of you not to reveal any of this to me on the day. No doubt the shock of the situation took it out of you, and you were unable to piece together what had happened until days after the event."

"No doubt, no doubt," said Fabián. "You're the medical man."

Suarez beamed. "Funny that I didn't see any distressed children near you at the time. All I saw was a little *huahua* lying in the gutter, gazing up into the air, with all the stuffing knocked out of him. I must get my eyes tested."

"Maybe you should," said Fabián. "You're getting on a bit, Uncle."

———

There was no late-night storytelling session with Suarez that evening. He went out, leaving us alone in the library with a couple of beers and Jerry Lee Lewis.

I knew there must be more to the story of Fabián's arm than what I had already heard. Or, more likely, that there must be less to it. In its current form, the portrayal of Fabián as hero was all very well, but I knew the truth would come out before long.

It will be apparent that "the truth" was something with which Fabián and I were fairly free. The best story was usually the one we believed. It was what defined our friendship. But there was also an unspoken understanding—or at least there was as far as I was concerned—that we both knew when things had gone too far from the realm of the plausible.

He might be telling me all about a steamy clinch with Verena in a stationery cupboard, say, and I would go along with the story right up to the point where things started to stray too far. We had an accepted technique for establishing the truth without subtracting from the credibility of the storyteller, which went something like this:

"So, there you are, with your hand up her skirt, and she's begging you to go further," I would say, "and the teacher walks in. What a nightmare. No wonder she was looking so hot and agitated when she came back to the class."

"I know," Fabián might say. "I was pretty agitated myself, I can tell you."

"Terrible," I would say. "Well, maybe next time."

"Sure. One day."

There would be a pause, and then I would say:

"Anything could have happened in that cupboard, couldn't it?"

"You're right," Fabián would say. "Anything could have happened. Anything from full penetrative sex through to a bit of harmless flirting followed by a kick in the balls."

"So, on that scale of possibility, what would a really unimaginative person say had happened to him in that cupboard?"

"The unimaginative person would probably say that he followed Verena into the cupboard hoping to cop a feel, but that she bashed him round the head with a foolscap folder before making him carry about three tons of paper back to the classroom for her. Something like that."

"How unimaginative."

"Quite. How disappointing," Fabián would say.

As we had already had one version of what had happened at the *Semana Santa* parade, I was expecting the true story to come out in a similar fashion. What I didn't expect was that "the truth" would far outgun the story.

"Are you going to tell me what really happened with the arm?" I said.

"It's not what really happened with the arm that's the best bit," he said.

And he told me how he had seen a vision of his mother looking down on him from within the glass case of the Virgin during the Easter parade.

I didn't have a clue how I was supposed to react. In all of our two years of banter, not once had the idea of a *religious* experience come up. And, as I said, we had never, even remotely, touched on the subject of his mother.

I stayed silent, trying to disguise my growing unease, while he went on talking, apparently rationally, about the reasons why he thought his mother had chosen to appear to him from within the glass case.

"I'm not sure, but I *think* it means that she must be trapped somewhere," he said. "What do you think?" He looked at me with a calm smile.

"What do I think?"

"Yeah."

Putting my beer down on the table, I then said something very stupid:

"Fabián. What would the unimaginative person say had happened here?"

His eyes jabbed in my direction.

"I'm not fucking around, you know," he said. "I really did see my mother in that crowd."

One of the pitfalls of being Fabián's friend was the occasional moment of panic and uncertainty as, halfway through a game, he changed the rules without telling you. I was used to it. I'd done it to others myself alongside him. But at this moment, I felt more at sea in his company than ever before.

"I thought—"

"You thought what? This isn't something I would go round telling at school. I'm speaking the truth."

"I know, but I thought . . . Your mother's dead, isn't she?"

Fabián took a slurp of his beer and stared over at the bookshelves on the other side of Suarez's desk. The jukebox switched records clumsily, from "Great Balls of Fire" to "Roll Over Beethoven."

He seemed about to say something, and then turned his head back to the beer. He finished it in a few gutsy gulps and, with his good arm, chucked the bottle at the wall. He wasn't left-handed, but it was a powerful throw. The bottle shattered right on the beat, in time to Chuck Berry, sending shards skittering across the checkerboard floor and leaving a round, foaming blotch beside the jukebox.

"Just believe me, will you?" he said.

"Okay. I believe you," I said.

"If I'm going to tell you about my parents, I'm going to need to get a lot more drunk than this."

"Fine by me," I said.

A Fabián I didn't know was dangerously near the surface. While the voyeur in me wanted to expose that person once and for all, I was conscious nonetheless of the need to tread carefully.

"What about getting out Suarez's shrunken head?" said Fabián, getting up and swaggering over towards the safe. "I wouldn't mind having another look at that. Do you believe all that stuff about the curse, and the lover's finger?"

Okay, I thought. *Okay, we'll leave it for the moment. I can play this game.*

"I don't know. I suppose so. I know he builds things up sometimes to make his stories better. But do you think he'd lie to us?"

"Of course he would. He probably just bought that *tsantza* himself from a junk shop. Stupid old bastard. He thinks we're still kids. He thinks he can tell us anything he likes. I looked it up, you know—there's a massive black-market trade in fake shrunken heads, just made out of pigskin and stuff, sold to tourists. The Shuar even make fake ones for themselves to perform their rituals, because they aren't allowed to cut people's heads off any more. There's hardly any cocking chance it's the real thing. The book I looked at even said how the real ones are made—they shrink the skin over a fire, then fill it up with pebbles so they can remold the face with their fingers. It's got dick-all to do with shrinking it in the sun around a stone."

"Well," I said, "I suppose you just have to ask yourself whether it felt real at the time; I mean—"

"I asked him whether if I went traveling with my mother's finger I would feel better about her not being here," said Fabián, perusing the bookshelves. "Unfair of me, probably, given that he's her brother. He said it was up to me. He just came out with that same stupid line he always says: 'Grief asks different questions of us all.' He's an idiot."

"Hadn't we better clean up that glass?" I said.

"No, leave it. Come over here. Look at the *size* of this encyclopedia. Look at all the stuff there is out there. We have to go and see some of it. Otherwise we might as well be beaten to death up a mountain like poor fucking Juanita. I want to get away from Suarez and his fake shrunken head. I want to find my *own* shrunken heads."

"What about finding something else to drink?" I suggested.

"A noble suggestion!" said Fabián, turning away from the encyclopedia and pointing his finger at me. "First sensible thing you've said. You stay here and watch the driveway for Suarez. I think I know where he keeps a bottle of tequila. Otherwise, I'm going to break into Byron's house and steal from him. Let him try and shoot me if he dares."

Forgetting that Byron was driving Suarez, so wouldn't be

there to shoot Fabián even if he had wanted him to, Fabián left the library. I moved over to where he had been standing, near the bookshelves, from where I'd be able to see the lights of Byron's car if he and Suarez came back.

Let's get a few things clear here:

The set of encyclopedias was not made of ancient cracked leather, or trimmed in gold leaf.

The binding of the volume did not billow out centuries-old dust as I opened it.

I did not find myself gazing in fascination at descriptions of a forgotten continent.

The twenty-two-volume family edition of the *Encylopaedia Ecuatoriana* was backed in leather-effect brown plastic, illustrated with faded 1970s color photographs and printed on cheap, almost translucent, paper. It sat in Suarez's library, between his imposing medical textbooks and a collection of old-style, red-spined Everyman Classics. You could have gone into any other middle-class home and found the same publication. In a belated effort to follow my mother's suggestion, I pulled down the S–T volume and opened it at "Stonehenge."

Just reading the name again was like throwing back the dustsheet on a stockpile of drab English memories: drizzle and anoraks, motorway cafés, a dismal visitors' center. But as I read the entry, I began to see the place in a different light. Why hadn't I been told this stuff before? Here were druids and solstices, and great, hefty unknowns. I'd opened the encyclopedia expecting it to be a boring, factual reference book—the sort of thing you were *supposed* to consult—but in frank, unashamed prose, this one explained the cosmic felicities in the location of the site, detailed the mystery of how the stone had been transported there from Wales, and referred me to an entry in another of its volumes relating how Joseph of Arimathea had visited Glastonbury and planted a spear there that became a rose-bush.

Something began to make thrilling sense to me. When I had first met Byron two years previously, he had asked me where I was from, and I had said England.

"Ah, Londres," he said. "City of the kings."

"What?" I said.

"London is the city where you still have kings and queens," he said, wistfully.

At the time, the remark had merely struck me as naive, but now, faced with this encyclopedia and all its entries, his words seemed defining, iconic—a lesson in how removal could enable re-imagination, how looking at things in the right way could breathe warmth into the palest of truths. If such a simple re-expression of the facts could do that for gray old England, then what could it do for Ecuador, where princesses frozen in mountains made the headlines on a day-to-day basis?

I took down an earlier volume, and turned to the entry for Inca:

Lots of dates; lots of facts; a terrible photograph of Machu Picchu; a woodblock print of the great feuding brothers, Huáscar and Atahualpa. Some juicy details about brain banquets and the massacres of Spanish Catholics, which were promising.

Further down, another entry, "Isla de Plata":

Known as the "poor man's Galápagos"; profusion of endemic species; humpback whales migrating from Antarctica to Colombia; named Island of Silver (or Money) on account of being site of (as yet undiscovered) treasure of Francis Drake;

seventy-two tons of silver thrown overboard; nesting ground for albatross and blue-footed boobies.

As yet undiscovered.

"Okay then," said Fabián, charging in with a tray. "Here it is: tequila, limes, salt. I sense a quest coming on."

"Have a look at this," I said, bringing the encyclopedia over to the table.

"Are you mad? Look at *this,* man! Whatever it is, it can wait. Sit down."

"But this—"

"I thought you wanted to hear about my parents. Take the chance now before I change my mind."

Fabián unplugged the jukebox, turned off the overhead lighting and switched on the set of antique disco lights that Suarez had installed in the library. This story was to be told not by firelight, but by roaming spotlights of phased red and blue.

Before putting the book back on the shelf, I committed a place name from the map to memory: a small town, on the coast, not far from the Isla de Plata, with a reputation for surfing. There were other, bigger-looking places, some of which I'd heard much more about, but this name leapt out at me and stayed in a negative image on my retina after I had closed the covers—even after the room had been thrown into a silent dogfight of scrolling primary colors.

The name was Pedrascada.

Fabián positioned himself in front of the tequila tray and poured two pairs of shots. Solemnly, we each threw back one, then another. Our winces turned into nervous smirks after the second, but Fabián said, "No laughing. These ones we can sip."

He poured out two more, and we sat staring at each other across the table as if an accusation of cardsharping hung in the air. The only sound in the room was the gentle creak of rusting disco hinges.

"Are you sitting comfortably?" said Fabián.

five

Something you don't know about me is that my dad was a mestizo (said Fabián). He would never have admitted it, but he was. His grandmother was an Indian, from Peguche. He used to claim that even she was technically a mestiza, and that his Indian blood was so diluted as a result that it didn't exist.

"*Mestizaje* is relative," he would say. "In Europe, maybe I would be considered a mestizo. I have enough Indian blood in me to be seen as different over there. In Ecuador, I am not. Here, I am white. I am basically a Castilian." What he really meant was that he was ashamed of his own grandmother. Suarez would never approve, with all his crap about ancestry and the way he loves all that indigenous stuff, even though *he* is about as pure a conquistador as you can get.

But my father—that's Señor Félix Morales to you—well, he would never admit it. He tried as hard as he could to be what he thought was a European: he would listen to classical Spanish music, and try to dance the *pasadoble* like some flamenco expert. He even wore this crazy red and white spotted neckerchief the whole time, imagining it to be somehow sophisticated. My mother, who had no Indian blood that we know of, loved dancing and listening to all that terrible pan-pipe music. She even spoke quite good Quechua.

Papi had grown up hearing folk-tales about women who had given birth to calves, and men who turned into condors—some great stuff. But he would never tell them. My mother would ask him sometimes to tell us his grandmother's stories, and he would say, "If you want to hear a load of peasant rubbish you can look it all up in a textbook, or go and ask the first *campesina* you find grinding barley in a hut in the mountains."

He read nothing but Spanish literature, and even put on a hint of a lisp sometimes, like in a Madrileño accent. He'd only ever been to Spain twice in his life, and even then only on business trips with the construction company.

All this revolution stuff is bullshit, you know. Mestizos might make up a third of the population but it's not the top third—and that's before you even get to the full-blood Indians. I mean, look at the people who live in the New Town. Ask the kids at school, or any of your parents' buddies at that stupid sports club: they still think that one Indian is like every other Indian. They might just as well be animals.

So, Papi was embarrassed by who he was—and yes, he was impressed by my mother's money. Look at all this—you don't think all this came from doctoring, do you? Suarez and Mami come from a wealthy family. My father liked that.

I'm only telling you this so that you can see what kind of man he was. He was scared of himself, scared of being found out, scared of not being real, or something; I don't know.

Here, have another tequila.

Arriba, abajo, a centro, adentro. Mother of God, this is strong stuff. Sit up straight. Are you listening to me?

It was just over seven years ago. I was eight years old.

We used to go on these driving trips at weekends. My parents liked to disappear into the mountains, eat at village cafés, maybe go for a walk, that kind of thing. It was fun, even though I bitched about it at the time.

One day, we were somewhere really high up in the cordillera. We were meant to go for a walk, but it was raining hard, so we drove up to have a look at this hacienda instead. The Hacienda La Reina, it was called.

It was one of those farms that are so huge that whole villages grow up around them: there was a school, a church and even a little post office shop for the workers and their children. It was a beautiful place. The houses and fields were set against these massive green mountains. The air was wonderful.

When we got up to the hacienda we found a fiesta in progress. I think it's called Zaparo—some Indian harvest festival. An excuse for people to let their hair down and get messed up.

The farmworkers had been drinking homemade *chicha* and *aguardiente* for hours, and they were falling around all over the place. A band was marching round the fields, playing music. People were wearing bright red head-dresses made of feathers. Lanterns were being lit.

My parents weren't the sort of people who just got back in the car in a situation like that, and soon they were eating the food, drinking the booze and chatting to the locals. There was a suckling pig on a spit, and kids sitting around playing. It was pretty cool.

I don't know how my father got so drunk so quickly—I guess he wasn't used to the home-made *chicha* they drink up in the mountains. It's gross, man. You know they make it with saliva? The women spit in a bowl with a load of maize and then ferment it. Sick shit, but the *indígenas* love it.

There was a paddock in the middle of the area where the festival was taking place, with a separate, smaller pen full of bulls to the side. I can't remember how it started, but soon most of the party was crowded round this paddock, cheering and singing. There was a group of Indian farmworkers in the field, and they had started doing some amateur bullfighting for the crowd.

The bulls were little—they wouldn't have been any problem for a proper *torero*. But these weren't *toreros*: they were very drunk *campesinos* wearing rubber boots that slid around in the mud after the rain.

We stood around, getting into the spirit of the occasion, cheering and laughing when someone made a good pass. Messing around. Nobody was really going to hurt these bulls—the idea was just to get out of their way.

You know how it works. Normally, you hang your *muleta* on the *estoque*, the sword, to create that cape that the bull chases. All that *olé* crap. These guys were just pretending—running around waving their ponchos in the air for a laugh, then coming out of the paddock to high-five their buddies and try to impress girls into going back to their cottage for a fuck.

Papi secretly loved those Indian festivals. He was taking more and more from the *chicha* bowl, and swaying around to the music. It was when he was in moods like this—in other words, when it suited him—that he used to let his mask drop and go on about how great it was to be an Ecuadorian, that you had the best of both worlds. The sophistication of Europe, the spirituality of an Indian, blah blah blah. But then he started to get angry about the way the men in the paddock were treating the bulls.

The bull they were fighting was white, I remember. All the bulls were young, and very scared. No wonder they started running at these guys in the pen with them. It was totally disorganized.

It was getting dark as well, and this wasn't helping. People were sliding around more than ever. One guy nearly got trampled when the bull came in low and he slipped under its feet, but he managed to twist his head and shoulders away into the mud at just the right moment.

The crowd was starting to lose interest and move away. There was no reason for my father to do what he did.

He said, "These people don't know what they're doing. This is an insult to the tradition of bullfighting. I've got a good mind to get in there and show them how to do it properly."

And damn it if he didn't go down there and say he wanted to go next in the ring.

Right. Tequila break.

Your turn.

Get it down.

Where was I?

Oh, yeah.

"Three cheers for the *forastero*!" said the Indians. (It's the word they use to talk about outsiders.) "The *forastero*'s gonna show us how to do things properly. Give him another drink!"

My mother was getting nervous, but was still smiling—she

would never have suggested that he couldn't do it. He'd have gone crazy.

They held the bottle to his lips for a long time, until he was virtually choking on it. "Give him some *cojones,*" they said. Then they all slapped him on the back and pushed him towards the railing.

He stepped through into the paddock. Now, the bull they'd been working previously was tired and had been danced around by four or five men, easy. But some Indian guy, who I guess must have been a big cheese on the plantation, said, "No, no, no, this won't do. We'd better give this grand *torero* a worthy opponent! An animal that stands up to his big talk!" And they penned up the tired white bull that had been running around.

I can remember watching it as it went back in, thinking, *Shit—Papi could have seen that one much better.* It stood out in the dusk, you see.

Three or four of them got in the pen for a while, arguing about which bull to send in. Then they decided, and started moving this bigger, fresher and blacker one towards the paddock. I nearly shouted out that it wasn't fair because this one could hardly be seen, but my father wouldn't have stopped, and I didn't want to embarrass him.

He was standing in the center of the paddock, getting mud on his loafers and up his chinos, trying to pretend he was a real *torero.* The crowd got into it and cheered as he did all his warm-up exercises. It was quite funny.

Anyway, this bull wouldn't come out. The Indians pushed and pushed it, but it wouldn't come. My father got braver and started shouting at the man who had challenged him.

"I see your bull knows what's good for him, my friend!" he said.

"You're gonna pay for that remark, *forastero*," said the Indian. And in front of our eyes he went right up to the bull, took the end of his cigar in his fingertips, and stabbed the lit end into its leg.

It screamed and came flying into the paddock, kicking up earth all over the place. I still have this little blue T-shirt I was wearing then. I kept it even though it would never fit me now. You can see, between the bloodstains, some of the specks of dirt kicked up by the bull as it charged towards my father.

That moment is fixed in my mind: the bull's horns down; the spray of earth behind it lit up by the lanterns; the band marching around in the background; an Indian guy passing out in front of me 'cause he was so drunk.

Papi wasn't bad at all, I have to admit. He pulled some good moves. He started showing off, turning to face the crowd away from the bull, kneeling down in front of it and stuff.

Then my mother noticed some kids fooling around near our car and asked me just to go over and make sure it was locked. There were a lot of drunk people around.

I looked up at her.

"He'll be fine," she said. "Just go and check the car quickly. He'll be out in a second, and imagine how angry he'll be if someone's broken into it. Don't worry, Fabi. Look at him—he's doing great." She gave me a kiss on my forehead.

I'd gone maybe ten or twelve paces towards where the car was parked when a massive cheer went up, followed by a shocked gasp, and then the sound of a woman screaming. By the time I'd turned and was sprinting back as hard as I could to-wards the paddock, the crowd had fallen silent.

I couldn't see what had happened at first, because it had got so dark, and because there were so many people crowding round the fence.

Papi had been lifted right off the ground and tossed about like a rag doll on one of the bull's horns, which had penetrated his ribcage and punctured a lung. There was blood coming out of the hole in his chest in time with his breathing. It sounded like he was drowning—which he was.

Pass the bottle. Aren't you having another one?

Suit yourself.

Well, after that, things got pretty out of control. My mother was going crazy. She was screaming at the Indian guy who'd been arguing with my dad at the same time as trying to talk to him and hold his chest to keep the blood in and hollering at people to call an ambulance. The bull had gone even more crazy and had smashed up a part of the fence around the pad-dock. They had to get a load of gauchos on horses to come and shepherd it back into the pen so nobody else got hurt. I even re-member one guy running around panicking 'cause his car was red and he thought the bull would go for it if it got out.

Me?

Hang on a minute. Sorry. I'll be all right soon.

Must have gone down the wrong way.

That's better.

I got into the paddock, went over to where my mother was and knelt down to help her hold him together. I put my hands on his chest. He smiled at me, and winked. He said, "Fabi, did you see how scared that bull was? Can you see I'm not scared? I'm gonna be fine."

Then he coughed, in this bubbly way, and said, "I need a drink of water." You know when we used to go swimming, and hold our breaths, and then shout as loud as we could at each other under the surface? It sounded like that. His voice was all liquidy and gurgling.

"Fabi, go find some water," said my mother.

I didn't move.

She screamed.

"Fabi, go! You aren't helping. Go get some water from somewhere then come back here. Has ANYONE called this ambulance?"

I ran off without looking back, away from the field, away from the car, towards the church and the cottages. I ran so fast, I almost forgot why I was running at all.

Of course, all the houses were shut up. Why had I come over here? It was stupid. Everyone was over at the fiesta. The street by the little whitewashed chapel, with its simple wooden cross on top, was dark and silent. All the huts where the workers lived were shut up and bolted. There was nothing alive over there but a tethered llama, and a dog lying behind a cactus eating a bit of pork fat he'd scored at the party. I looked back and saw people running around in between all the golds and reds of the fiesta.

I heard the noise of cars revving off down the mountainside.

I think I went into the chapel because I thought I might be able to bring him some holy water. If he didn't want to drink it he could put it on his chest, and then he'd be okay, I thought.

The door slammed shut behind me and I could hardly see

anything, apart from a couple of fold-up wooden chairs, and metal shining in the dark where the altar must have been. My breathing was loud, and echoing. The air was wet and dusty.

I heard a massive bang, and the windows came to life. There were streaks of red and yellow lightning in the sky outside, and the walls of the chapel lit up like a flash bulb. My eyes weren't ready for it and it seemed incredibly bright.

The light illuminated a pair of eyes inches from my own. I gasped, and stepped backwards in shock, then saw a painted tear on a cheek and realized that I'd been standing right in front of a wooden statue of the Virgin. Red light sparkled on her silver crown.

There was another flash. I knew what was happening now. Some asshole had started letting off fireworks outside, even though my dad was lying there wounded.

This time I saw something else. A man and a woman standing holding each other in a corner. The guy had a long black ponytail, and wore a wide-brimmed hat. I glimpsed the girl's scared face behind his shoulder. His bare arse in the red light. Her arms in their frilly white blouse across his back.

I turned away to the door. I fell forwards through it and left it open, running back towards the paddock, slipping around in the mud as I went. I was frightened, but more about not having found any water for my dad than anything else.

I got back to the paddock and climbed over the fence. I ran towards the crowd of people and pushed through them to get to the middle.

They weren't there.

I started shouting: where are they? Where are my parents?

Some Indian woman came over and said they went. They

looked for you. Your Papi is hurt, so your Mami drove off to meet the ambulance halfway up the mountain. It's a winding road. She's going to meet the ambulance as it comes up, put your Papi in it, then come back up here to get you. Then you're gonna go back down with her and see your Papi, and it'll all be okay. Stay with me, *cariño*. We'll wait for them to come back. Won't be a minute. Won't be any time at all.

She had a kind face, all beaten up with the wind like the older Indians. She put a cold hand on my cheek.

Pour me another.

So we waited.

I sat in the old woman's front room in her little cottage. She showed me how her loom worked. We sat there for hours. She made me tea, and put *MacGyver* on the TV for me. Funny. Why do I remember that?

They never came.

Never came.

Car flew off the road, and pheeeeeeuuuuuuw . . . Poof.

Burnt right on up. Lucky they'd called an ambulance, huh? Lucky one was already on its way. Not much they could do about it though. All gone.

Just like that shot of tequila.

They found the car at the bottom of a steep valley, all burnt out, upside down. My father was inside it. But they never found my mother. She wasn't in there.

And everyone says she's dead but me.

Sorry.

I've never told anybody this before. Oh, fuck. Shit.

This isn't going to happen. I never cry, man.

I *never* cry.

'Nother tequila's what I need.

Fuck you. I can take it. Shit on you, you mother-pricking English asshole fuck.

Suarez is a bastard. He says there's no way she could've survived. But anything could've happened to her. She could've been kidnapped by *guerrilleros.* Anything. Could be anywhere.

Anti, I'm gonna throw up now.

Well, looky what we have here.

Talk of the devil.

Here comes Suarez now.

Shi—

six

Fabián leaned sideways as pale vomit leapt out of him like a jaguar. The headlights of Byron's car lit up the walls as brightly as any firework flashes inside a hacienda chapel. Any second now, the key would be in the lock. But Fabián wasn't moving, and there was nothing to be done.

When Suarez ambled in, he seemed momentarily delighted to see us enjoying ourselves. He started to say something like why didn't we have any music. Then he must have smelled the metallic edge to the air, seen the bottle on the table, noticed Fabián slumped in his seat. He stopped in mid-sentence and slowly brought up the house lighting on what was a pretty ghastly scene.

There was a horrible pause. The disco lights were still stuck in their meandering cycle. Suarez turned them off before speaking.

"You should never leave two male dogs on their own. They always have to go out looking for trouble," he said. "Dog and a bitch, fine; bitch and a bitch, no problem; but never two dogs."

He walked over and peered at Fabián, who was pretending to be out cold.

"You are a pair of dogs," he said, in conclusion. "Well, I won't be asking Eulalia to clean up all this glass and puke, so you can do it yourselves in the morning. I think I will, however, ask Byron to carry this degenerate up to his bed. Wait here, Anti."

Suarez left the library.

I sat staring at a slick coating of drool on Fabián's cheek, which shone in the unfamiliar light of the room. He mumbled, and a pendulum of slobber waggled beneath his chin in time to its movements.

Suarez reappeared in the doorway. Byron's massive face loomed behind him, wearing a broad grin of anticipation. He was going to love this.

Byron walked across the library and spread himself on his haunches in front of the sprawled Fabián. With one arm under his thighs and the other holding the scruff of his neck, he heaved Fabián over his shoulders. His plaster cast knocking lightly against Byron's back, Fabián was surprised into conversation.

"What? Jesus," he said. "Oh hello, Byron, you big bastard. Don't shoot me."

I could hear Byron talking to himself as he ferried his burden up the stairs. "This one's always been a puker," he said, chuckling with every step. "Always puking."

Suarez and I were alone.

"Suarez, I'm so sorry . . ." I began.

"Don't worry," he said. "I know it wasn't your fault. It's my fault for being so liberal with my alcohol."

He sat down, taking Fabián's place at the table. The story-teller's chair.

"Have you had enough to drink, Anti?" he said, inspecting the bottle.

I said nothing. Suarez picked up a shot glass, messy with Fabián's drunken fingerprints, and poured himself a tot of tequila.

I was about to launch into another apology, but Suarez seemed more sad than angry.

I waited for him to speak first. He sat, curling his lower lip, gazing at the spray of vomit on the floor, evaluating the problem.

"Fabián is quite unhappy at the moment, isn't he?" he said, finally.

I paused, then said, "Yes, he is."

I was too drunk to think of anything but the truth.

"It's difficult for me sometimes to tell when he's going through a bad patch. I do try to let him have time with his own thoughts. I don't believe in smothering people—especially given that I am his uncle and not his father."

"We were talking about his parents tonight. That's why he drank so much."

"Tell me what he told you," said Suarez, sitting up straight. "It's been too long since I talked about it with him properly."

I paused. This was an uncomfortable enough conversation already, and the smell of vomit had begun to dominate the room.

"He thinks that you don't care what happened to his mother. He thinks she has disappeared, or been kidnapped, or is wandering in the mountains with amnesia," I blurted out.

Why I added that last possibility, I don't know. It was an explanation that had popped into my head while Fabián was talking, not something that he'd ever suggested.

"Sorry," I added, uselessly.

"Believe me, Anti, there is nothing that would bring me greater joy than to see my beautiful little sister again," said Suarez. "It quite destroyed my life when she died."

I felt awkward hearing this degree of honesty from an adult, and particularly from Suarez, who was normally so in control.

"But have no doubts," he said, looking directly at me. "She is quite definitely dead."

I swallowed uncomfortably. Suarez went on talking.

"If I thought even for a second that she was alive, then believe me, I would be ripping up the Andes from their roots, spending every penny I had, in order to find her. But guerrillas don't just kidnap people without asking for a ransom. She isn't some *desaparecida,* you know. She isn't like your Lord Lucan." First Lord Byron, now this. Suarez seemed to have a thing about English lords. "My sister is dead. That is a fact. I wish it wasn't as much as poor Fabián does, but it is the case. He just doesn't like to believe it because they never found a body."

"What happened to her?"

"I thought he told you. His parents' car went off the edge of a cliff in the mountains, and they both died. There is no way that his mother could have survived. He thinks she is missing because her body was never recovered from the wreckage. But these things do happen. The car turns itself over so many times that a body is thrown from it on the way down, into the undergrowth, and . . ." He cleared his throat and looked away.

"I'm sorry, Suarez. I'm really sorry," I said, feeling young, embarrassed, inadequate.

"It's fine, Anti. Really. You can see why he wants to think otherwise, but there is no other possible explanation. There were eyewitnesses who saw the car go off the road. It was only a dirt track, and the rain had eroded the edge of it. The police think the passenger door wasn't properly closed when they went over the edge, and that is why my sister fell out. They scoured the mountainside for her, but the car had fallen a long way and the hill was thickly covered with vegetation. That's the only reason. But you can see that there is no chance that she survived."

He drained his glass of tequila, took out a wide, red and gold packet of Dunhill International and lit one. Then he pushed the packet across the table towards me, a cigarette extended from it. I took one.

"Just for tonight," he said. "I doubt your mother would be pleased if she knew I was offering smokes to her asthmatic son. Starting from tomorrow, I'm starting a new regime with you boys." He winked at me before continuing. "No, Anti, my sister has not been kidnapped. She has not lost her memory. She won't be coming back. I prefer to see it that she decided halfway down the mountainside not to continue with the car, but to fly off on her own to someplace new. And I think that she's still flying around there, very happy indeed. That is why we haven't found her. That's how I like to see it."

He sat, apparently gazing at his flying sister amid the dance of cigarette smoke above the table, relishing the vision.

"Suarez," I said. "Did you say she fell out of the passenger side of the car?"

"Of course. Fabián's father always drove them everywhere. My sister never even learned how to drive."

"But surely his father was too hurt to drive a car?"

"Too hurt? What's he told you? They'd gone up to the mountains on a hiking trip. That's all we really know. It's that not-knowing part of things that makes it so difficult for Fabián to understand. He was staying with me for the weekend when it happened. They left him here because he'd been ill and was too weak to do the walk they wanted to do that day. The next thing either of us knew, they were gone. That's very often the way it happens, Anti. People just aren't there any more."

Suarez twisted the end of his cigarette against the plastic of the tequila tray to get rid of some ash. He looked at me again, gesturing with the glowing cone.

"If Fabián hadn't been sick, he would have gone with them in that car. That's what I always tell him. He should feel happy about that, not guilty. It means that his parents are living on through him."

"There was no bullfight, then," I said, almost to myself.

"Bullfight? Fabi has never even been to a bullfight. I took him to a harvest festival once in the hills where there were some kids fooling around with bulls, but he's never set foot in a proper bullring."

"I see. That makes sense," I said.

"Would you like to go?" Suarez continued. "Would that cheer him up, do you think? I'm not sure he enjoyed it when we went before. One poor boy got spiked by the bull, and it quite upset Fabi at the time. But if you think it's what he would like, I would happily take you both."

"No, I don't think so. I don't think it would help," I said.

"I think it might remind Fabián too much of his father, somehow."

"Ha. A likely story. Good old Félix Morales. A nice guy, but no bullfighter." Suarez drove his cigarette end into the tray in front of him and dusted his hands free of ash.

"What was he like, then, Fabián's father?" I asked, not wanting to expose Fabián's story any further than I had already.

"Well," said Suarez. "Some thought he wasn't right for my sister—they said he was too obsessed with class, too paranoid. What you would call having a chip on your shoulder, right?"

I nodded dumbly.

"But I always disagreed," Suarez went on. "As far as I was concerned, all that fear made him stronger." He poured himself more tequila. "My own father, God rest his soul, once said of Félix, when it became obvious that he was going to marry my sister, that he was 'the kind of kid who lies awake at night, terrified that all of his toys are going to come to life.'"

He drained the tequila, wincing slightly. "The trouble with Félix's son, of course—the trouble with my nephew—is that he lies awake too much as well. Not because he's afraid of his toys coming to life, but because he's hoping as hard as he can that they *will*, and he wants to catch them in the act."

I got up.

"Suarez, I'm going to clean this up now. It stinks. We shouldn't leave it till the morning."

"You can leave it for Fabián if you want. I know it's his mess more than it is yours," said Suarez, waving a vague hand in the direction of the vomit.

"I'll do it," I said.

———

Having fumbled around trying several wrong doors, one of which opened on to a startling menagerie of stuffed animals that I'd never even seen before, I found Eulalia's cleaning cupboard. I took out some blue rubber gloves, a bucket and some disinfectant, and was on my knees scrubbing the black and white squares of the library floor when I heard a sound at the door. Suarez, it seemed, had returned for another drink before he went to bed. He'd changed into a plush red dressing-gown. As he crossed the room to sit back at the table, I thought I noticed him stumbling slightly, although it might just as easily have been my intoxication as his own that gave me that impression.

"You better just tell me what Fabián said to you tonight," he said. "This whole episode has worried me considerably, and I think I need to know what's going on in his mind."

I was cornered. I pulled off the rubber gloves, dropped the scrubbing brush back into the bucket and sat back down at the table.

I gave him as good an account as I could of the bullfight story. Again, in my drunken state, I developed the ending to include the possibility of Fabián's mother being missing with amnesia. I was losing track of who had said what.

When I finished, Suarez said nothing, and I worried that I had got Fabián into trouble.

"I'm sure," I said, hoping to limit the damage, "that Fabián doesn't really believe all of this himself. It's probably just a way for him to make sense of what happened, and to tell me a good story. I don't think you need worry about it that much."

"The problem with Fabián," said Suarez, "is that you never know whether or not he believes what he says. I sometimes worry that he's so good at talking nonsense that he deludes even himself." He frowned down at the table. "Perhaps I should have a word with him. It sounds to me as if this is getting out of hand."

I began to panic. If this conversation got back to Fabián, he would be furious.

"Do you really think that's necessary?" I ventured.

"Don't you?" said Suarez.

"I'm sure that deep down he knows the truth, even if he does let some details run away with him at times," I said. At this point I would have said anything to stop my betrayal being exposed.

"As you know, I'm the last person on earth who would tell people what they can and can't believe," said Suarez. "So long as you think he isn't deluded in a way that is *dangerous*."

I wondered what Suarez would make of Fabián's belief that he had seen a vision of his mother on a carnival float at the Easter parade. But mentioning that was out of the question. I felt in enough trouble already.

"I don't," I said.

"You're sure?"

"Positive."

My certainty cheered him. He just wanted *someone* to tell him things weren't serious, and, inconceivably enough, he appeared to have allowed that person to be me. The responsibility made me feel even more uncomfortable.

"You're right, of course," he continued. "Sometimes it doesn't hurt to let people believe what they want to believe. I haven't forgotten how distraught I was myself at the loss of my sister. It took me some time to accept that she was gone when they couldn't find her body in that car." He sighed. "Real life can be so very *disappointing* at times, don't you think?"

I thought of Fabián. *What would the unimaginative person say?*

"Looking back," said Suarez, "I am probably in no small part to blame for Fabián's state of mind. If I couldn't admit it to myself at the time, then I doubt I was capable of admitting it to him."

"But you accept it now," I offered, feeling more out of my depth than ever.

"I accept it now. Fabián does not. It may take some time. But let us not forget the words of my friend Miguel de Torre: 'Grief asks different questions of us all.' If, as you say, I have no need to confront Fabián about all of this," said Suarez, who now, strangely enough, appeared to be smiling, "then I suggest that you allow him to continue to believe what he wants. Up to a point."

I started to speak, but he cut me off.

"Right now, however, it is *my* belief that you should forget about this conversation altogether, and go to bed. You have a lot of tequila to sleep off." He tousled my hair with fat, splayed fingers.

"You won't tell him, then?" I asked. "You won't tell him what I told you?"

"I promise not to mention it. I am trusting you when you say that I don't need to. *And* trusting you to tell me if the situation changes."

At the foot of the stairs, he turned, gave me a playful punch on the arm and said, "You never know. There's always the chance that what Fabián says about his mother may be right!"

My last memory before I passed out was of his eyes, sparkling insanely in the gloom.

The following morning, I woke, impacted into the sheets, to bright light and hideous noise. I had forgotten to draw the blinds, and Eulalia was vigorously cleaning right outside my door. The plastic pipe of her vacuum cleaner clattered and chimed against the metal banisters with all the discord of a child systematically thumping piano keys.

Suarez was in a spry mood. When I made it downstairs, I found him sitting in a bright pool of sunshine at the kitchen table, wearing a lurid short-sleeved shirt and smoking a Dunhill over his coffee. Fabián cowered beside him and barely lifted his head when I walked in. He probably knew that I'd heard him retching through most of the early hours of the morning.

Suarez took pleasure in presenting us both with a huge and traumatizing breakfast: a tray of wobbling poached eggs and blood sausage, drenched in bright-red chili sauce.

"If I remember rightly from my days as a party animal, you must both be starving after last night," he said. "No, nothing for me, thank you. You boys dig in. Eat it *all.*"

He sat grinning, and continued to smoke throughout the ordeal. Nor would he allow us to open a window in spite of the heat. There was to be no escape. His anger from the night before had apparently vanished, but at a price: eating the breakfast, it seemed, was the debt we owed to Suarez for the fun we'd had at his expense.

The eggs looked up at me like prized-out eyes. The sausage was heavily spiced. I barely made it through, but I fared better than Fabián, who got halfway through his plateful before mumbling, "No one should be subjected to this," and taking flight to vomit once again.

When it was over, I got the bus home as arranged, took the service lift up to the apartment and went straight to bed.

seven

The week passed, and Fabián barely spoke to me. I assumed he was embarrassed about what had happened and would re-establish contact when he was ready. But it turned out that I wasn't the only victim of his volatile state of mind. On Wednesday, he caused an incident during a science class. We were usually partnered up randomly to do experiments, and Fabián had been put with Verena Hermes. I was on the other side of the room when it happened, so all I was aware of was an explosion and some shouting, but afterwards, I asked her about it.

"He's so weird these days," she said. "He just started zoning out while we were doing the experiment, inhaling the ammonia, then looking out of the window at the sky and whispering. Crazy stuff. I tried to ignore it but he was saying it right into my ear, and we were supposed to be working. I got a *zero* because of him."

"You'll bounce back. What was he whispering?"

"He just kept saying, 'Can you see her?' What a freak."

That wasn't all. I heard he'd got into a fight with someone

during a football match after school and hit the guy over the head with his plaster cast. And I'd seen him from a distance, striding round the outskirts of the playing fields, gazing up at the mountains as if he were seeing them for the first time.

On Friday afternoon, we ended up waiting outside the school gates together, and I came to the point.

"Are you going to stop this weirdness, or let me in on it?"

He ignored me.

"Well?" I said. "What's going on?"

The hostility took me by surprise. "What do you mean, *what's going on*? Why are you only interested in how I am on Fridays? Are you trying to get another invite back to my house?"

"Jesus, no. What's the matter with you? I just thought I'd see how you were."

"I'm fine. Don't worry about me."

I crunched pistachio shells listlessly under my foot.

"I'm going back to school in England soon," I said. "I just thought you should know."

He continued to scowl.

"Listen, I spoke to Suarez after you'd gone to bed—"

"Good for you. Next time you want to come over, why not just call him directly, seeing as he's such a big buddy of yours."

"Wait a minute—"

"Byron's here," said Fabián. "I'll see you Monday."

Waiting to be collected from school had never felt lonelier. I had to do something to make things right.

That weekend, my father walked into my room holding an envelope with a UK postmark. From the mollifying look on his face, I knew it was bad news.

"Aptitude tests," he said, with a shrug. "I have to time you while you do them, then send them back to the school in a special sealed envelope. All very official and self-important."

My mother was out playing tennis, so I would have to remonstrate with him. I sighed dramatically and threw my hands in the air. I hated doing this sort of thing to my father, as he was much worse than my mother at working out when I was acting up and when I was genuinely unhappy. But, unfair as it may have been, my displeasure had to be registered.

"Listen," he said. "If you really don't want to go, we'll see nearer the time. But I'm not sure if even *you* know yet what you want."

I raised an eyebrow in what I hoped was a scornfully skeptical fashion.

"Come on, mate. It's a beautiful day—you can do the tests right now out on the balcony, and I'll bring you lunch."

My shoulders were slumped as we trooped out of my room, and I walked as slowly and painfully as possible, wheezing a little as well for good measure.

"Okay," said my father. "Here's a thought. If you really want to make sure you don't have to go to this school, you could always just . . . flunk the tests."

I stopped in the corridor and looked back at him.

"You didn't hear this suggestion from me, obviously. But it strikes me that the only reason they've sent you these tests is to make sure that what they're about to take on isn't some halfwit who's had his brain wiped by two years at the International School." He lowered his voice conspiratorially. "All you have to do is *be* the halfwit."

Smiling now, and breathing freely again, I slid open the balcony doors and positioned myself at the table.

"Got a crayon?" I asked.

"That might be taking the piss a bit, I think."

I sat, observing the city. A swallow dipped low over the eaves of a house down the slope below us. Beyond that, Quito spread in its muddled way towards the foothills and slopes of venerable volcanoes. My father had left a brochure on the table while he went to find me a pen. I opened it and had a look: kids with bad hair in tweed jackets sitting around a pool table; a geek with soft stubble and a huge mole wearing unfeasible safety goggles as he squinted into a Bunsen burner; some poor myopic boy limping along with a rugby ball against a desolate backdrop of mud and bare trees. I looked up again. Sunlight ignited the crest of Cotopaxi, sending it back for magnificent reflection in the glass doors that fronted our balcony. I coughed feebly to myself and poured a cup of coffee from the pot on the table.

When my father returned, I made one final plea for clemency, but it fell on deaf ears. (If I remember rightly, it culminated in my saying, "Then my father is truly dead," the pivotal line uttered by Luke Skywalker when Darth Vader refuses to renounce the Dark Side. My father's response was both predictable and justified: "Stop being so melodramatic.") Pen poised above the paper, breathing in rarefied air tinged with sweet smog, I gazed again across the city as if it were for the last time, towards the volcanoes in the distance, and thought of Juanita. She never had problems like this.

———

My father was right, of course. I could easily have fixed my answers. Been the halfwit, and been sure of staying put. But he knew me far too well to think I would ever take that suggestion seriously. And much as I would like to say that at the time I was so concerned about Fabián's welfare that I overlooked any course of action beyond just getting the tests out of the way, that isn't what happened either. In the end, my pride won the day and, by the time I had finished the first test, I knew that I was in the process of consciously writing myself out of Ecuador. There was even—I can say it now, with the benefit of hindsight and greater self-awareness—there was even a certain masochistic pleasure to be derived from completing my own extradition document with everything that I would miss lying right there in front of me. I was deliberately expelling myself from the land of giant turtles and ice princesses, and I only had myself to blame.

That said, the problem of Fabián began to resurface in my mind before I'd even finished writing. I had to find a way of regaining his trust, especially if I was not long for this country. And no matter how much I thought about it, every course of action I considered seemed to bring me back to Miguel de Torre, and to a half-remembered, blurred image of Suarez the previous weekend. *Sometimes it doesn't hurt to let people believe what they want to believe. Real life can be so very disappointing at times.*

The tests done, and safely packaged up in their envelopes to be sent away, my father and I sat together on the balcony, eating a lunch of salty, buttery corn on the cob and playing a favorite game. It involved waiting in silence until an interesting sound came up off the city, then competing with each other to arrive at the best explanation of what had made it.

"That was a taxi driver screeching to a halt when his client wouldn't pay the bill, followed by the shot as he dispatched him using the silver-plated pistol he keeps strapped to his ankle in case of such problems," said my father.

"Bullshit," I said. "The screech was the sound of a condor that escaped from the city zoo this morning hoping to fly back to his family in the hills, and the bang was the sound of a tranquilizer dart being shot at it by his keeper, Pepe, who is terrified of being fired because he's lost two condors already this year and they are hard to come by as it is."

"Did Pepe catch the condor, then?" said my father, wiping his chin with a paper napkin as he stared distractedly ahead.

"No. It got away."

"Good. That's good."

"Subconsciously, Pepe is allowing the escapes to succeed because he believes he was a condor in a previous life."

"Pepe is a fool."

We sat in silence for a while, listening to the city's equivalent of white noise: the steady exhalation of traffic, punctuated by the occasional, submerged blast of a car horn as some distant, chaotic moment unfolded.

"I've got something I've been meaning to ask you," I said.
"Shoot."

"Where do you think someone would end up if they were found, say, wandering around in the mountains with amnesia, and nobody claimed them? I mean, if it were back home, they'd end up in some hospital, and there'd be all that missing-persons stuff going on, all that, right? But there are still some pretty wild areas of Ecuador, aren't there?"

"Sure are."

"So it's possible that someone could be missing for quite a long time—years, even—up in a mountain village or something, without anyone knowing where they were and thinking they were probably dead. Can you remember any examples of that sort of thing happening?"

"I've read stories about people being found living whole new lives because they lost their memory, but mainly in books. I'm not sure if it happens much in real life."

"I'm not interested in real life. It can be very disappointing. You would say, though, that in *theory* at least, it's possible?"

"It's possible. Why are you asking me this?"

"It's for something I'm writing for school," I said. "A story."

"A story? Didn't know that was your kind of thing. Well, I don't know if there's any set procedure when someone is found. But I think . . . What I think is that there *should* be a special hospital set up somewhere especially for all the people with amnesia. They could stay together in safety, and then if you thought you'd lost someone, all you'd have to do would be to go along and see if they were there. That would be good, wouldn't it?"

A plane came in to land right down in the throat of the city—one sight I had never properly got used to.

"Yes, it would. It would be very good. Do you reckon anywhere like that exists?"

"I doubt it—it would be pretty specialized. Besides, who's going to pay for the upkeep of the patients if nobody knows who they are?" He chuckled. "You know, I think your mother might have a point about how being educated out here isn't doing you any favors . . .

"Aha," he said, springing up as he heard her key in the lock, "now *that* sounded to me like the return home of a triumphant women's tennis champion. Do you want to tell her the good news that you've done your tests, or shall I?"

"I'll leave that pleasure to you. One more thing, though: can you get hold of blank newsprint paper?"

My parents knew about Fabián and his missing parents but, luckily, I hadn't yet updated them on the various recent goings-on—mainly because I hadn't reached any firm conclusions myself about what I believed. Consequently, when I outlined to my father the story of a bullfight, followed by a car coming off a road in the mountains, he wasn't suspicious in the slightest. Quite the contrary. In fact, all he said was, "Sounds a bit fantastic to me." Eventually, though, with his help, and without arousing too much suspicion, I wrote something vaguely journalistic. Then I just had to make it look right.

Getting hold of the right paper was only the first step. I then had to try to print on it in a convincing typeface. I was no master forger, but it's surprising how much you can accomplish with a good printer, the right sort of paper and the spillage of a mug of tea (that particular trick was something I knew about having read about the forgery of the Hitler diaries). I even managed to photocopy an old car advert on to the reverse of the page so it looked as if it had been taken from a real newspaper, so that by the end, I had made a pretty convincing simulacrum. It wouldn't have taken an expert very long to work out that it wasn't real, but I reasoned that I didn't have to work too hard: the Emperor's new clothes were never described to him in detail because he was so ready to believe in them.

Luckily enough, Fabián approached me himself to make his peace on the day it was ready, which meant that I didn't even have to think of a pretext to show it to him. He walked over as we were breaking for lunch after the morning's lessons the following Thursday.

"What's all this about you leaving, then?" he said.

"It might not happen. But even if it does, I'll be back for the holidays—just not for the boring bits in between."

"I see." He sniffed absentmindedly. "Sorry about last week. All this shit with my parents. It gets frustrating."

An apology. That was new. Perhaps there was no need to go through with the plan at all. But I couldn't lose my nerve now.

"I wanted to talk to you about that," I said. "I found something, and I think it might be important. It was in a stack of newspapers Dad brought home from work."

We were in the canteen by then, which was hot and steamy from great vats of rice and beans on the counter, and when we had got our food and were sitting at an isolated table in the corner, I got out the press cutting and laid it out for him on the table. It was creased and stained. It looked as if it had lain in a folder somewhere for a few years.

Fabián read it through several times. For a few moments, his eyes were spyholes on the struggle in his head. They flared from anger to incomprehension and back again. Then he must have realized that he was losing too much cool, because he checked himself and organized his features into a less vulnerable expression, closer to touched amusement.

I was taking a big risk here. In spite of whatever outward reaction he chose to manifest to the cutting, I could have no idea what its real effect on him would be. For all I knew, it could have meant the end of our friendship.

He looked back at the cutting, then up at me.

"What the fuck are you doing?" he said.

"I—"

"You've been checking up on me?"

I paused.

"I wanted to show you that I believed you," I said, carefully. We looked at each other for a while longer, uncertain of how to proceed.

"I see," he said.

This is what was in front of us:

El Diario, February 29, 1989

DOUBLE TRAGEDY AT ZAPARO FESTIVAL

IBARRA: A man and his wife may both have perished on Friday when their car plunged from the road to the Hacienda La Reina. They were rushing to the hospital to attend to the man's injuries following a freak mauling sustained during a bullfight at the hacienda's Zaparo Festival celebrations. The man did not survive the accident, and his body was found in the wreckage of the car. His wife is yet to be found, and so it is not known whether or not she also lost her life in the tragedy. The couple has not been named.

OPENING OF NEW AMNESIA CLINIC DIVIDES BEACHSIDE COMMUNITY

GUAYAQUIL: Mixed reactions yesterday greeted the opening by local eccentric Dr. Victor Menosmal of his new, privately funded Amnesia Clinic on the outskirts of the coastal town of Pedrascada. Menosmal, who has no formal medical training beyond a master's degree in psychology, has long been obsessed with the problem of memory loss, and upon receipt of a large inheritance following the demise of his father, vowed to dedicate himself to the study of the problem. The clinic, says Menosmal, will be part research institute, part safe

"Yes," said Fabián. "I see."

I looked down at the congealing beans on my plate.

"You say you got this through your dad?" Fabián went on.

"That's right," I said.

"I never saw the newspapers at the time. I didn't know it had been reported."

"Well, it was. There it is, in black and white."

"Yes. There it is."

"Yes."

I swiveled the cutting round in my favor and pointed with a fork.

"Interesting about this Amnesia Clinic, too," I ventured.

"Yes," said Fabián, staring at his food. "Although that name is a bit ridiculous. 'Menosmal.' Can anybody really be called that? It would be like an English person being called, I don't know, 'Justaswell' or something."

"I think I've heard it somewhere before. It might be French."

"Right. I see. Thanks for showing me. Can I keep this?"

"Of course. It's for you."

He folded up the cutting and slid it carefully into his wallet. Then, after silently shoveling in his food for a while, he said, "So. What are we doing this weekend?"

eight

I meant it as a gesture. An elegant, understated way to apologize to Fabián for having doubted him, and an endorsement of the stories he'd told me. Nothing more. I thought I'd left so many holes in the articles, not least the absurd name I'd given to the doctor, that both my authorship and the intentions behind it would be quietly obvious—although, of course, to have said this out loud would have been against the spirit of the exercise and destroyed it in the process. So when his reaction to the cutting was one of apparent vindication, and when he didn't question anything about its contents beyond the doctor's stupid name, I assumed that my apology had been both identified and accepted. Privately, we would pretend it was real. It would be taken as read that Dr Menosmal and his Amnesia Clinic existed, and he would enter the pantheon of fictional heroes who'd lived side by side in our minds with real, historical figures when we were younger. Churchill, Bolívar and Pelé were all very well. We believed in Dracula, Batman and Han Solo just as much—not because of any assessment of how real they were, but because of how much they seemed to us to *deserve* to exist.

For a while there, it seemed, we had come dangerously close to growing up, but thanks to my tactical bit of forgery we could fall back into our old habit of cheerfully talking rubbish. I was so busy being relieved about this that it never occurred to me for a second that he might *believe* any of it.

On Friday, Suarez arrived late and brimming with sarcasm about the events of two weeks before. True to his word, he made no reference to our exchange in the library after Fabián had been hauled off to bed.

"Anti, how wonderful to see you again. If I had known you two hell-raisers were getting together, I would have ordered in another case of tequila, or some whores. Well, it's short notice, but we might get lucky. Hand me the telephone directory, will you?"

After several remarks of this kind, we escaped to watch television in Fabián's room.

On the surface, it was a normal evening—exactly what I had feared lost following my fall-out with Fabián, and exactly what I knew I would miss most when I left the country. We discussed the merits of a low-caliber horror and soft-porn film on cable TV and traded a couple of lame lies about girls at school. But there was something listless about our behavior, as if we had been asked to act out our customary roles and lacked enthusiasm for the task. I'd already felt the urge to escape this familiar room, with its well-worn videotapes and its over-ogled pin-ups, even before I noticed that Fabián was leafing through a road atlas.

"So," he said, "where shall we go?"

"What do you mean?"

"I thought you were planning to live a little more before you get locked away for ever in Englishness."

I had relayed to Fabián some of the details of my experience during the power cut in the lift. Not the full amount—not the tears, for example—but some.

"Hand me the atlas, then," I said. "I'll have a look."

I envisaged a day trip in the company of Suarez to climb Cotopaxi, or at best an illicit afternoon's boozing in some highland bar. I leafed through the atlas and suggested to Fabián a few places we might go within easy reach of Quito. Otavalo. Baños. Cayambe. This amused him.

"Isn't it obvious?" he said. "We should go to Pedrascada."

There were plenty of reasons why I had chosen to position my made-up Amnesia Clinic in Pedrascada. It sounded like an exotic, faraway place. The fact that it was a surfing beach seemed cool to me. The prospect of Francis Drake's sunken treasure had fired some youthful corner of my imagination. But a fourth, less obvious reason was that in spite of having seen it mentioned in Suarez's encyclopedia, I had been unable to find it on any of the maps of Ecuador we had at home. It had seemed to be a neat solution: put the imaginary hospital in the place that doesn't exist. I had been pleased with my ingenuity. I would soon learn that there are many places in South America that don't make it on to maps.

"You think we should go to Pedrascada."

"Why not? Why choose somewhere random?"

"Well, okay, but . . . it doesn't seem to be in this atlas."

"I know where it is. I've heard about the surfing beach there."

"But—"

"Just think about it for a second. A whole hospital full of people who don't know who they are, or where they came from. Wouldn't you like to see that?"

My anxiety must have shown. He grabbed the atlas back and said, "I know what you're going to say. I'm not crazy. I know this place may not be there any more, if it ever existed at all. I know that even if it is there, the chances of us finding my mother there are virtually zero. But don't you think it's worth a look anyway? Hmm?"

He was testing me. He wanted to see if my resolve would fall at the first hurdle, and I couldn't let that happen. It would invalidate all the effort I had made to show faith in him in the first place.

"Yes, I do," I said, carefully. "That's why I showed you the article to begin with."

"There you go. We should go to Pedrascada. We've got to go *somewhere* before you leave, and it might as well be there. Besides," he said, lowering his voice, "I'm sick of being stuck here. Suarez has been driving me crazy ever since that night we got drunk. Asking me if I'm okay, if I want to talk about anything. He even invited me to go see a *bullfight,* the weirdo."

I felt blood rushing to my face and looked away in embarrassment, but Fabián carried on talking. Either he hadn't made the link between Suarez's bullfighting question and me, or else he had unearthed my betrayal and was using it to lever me into going along with his plan.

"I want to get away from him for a while," he concluded. "It will be great. We can go whoring."

So I wasn't off the hook after all. I could only hope that, like so many of the plans we made together, this one would wither in the light of good old feasibility. Skipping school was easily done, but to justify a long absence from our respective guardians we'd have to do something virtually impossible. We would have to lie to Suarez. Given what a connoisseur of bullshit he was, he would be as alert to a bad fib as a gourmand to a duff cut of meat. With that in mind, I decided it was safe to play along with Fabián for now without fear of having lost face later on when the plan died anyway.

"Okay. Let's say we do go. How the hell do we get down there?"

"I know how to do it. Bus-train-bus. Or possibly bus-train-bus-bus-taxi-boat, depending on how lucky we get. Don't worry about that. You can get anywhere if you have the money. Leave the logistics to me."

There was a rap on the door. Fabián thrust the road atlas towards me and I bundled it under his duvet before leaping into what I hoped was a nonchalant position in front of the TV. Suarez came in, amused at how obviously we were hiding something, and gave us time to relax into our assumed poses more convincingly before he spoke.

"I am prepared to offer you a truce. There are two cold beers downstairs. They are yours if you want them. But at least come and tell me about whatever vicious scheme it is that you are hatching up here."

We trooped down the stairs behind him.

Back then, I thought Suarez was the sort of person we could tell anything to. I also imagined that he would love the concept of the Amnesia Clinic as much as we did, and for the same reasons: for its appeal as an idea; for the fact that such things should exist in the world. If we'd simply told him what we were planning to do, he might even have sanctioned it. But Fabián did not perceive his uncle as I did. Even though I was the person who had given it to Fabián, the idea of the Amnesia Clinic was his now, and he would hoard it, away from Suarez, alongside every other secret he'd manufactured to obscure the dreary, awful truth. In spite of this, I thought that being confronted by Suarez and his chilled, conciliatory bottles of Pilsener would make it very difficult for Fabián to try to deceive him. I expected that Fabián would relax as usual into the cozy fug of stories in Suarez's library and let his mind wander from Pedrascada, as it had from so much else. It was not the last time that I would underestimate him completely.

"So, boys," said Suarez, his beetle-crushers pounding across the polished hall floor and into the kitchen, "what are you planning? If it's a military coup, then let me tell you, there are some very important dos and don'ts."

"We weren't going to tell you," said Fabián, suddenly downcast as we entered the kitchen.

"Weren't going to tell me what? Sit down, sit down," said Suarez, setting the beer bottles down on the table for us.

"We—" Fabián looked miserably towards me. "We might as well tell him, I suppose."

I shrugged. It was genuine. I had no idea what he was up to.

"We're supposed to be going away on this school trip next week. Visiting Inca ruins. Participating in an Indian festival. Some stupid cultural awareness trip. We were just trying to work out what we could do to get out of going. Anti says his parents would never write him a sick note, but I told him you've done it for me before. Couldn't you find some way to get us out of it?"

Even by Fabián's standards, it was a spectacular double bluff, and Suarez's response couldn't have worked more in our favor. First, he reproved Fabián for blowing his cover on the sick notes, and said that he would think twice before writing him another one. Then he really got into his stride. As he spoke, he paced the room and poked a plump finger repeatedly in our direction. His words were punctuated by tiny flurries of cigarette ash that fell in time to his emphatic hand gestures.

"A word of advice: next time, don't try and get me to lie for you on the basis that staying here to fester in front of American television is a more worthwhile pursuit than exploring one of the most extraordinary cultures the world has known—and, what's more, the culture that still defines the country you live in, contrary to many people's best efforts. Really, for two imaginative boys like you, I find it pathetic. I'm being perfectly serious about this. You have to take a more active role in your own education, Fabián, otherwise you might as well leave school now and graduate straight to washing dishes. As for you, Anti: when you go back to England, people will ask you, 'What was it like in South America?' Do you really want to tell them that the most interesting thing you saw when you lived here was on the HBO network?"

By the time he was finished, he had told us in no uncertain terms that we would go on the school trip, that we would enjoy it immensely, and that he expected a full report from both of us when we got back on the reasons why we had found it an enriching experience. He asked us when we were leaving.

"This Wednesday, coming back Sunday night," said Fabián, almost grinning. He was so pleased with himself that he was barely able to maintain his moody, adolescent façade, but just as Suarez looked back in his direction he managed to reassemble it. As for me, my only problem was not looking as terrified as I felt about the direction in which things were going.

"Oh, please. Stop looking so pathetic," said Suarez, to both of us. "You'll have a great time."

"If you say so," said Fabián. "We'll try."

There are plenty of ways I could defend not having spoken out at this point, before anything dangerous happened.

I could say that I didn't think we'd ever actually make it down to Pedrascada.

I could say that I still believed Fabián saw the newspaper cutting as another act of the ongoing pantomime between us, and so wouldn't mind even if we did get there and he found out that the Amnesia Clinic didn't exist.

I could say that my friend seemed happy again, and that was enough for me.

I could even say that I thought I was in some way following Suarez's drunken advice to me on the night of the tequila incident.

Any of these statements might hold water to some extent, but I know now that none of them is the real reason why I said nothing and allowed the trip to go ahead. The truth is that I envied Fabián the world he had created for himself, with its Easter visions and its bloodshed in misty mountain bullrings. This would be my last opportunity to take a proper excursion to that world. I wanted to break in and inhabit it while I could, before it was lost to me for ever.

And I was terrified to the point of paralysis.

nine

Names seem more and more important to me the older I get. Take, for example, the shipping region of Finisterre, which no longer exists. Its name is derived from the Latin, *finis terrae*, because early sailors thought they had reached the ends of the earth when they strayed into its waters. The bus station in Old Quito is called the *Terminal Terrestre*, which strikes me now as an interesting echo of the same idea. That name is derived from the cozier notion of reaching your final destination, but when Fabián and I arrived there after school on Wednesday afternoon, and I saw it for the first time, I wouldn't have questioned the suggestion that I was reaching the end of the world as I knew it. Young Indian girls and their siblings, or children, sat in corners, hoping for food or sucres. Beggars plaintively waved leprous stumps. Travelers and businessmen ignored them as if they were drawings on the walls. As if in response to this indifference, one girl of about my own age sat against the wall with her turquoise skirt spread before her, tapping monotonously with a coin on the greasy but empty metal meal-tray in her lap. I couldn't decide whether this small but determined assertion of power over her environment was intended to attract the attention of potential philanthropists, or just to remind herself she was still here. Or maybe it was no announcement at all—maybe she was just passing the time. I realized that, in fact, I was in no position to draw any conclusions about this place, which made being there seem all the more exciting and dangerous. We were about to jump.

That name, *Terminal Terrestre*. It could mean more than the ends of the earth. It could mean "the end of all things earthly." There's life in that name, and possibility. It's a hub, a convergence of threads, a decision yet to be made. The air felt as thick with possibility there as it was with the smells of frying, with dirt, with voices.

Plenty more good names could be found within the building itself: bus companies called *Flota Imbabura* and *Macuchi,* their syllables evocative of condors and volcanoes, operated out of concrete kiosks that lined the interior walls. Ticket touts bearing the different company logos on their short-sleeved shirts prowled the concourses, stalking customers. They bellowed the destinations they peddled as if they thought their enthusiasm for a particular place might actually influence your choice of where to go. Tulcán. Riobamba. Guayaquil.

Fabián had gone off to buy tickets. I stood nervously in the center of the concourse, wondering whether we really were going to do this but not quite panicking. If we decided tomorrow, halfway through the journey, not to go through with it, then we could still come back, and all we would have to do would be to formulate a satisfactory explanation as to why our trip had been curtailed. My parents had accepted without question the story that we were going on a school excursion; all that was left was to make sure the alarm wasn't raised at school when we didn't turn up on Thursday and Friday. Fabián had forged a sick note that Verena would deliver, and I had pleaded a family trip away. I think I remember saying it was the Queen's birthday, although looking back now I can't believe anyone swallowed that. Whatever reason I had given, with surprising ease, we were now covered until Monday. We could go anywhere we wanted.

It would have been easy for me to borrow a proper duffel bag or suitcase for the trip from my parents. But for some reason, thinking I would be giving too much away if I involved them in my packing, I had decided instead just to stuff a few changes of clothes into my canvas school bag. Fabián, on the other hand, had appeared at school that morning with a serious-looking rucksack, and I felt badly prepared as a result. Nevertheless, there was something exhilarating about embarking on a journey with so little baggage—it was an early sign of what has become an almost obsessive desire in me to shed any dead weight I might be carrying and travel light.

An Indian woman approached me. She leaned forward under the weight of a baby she carried in a bright green shawl across her back. Her face was flecked with dirt, her skin ruddy from exposure to open air. I grasped inside my pocket for some change to give her, before realizing that all she was asking me for was the time. I took out a handful of sucres anyway, and went to buy myself a coffee. As I walked towards the café, a tout stood in my path, brandishing his sheaves of tickets like a street conjuror with cards.

"*Aaaaaaaa Ibarraibarraibarraibarraibaraaaa!*" he roared, maintaining furious eye contact with me throughout, as if I might fail to catch his drift if I didn't concentrate.

"*No voy a Ibarra,*" I said, without stopping, though giving the man an apologetic smile, in case I had offended him by not wanting to go to Ibarra. I could hear him promoting the destination to others behind me with undimmed passion as I walked up to the café counter. The coffee was instant and bitter, but warm. I went outside again, and saw Fabián moving through the crowds towards me. He seemed to tower over the people in the bus station, as if the excitement about finally being on the road had added to his presence. He had been waiting for something like this to happen for a long time.

"The bus leaves in ten minutes, and we're gonna be on it," he said. "And thanks for getting me a coffee, fuckmunch."

"You can have this one," I said, giving it to him.

He tasted it.

"See what you mean. Let's get some Cokes and stuff for the journey. It's going to be a few hours."

I was expecting, and hoping for, one of the bright, chaotic buses you saw everywhere, struggling along on the brink of collapse, belching diesel smoke and dripping with people. However, when we got outside, Fabián marched towards a brand-new monster Mercedes cruiser, with dark windows, two sets of massive rear wheels and low-slung, predatory headlights. It wasn't what I had in mind. I looked over wistfully at the real buses, where Indian men in hats and ponchos crowded together, carrying live chickens and passing their battered suitcases up to be lashed to the roof rack.

"Thought we'd travel in style," said Fabián. "We need to do this bit quickly if we're going to find somewhere to stay tonight."

I suspected that Fabián had brought more money with him than the sum we had agreed. I had virtually exhausted my savings for this.

The doors of the Mercedes hissed open.

"Bring your bag on," said Fabián, doing the same in spite of the driver, who was gesturing towards the baggage area in the coach's belly. "Then we won't have to worry."

I looked back into the terminal as if down a tunnel, at stalls selling chubby green bananas beneath a yellow electric light that seemed to shine brighter as the daylight began to fade. The cold air of the coach was making me nervous.

"Hey," said Fabián. "Get on."

I walked through the wall of air-conditioning and on inside.

We settled into gray seats of imitation leather, the bus filled up and the doors closed with a hydraulic sigh. We pulled out into the pandemonium of Friday night traffic, glided between the red roofs of Old Quito and accelerated on to the motorway. I stared at a plastic cup-holder positioned in front of me beside a pristine ashtray. It jolted up and down as we moved, as if waving goodbye. The metropolis deteriorated around us, finally dwindling to nothing, via a few shanty efforts at reassertion, and within half an hour we were in open countryside, cruising swiftly along the part of the Pan-American Highway known as the Avenida de los Volcanes.

"Sounds like someone's address," I said. "66, Avenida de los Volcanes."

"Yeah, well. It's our address from now on," mumbled Fabián, who was already dozing.

We sped south. A frantic salsa horn section played over the coach stereo at a discreet volume. The tinted windows acted like great plate-glass sunglasses, both obscuring and improving the reality outside, turning everything into an image of itself. As the sun set, the coach was flooded with red light. We shot through roadside villages of breeze-block homes. Pale dogs scrapped in the dust; Indians walked hunched over with grain sacks—the scenes whipped across the glass and receded quickly into the distance behind us. The volcano peaks remained constant, towering behind the scenery that flew past, operating on their own massive scale. Our fellow passengers read magazines, slept and chatted to each other. The windows, like giant television screens, flickered with information regardless.

I glimpsed patches of increasingly barren ground in the darkness as we climbed, and the lights of what towns I could see sank further and further below us. The villages we passed through became more and more desolate, often little more than a few wooden huts clustered by the roadside in the mist, with a dog, dead or sleeping, under a single street-lamp. And still we climbed. More than once, I looked out of the window to see a dizzying downward drop. I tried not to think about Fabián's parents.

We saw the lights of the town first, in a valley beneath us, and the coach began to thread its way down a giant corkscrew of a road. Some of the hairpins were at such an acute angle that the bus was forced to reverse just to get down. The bell-tower of the church in the town center was lit yellow from within, and watching it zigzag up the bus window was the only way I could tell how far down we had got. It blazed so brightly, and everything else was so dark, that it seemed unreal, a toy tower. After a descent that seemed to go on for ever, we sped through a few deserted streets in dusty monochrome and the coach stopped.

"Are you sure this is the right place?" I asked Fabián. We were the only passengers disembarking.

"Of course. It's only because it's late that nobody's getting off. If you came here during the day this place would be packed with tourists."

We stood alone in a deserted marketplace that reeked of passion-fruit and mangoes. The height of the surrounding mountains could only be gauged in the darkness by the cross of a hilltop shrine, lit brightly, suspended a mile in the air behind us like a vision.

"The Light of God," said Fabián, looking up. He took a deep, satisfied breath. "Smell that highland air. Nothing like it. I like this place."

"Me too," I said, looking around us at the square. Some grand colonial constructions fronted on to it, with elaborate wrought-iron balconies and patterned wooden window-frames. Cats squealing in an alley behind us broke the silence: perhaps a dispute over some spoil from the market.

"This place looks shut up. Where are we going to stay?" I said. But Fabián was already making confidently across the square towards a side-street. I followed him.

Studded doors faced cobbled streets in which disused tram-rails lay rusting. A lone radio squawked from behind a set of darkened shutters. The air was fresh after the bogus environment of the bus, but thin with the altitude. I walked slowly, feeling the tightness in my chest.

"Ha! My research paid off," I heard Fabián say up ahead.

As I rounded a bend in the street I saw a white neon sign poking out into the street above an enormous set of wooden doors. Although not illuminated, it did say, in red lettering, *Hostal.* Fabián battered imperiously on one of the doors and stepped back into the street to look back up at the windows. Nobody heard him: the wood of the door was so thick that his efforts had simply been absorbed by it. On my side of the door, I noticed an old metal bell-push, painted shiny black, and beneath it, a modern, plastic button. I pushed it. Presently, the clink and scrape of locks sounded from within, and a middle-aged woman wearing a tabard and pink slippers trundled to the door.

I had expected people to question us on account of our age. But Fabián looked older than he was, and, as I was to discover, my European appearance tended to trigger a sequence of stock gringo responses in people that bypassed my youthful appearance. The first thing anybody saw in me was the potential for money. We paid Pink Slippers in dollars for our room, and then asked her to wake us in the morning in time to catch the train south. From her wordless nod of assent I guessed this was a common request.

We followed her through a gloomy interior courtyard decorated with potted ferns but dominated by a fig tree decked out with cages of tiny, twittering songbirds. Guano streaked the terracotta floor tiles, and I wondered whether our hostess was in the habit of letting her birds out periodically to relieve themselves. Then, as we followed her up a flight of tiled steps towards the first floor, I looked up and saw the real source of the floor stains. Above us, suspended upside-down like bats, in the shadows where the whitewashed walls met the rafters, thirty or forty pairs of wild birds were roosting for the night. Newspaper had been spread out on every step, near the wall, to catch their droppings.

The layout of the building was reminiscent of a prison. Each room led out on to a balcony that overlooked the central courtyard, and from any one door you could look up or down at any other. The noise of the caged birds rose constantly from the central well, whilst up in the rafters, the silent, wild birds oversaw things. What had this building been in its first life? A grand house built—when? During some banana boom? Now it was an aviary, and a backpackers' guesthouse—in that order.

"What happened to your arm, *cariño?*" said Pink Slippers to Fabián as we climbed the stairs.

"I fell over," he said.

Our room had yellow, peeling walls and high ceilings, and it was furnished with two iron bedsteads, a battered wardrobe and a cracked porcelain washstand. Water could be fetched from the bathroom down the hall if we needed it.

"That is, if you boys are shaving yet," said Pink Slippers with a grin. Fabián scowled at her. She gave us a key, which I pocketed, and one for the outside door if we were going to be out late.

When she'd gone, I lay down on one of the beds, but Fabián was ready to go out straight away.

"I'm starving," he said, "and we're on holiday. Let's go."

The café to which Pink Slippers directed us was in a white-washed building with a pock-marked Coca-Cola sign and a veranda. An entire pig hung outside the door, suspended by a shiny metal hook sunk into its jaw. It looked whole from the outside, but as we walked in, I saw that the flank facing into the restaurant had been carved into. Red, raw flesh sparkled in the strip-lighting against hairy, pale skin.

"You are what you eat," I muttered.

"*Chancho*. Excellent," said Fabián.

Beer and soft-drink crates stood piled high on the concrete floor at the back. Pilsener. Sprite. Inca-Cola. An aluminum pot simmered on a gas ring. Three Indians were playing cards at a table in the corner. We ordered the two-course menu of the day. When it arrived, the soup was a watery concoction flavored with large handfuls of coriander and one wrinkled chicken's foot carefully placed in the center of each of our portions. Fabián picked up his immediately and munched it, bones, talons and all. Silently, I transferred mine to his bowl. When this was out of the way, we were given forks and sharp, serrated knives for the main course—a delicious meal of rice and pork, accompanied by bottles of beer, fried slices of banana and bites from a great raft of brittle crackling that arrived on the side.

Contented, Fabián sat back in his chair and said, "I'm glad we're staying here for the night, for two reasons. First, it isn't too far from here that my mother vanished. And second, I've heard that there is an excellent brothel."

"I wonder if there's any coincidence there," I could have said. It was the sort of joke he'd have appreciated, and it would have been far less provocative than what I *did* say.

"You're not going to a prostitute. You're too young, and besides, you haven't got the balls."

"Is that right?" he said. "It's totally legal. Why shouldn't I go?"

I lowered my voice.

"You don't seriously want your first fuck to be with a prostitute, do you?"

"First fuck! Please. I've fucked more people than you could imagine. And why the hell shouldn't I start with a prostitute, anyway? You're so naive. I don't know anyone whose first fuck *wasn't* with a *puta*. It's the best way to do things. They know what they're doing, you get it out of the way, and then when you find the right woman later on you don't make a dick of yourself."

"Keep your voice down, will you?" I said. The Indians at the next table had glanced over more than once as Fabián raised his voice.

"Don't worry about them, they can't understand us," said Fabián. "No, in many ways, brothels provide an extremely valuable service. Look at Suarez. He loves them so much he never even bothered getting married."

"There's no brothel here. This isn't exactly a bustling city, is it?"

"My friend, there are whores in every little mountain pueblo up and down the Andes. Getting laid round here is as easy as picking sunflowers. You've been living in this country over two years now and still have no idea where you are, do you?"

"That may be true," I conceded. "But I don't believe Suarez goes round visiting prostitutes. He's a doctor. He knows better."

"You know that this is an election year in Peru?" said Fabián.

"Yes. Hence the war," I said.

"Precisely. And you know what one of the major election issues down there is? The abolition of brothels. The candidate going up against the current president has publicly said that one of the main reasons why he's against abolishing them is that he enjoys going to them too much. You can't assume that just because someone is a respected public figure they're going to be unrealistic about the things that really matter. Same thing with Suarez."

"You do not sit around comparing notes on brothels with Suarez. It's bullshit."

"Is it? How do you think I know what the brothel in this town is called, then? You don't have any idea what Suarez and I talk about when we're alone. It's not like having a parent. His attitude towards me is completely different."

"So what's this brothel called, then?"

"Ethel's."

I burst out laughing.

"Ethel's Brothel? That's good. That's brilliant. Let me buy you another beer." I was still chuckling as I got to my feet.

"You can buy me another beer if they believe you're old enough, *rubio*. And you'll be eating those words before this night is out."

"It's after midnight. Where the hell are you going to go? The whole of this town is shut up. And we have to be on that train first thing in the morning."

"What, you think brothels have nice sociable afternoon opening hours? I told you. I'm going to Ethel's. Just because it sounds like an English name. It's not so ridiculous in Spanish. Ethel was—"

"Fabián, don't bother with the story. It's hardly even a realistic name."

Fabián sighed. "When are you going to get over your expectations?"

"I might ask you the same question," I said, turning my back on him to request the beers.

The conversation moved on to how we would reach Pedrascada the next day, which would be complicated. We still didn't know exactly where we were going, and success would depend on finding the right bus to take us up the coast once we had descended the Andes by train in the morning. I assumed that the brothel conversation had died. It wasn't as if there weren't other exciting plans afoot. But Fabián had made plans all of his own for this trip, and the discussion of what might be in store for us the following day was not enough to dampen his ardor.

"Right," he said, finishing his bottle of beer and wiping his mouth with the back of his sleeve, "I am now ready for the arms of a loving woman."

He turned to the group at the next table and spoke to them in Spanish. I overheard the word "Ethel's." He pronounced it "Ettel's."

The Indians spoke to each other quickly in a mixture of Spanish and Quechua and then laughed uproariously.

"Fucking *campesinos*. All the same," he seethed as we left. "Whose religion was it anyway?" he shouted back, mysteriously.

There was more laughter from within the café.

I noticed that he had brought with him the knife he'd been eating with.

"Carry on," he said, "this won't take a minute." He scurried back towards the pig. I stood further down the street, waiting for him.

"What was that you said about me not having the balls?" he said, running back towards me.

I looked down and saw that he held the bulky, bloody scrotum of the pig in his right hand. Pulling his arm back, he flung it at the café window. It hit the glass with a dull thud and slithered on to the floor, leaving a slight mess on the glass.

Fabián ran off gleefully into the darkness, leaving me to face the music.

Nobody came out. They hadn't even noticed.

I walked slowly down the street after him.

I wasn't sure of the way back to our hostel, but it didn't seem to matter. I was happy to walk in this misty, unfamiliar place, following side-streets at whim, catching glimpses of The Light of God between buildings and allowing my mind to wander. There was no sign of Fabián, and that didn't matter either. After I had taken a few turnings at random, I could hear the sound of water and found myself walking towards it in the darkness, as if it were a beacon.

I reached the source at the point where the town gave up and the mountainside's lush cape of secondary rainforest began. A few basic dwellings poked their heads above the trees lower down, but mainly the slope was so steep and the forest so thick that construction would have been impossible. The channel of water spilled from the forest, out of the sheer side of the hill and into a man-made gutter by the pavement. I watched the harnessed waterfall for a while, allowing its clatter to drown out my thoughts like white noise. I put my hand in the flow, which was numbingly cold. It had been a glacier not long ago. I realized I was ready for my bed.

I found my way back and managed to ease open the great front door of the hostel without much difficulty. No lights shone in the interior of the building, and I couldn't see beyond my own knuckle in the darkness. It was almost 2 a.m., and I was nervous about waking people up. I took a step forward. The door closed behind me. As my pupils expanded, I could make out the gray light of the central courtyard. I stepped towards it, trying to reconstruct the position of the stairs in my mind.

Something crunched under my foot. In my mind, I had trodden on a monster cockroach—one of many. I stooped down, felt around my shoe and then lifted it up to see what was underneath. Something chalky. Just a cracked terracotta floor tile. I took another step forward. More crunching of insects.

I heard swift shuffling movements in the darkness. Tiny, efficient rustles. The songbirds were shifting in their cages. I moved past them and found the bottom step. Something wet and heavy fell on my left shoulder. Too late, I remembered the wild birds in the rafters. I moved to the outer edge of the stairs, away from the wall and the roosting pairs. According to some, it's good luck to be shat on by a bird.

Relieved to arrive at the room, I fell on to the musty, yellow sheets to allow the adrenaline generated by my stealthy entrance to dissipate. It didn't occur to me until I was almost asleep that Fabián still hadn't returned.

ten

The saturated colors of a high-altitude dawn: Indians lugged produce across the market square against a backdrop of rich green mountainsides and a fierce blue sky. A piercing screech overhead put me in mind of condors, but when I raised my eyes towards the slopes that reared up above the roofs of the town, the size, the *clarity* of it all induced in me a kind of inverse vertigo and I couldn't keep looking. First light in the mountains is pretty intense anyway, but on this morning, in this place, the colors and textures seemed so tightly focused that the effect was almost agonizing.

Anger is another powerful sharpener, and I was fuming. Pink Slippers had woken me by pounding frantically on the door, and then ejected me so abruptly from the hostel that I had assumed there wasn't time for breakfast before the train left. Now, sitting beside the locomotive with our bags at my knees, I seemed to have plenty of time at my disposal, but no traveling companion. And a fat squirt of dried birdshit from the night before coated my shirt. I kicked Fabián's pristine new rucksack in frustration, and hoped I'd broken something valuable.

It wasn't a train station as such. The tracks were set in the cobbles to one side of the square where we'd been dropped the night before, so that the train could be approached from any angle, like a bus. This made the passengers seem vaguely opportunistic, as if they had just turned up with no travel plans, seen the train waiting and thought, *why not?* As the day bloomed and our departure time drew closer, more and more of these chancers flocked out from the town—foreign tourists strapped into gaudy backpacks, locals hauling their own, better-worn luggage—but still no Fabián. The engine pulling the train was a dull diesel-belcher, rather than the working steam locomotive Fabián had described to me, which was yet another reason to have a go at the bastard when he finally turned up. The last two carriages were more like it, though—antique wooden wagons, painted a deep claret color, with gold lettering on the side that said *Ferrocarriles Ecuatorianos: Primera Clase*—and these were filling up. Men and women wrapped in bright ponchos queued patiently for tickets, leaving their luggage to be loaded into the second-class wagons. These weren't painted, nor did they have seating. They were in fact just metal boxcars with sliding doors, but Fabián had anticipated this. He'd told me that the best ride was on top of these carriages, which cost next to nothing and gave you panoramic views. It was just the sort of thing Fabián would have said either as a boast or, more likely, as a practical joke. How like him to get me up on the roof of the carriage, then come along at the last minute laughing about it and asking me what the hell I thought I was doing up there. Well, no thanks. Nobody else was clambering on top of the carriages, and I wouldn't be the first.

The diesel engine coughed into life, sending a dense whoosh of smoke out over the square. I watched as the breeze whipped it into black, dissolving curls and felt my agitation build. Only one train ran every day, and if we missed this one, our plan to get down to Pedrascada was all over. My temper began to unravel. It was typical of Fabián to miss the train because he was out proving some point about his womanizing—as if simply turning up late would be enough to prove he'd been up all night with the non-existent beauties of Ethel's Brothel. I didn't have the luxury of an indefinite amount of time in this country, and now, just for once, the reality at our disposal was more exciting than the invented world he lived in. I bunched my hands into fists around the handles of our bags and stood up.

As I did so, a man in his twenties walked in front of me, lobbed his pack overarm on to the train roof and casually hauled himself up the ladder on the side. Although his complexion and coloring suggested that he was a local—possibly even with some Indian blood, given his broad features and straight, dark hair—his confident, almost contemptuous gait suggested someone from the outside, and his English, when he spoke, was impeccable, with a note-perfect New Yorker's twang. His teeth were capped and polished to an impossible bright white, although he had several deeply pitted acne scars high on his cheeks and he stank of aftershave. He wore preppy, American clothing topped off with a Yankees baseball cap and carried a portable stereo as well as a brand-new black rucksack. Not for him the plausible linen shirts or ethnic waistcoats worn by most of the other tourists boarding the train: this traveler might have just been spirited away from any campus in the world but for his physical appearance and absolute confidence in this environment. As I went to board the train, he leapt to his feet again and leaned over the side of the carriage to take my bags and help me up the ladder.

"You look young to be traveling alone," he said, after I had thanked him.

"I'm not traveling," I said. "I live here."

"Cool. Well, I hope you're enjoying my country. I *don't* live here. My name is Epifanio, but people call me Pif. I've been away studying, but I'm back down here now to check out the continent."

I was pleased to have stumbled on Pif, even though I knew that he was just the sort of fellow countryman of whom Fabián would be immediately suspicious: from a wealthy family, educated in the United States and returned (having adopted certain prevailing attitudes north of the border) thinking that his country of origin was little more than a theme park tacked on to the great project that was America. Fabián ranted about the type. He knew quite a few of them, he said, including some family or childhood friends only a few years older than him, and he claimed that what happened was always the same: "They go off to the States for a few years," he would fume, "then come back like fucking tourists."

According to the portrait that Fabián usually painted of such people, I could expect the following of Pif: he would cheerfully despise his country and find its inequality a source of curiosity and amusement; he would feel no solidarity with its people, or need to overcome its poverty, because he would no longer consider himself part of Ecuador but a resident of the greater *continent* instead. I didn't care. I knew, of course, that Fabián despised such people because he dreaded that he might one day become one. And for now, in Fabián's absence, I was very pleased to meet Pif. He was relaxed and friendly, and he immediately set me at ease. To a fifteen-year-old at large in a foreign country, I thought he would prove a tremendous asset.

The train began to fill up, both inside and out on the roof. The diesel engines upfront were revved up and belching. I looked around the square. No sign of him. A whistle gave three huge blasts, and slowly the train started to move.

"Problem?" said Pif, noticing my unease.

"I had a friend who was supposed to be meeting me to catch the train," I said, "but he hasn't turned up."

"That him?" said Pif, pointing over into the swelling crowds of the market-place. A brown cowboy hat cutting its way at great speed through the mass of people caught my eye. Fabián sprinted across the square towards the train, holding the new headgear in place with his one good hand. Pif laughed as Fabián came level with the side, shouting something incoherent up at me as he ran.

"Don't worry," said Pif. "We'll get him."

The train picked up speed. At the point where the tracks diverged from the road surface between the buildings of the town, Fabián flung himself at the ladder on the side of the carriage and Pif grabbed him by his bad arm. For a moment I thought there would be a comic cartoon scene in which Fabián would fall by the wayside, his legs cycling in the air, leaving only an empty plaster cast in the hand of his would-be rescuer, but then Pif pulled him upwards in a swift and confident movement and Fabián landed clumsily to cheers from the other passengers on the roof.

"Welcome aboard," said Pif.

"Thanks, man," said Fabián. He sat up.

"This is Fabián," I said.

"I like your hat," said Pif.

"Thanks," said Fabián.

"Where have you been?" I said.

Fabián smiled sheepishly. "I told you where I was going, didn't I?"

"This is Fabián," I said to Pif. "He almost missed the train because he was out all night whoring."

"Nice," said Pif, with the polite zeal of the connoisseur. "Anything good?"

"Is there any coffee in your flask?" said Fabián.

I felt acid-limbed from lack of sleep and the cold, and I still hadn't eaten, but as the train moved out of the town and the day got into its stride, I became more animated. It was impossible not to, in the face of such breathtaking scale shifts between us and the mountains around us. With each slope we skirted and each false horizon we shattered, the beast of an engine which had seemed so huge at the station felt less significant and more like a maggot browsing a mammoth. The train clattered through pine forests, across metal bridges and through dusty cuttings, negotiating its way through the fickle landscape of the highlands. On a couple of occasions we had to duck for tunnels. As the train passed through, the tunnel roof would whip over our heads like a near-miss from a guillotine blade and cool, moist air would stream over us inside, away from the sunshine. Screams and whoops would echo in the damp darkness for an instant before the light began to rush in as we approached the other end. Those who used the railway regularly knew precisely how low these were and stood in affectedly nonchalant poses, hands on their hips, the tops of their hats almost brushing the tunnel ceilings as the train shot through. I sat cross-legged and kept my head down.

After an hour, the train pulled into a small mountain stop. Those of us sitting on its roof were level with the upper-story window of a mint-green, one-up-one-down house that overlooked the station. A mestiza with ruffled black hair, woken by the train, stood on the balcony wrapped in a cotton sheet decorated with orange flowers. Rubbing one eye, she watched with the other what must have been a familiar tableau. I envied her the habit of watching that madcap express rattle through every day from the safety of her bedroom. I raised an arm to wave at her, then felt stupid. She wasn't nearly far enough away to justify a wave. I could almost have reached out and touched her if I'd wanted to. Beneath her window, a sequence of long benches lined a table under an awning, which formed a makeshift cafeteria at which ranks of Indians sat breakfasting. Their identical hats and different colored ponchos made it impossible to distinguish between the men and the women. Fabián jumped off the train to get food from the café. While he was gone, I watched as a live sheep was passed up to a man on the roof, who loosely tethered it to a railing on the top of the ladder but otherwise left it to roam about up there as he went off to sit downstairs for the remainder of his journey. The girl in the window saw me watching the sheep and smiled. Her face was creased with sleep. I wanted to wake up next to it.

Fabián reappeared with a bottle of water, a loaf of bread and a plastic bag full of hard-boiled eggs. I noticed he still had the knife from the café the previous evening. He ate his eggs by slicing the ends off and sucking at them in the shells. I had a different approach, painstakingly removing every piece of shell so as to have the entire egg at my disposal, then sinking my teeth in, enjoying the way the white resisted for a split second before yielding access to the smooth treasure of the yolk. I was so hungry, and so grateful for the food when it arrived, that I missed the girl leaving her window. When I looked back as the train started moving again, she had gone.

We passed a sign as we moved off: YOU ARE CURRENTLY AT AN ALTITUDE OF 2,347 METERS. THE JOURNEY YOU ARE ABOUT TO UNDERTAKE REPRESENTS THE LARGEST DROP IN ALTITUDE OF ANY RAILWAY LINE IN THE WORLD: 66KM ACROSS AND 2KM DOWN. HOLD ON.

The sun soared. We lay, comfortably fed, though I could feel the back of my neck beginning to itch with sunburn. I noticed that Fabián had taken a small plastic bottle and a packet of cotton wool from his bag. He was tipping the end of the bottle into the cotton wool and swabbing his face with it.

"Alcohol," he explained, raising his voice over the wind. "A trick Eulalia showed me. It's really good at removing grease and dirt from your skin, especially if you haven't been able to wash. Look."

He thrust the piece of cotton wool, smeary with gray grease and blackheads, towards my face.

"Charming. So tell me, was Ethel's everything you expected?"

"I'm not sure you want to hear about it," said Fabián. "I got into a bit of trouble. That's why I had to make a run for the train this morning."

"Tell me all."

"I think her name was Ana," he said, with a mock-dreamy look on his face. "Picture the scene if you will: a rusty bedstead and a naked light-bulb in a fly-blown attic room. Sitting in that squalid place, unaware of her own devastating charms, is a creature of the most wondrous beauty you could imagine. Cheap, too."

"I don't think I need to hear any more," I said.

"I don't need to tell you any more. I can *show* you, and leave the rest to your imagination," said Fabián, giggling. "What a fantastic girl she was."

He produced from within his pocket an enormous pair of blue knickers and opened them before me.

"How about that?" he said, with a suggestive smile. "She gave them to me as a souvenir."

"Well, I don't know what to say," I began.

"What's this, guys?" said Pif, who was picking his way along the roof towards us. "The spoils of conquest, I see."

"I stole the ten-gallon hat from her pimp," Fabián went on, more subdued now that his audience had expanded to two, though still having to keep his voice up over the noise of the train. "And I didn't have enough money to pay. That's why I got into trouble and had to run for it."

"That's quite a story," said Pif, plucking the pants from

Fabián's hands. "But I'm surprised you were even able to get out of her. You could park this train in these."

A couple of guys crouched near us who understood laughed. I couldn't suppress a grin myself.

"I'm not sure that's a ten-gallon hat you're wearing," Pif continued. "It looks more like a three-gallon to me. But the panties, on the other hand, now they gotta be ten gallons plus, easily."

"Who is this guy?" Fabián muttered.

"Your friend says he got lucky last night," Pif said to me. "I say his only luck was not being trapped in there for ever. What shall we do with them? Shall we make a hot-air balloon?"

"At least your jokes are amusing you," said Fabián. "Jealousy is a terrible thing."

"I'm not really jealous, pal," said Pif, throwing the pants back in Fabián's direction with disdain. "For one thing, they've still got perfect creases in them from when they were folded up, and for another, you forgot to take out the price tag. You bought these from the market this morning, didn't you?"

"Fuck you," Fabián snapped. As he spoke, he fumbled inside the pants to check whether or not Pif was right about the price tag.

"It's all right, I get it," said Pif. "You were in a hurry, and you didn't check the size first. But remember, in future: if you're going to be a good bullshit artist, it's better to take care of the little details."

Fabián stuffed his spoils back into his bag, pulled the hat (which, I now realized, he must also have bought from the market) over his eyes and pretended to go to sleep. Pif shook his head, settled down again and took out a camera.

We chugged on, through a scrubby landscape broken up only by cacti, grass and the odd adobe hut. Occasionally, an urchin or two sitting on a doorstep would wave at the passing train as their parents hung out washing or loaded up a mule in the background.

Presently, we stopped again.

"Aha, the Devil's Nose," said Pif.

Fabián pushed his hat back on to his head and sat up.

Like our bus the night before, the train was now covering such a steep drop that it would have to go down in stages, zig-zagging forwards and backwards down the side of the mountain. The descent was treacherous, hence the name *Nariz del Diablo*. Below us, in a dusty cutting so far down it looked like part of a miniature train set, I could see a station and a set of points. The idea that we would be going down there seemed ridiculous. The engine shuddered to a stop. I heard birdsong over the silence. It was going to be a long wait. Going down the *Nariz* was a serious business, Pif explained. The driver had to phone ahead and make sure that all the points were set the right way so the train could slalom its way down without accident. He said he'd read about it in a guidebook.

"Fucking tourists," said Fabián in response. Pif ignored him.

Our bottle of water was running low and there was no shade. The metal roof of the train felt like a hotplate.

"Where are you two headed, anyway?" said Pif.

"We're going to a town called Pedrascada," I said.

"Oh, yeah. The surfing beach. Cool. I spent a couple of weeks there last year."

"You've been there?" said Fabián, perking up.

"Of course."

"Maybe you can help us. Did you ever hear of or visit an Amnesia Clinic while you were down there?"

"A what?"

Fabián edged closer to Pif as he explained. "It's a sort of hospital, especially for people who have lost their memory. It's in Pedrascada. That's where we're headed."

I didn't like the way this conversation was going.

"Hey guys, I think we might be moving down the *Nariz* soon," I said.

"An Amnesia Clinic?" said Pif, trying out the expression. "Does anything like that exist *anywhere*?"

"Of course it does. It's where all the amnesiacs are put," explained Fabián impatiently. "Did you see it?"

"I've never heard of anything like it, either in Pedrascada or anywhere else," he said. "Are you sure it exists? It's not another one of your stories, hmm? Like the *puta* last night?"

"Listen, you fucking asshole—"

"Wait a minute," I said, stepping in. "It could be there, and Pif just didn't see it. Right? We don't know yet."

I was staring intently at Fabián as I said this, trying to make him see sense and back down. He couldn't seriously be expecting Pif to play along with him and pretend that something existed when it didn't. Pif didn't know the rules of the game, and had in any case already proved himself to be a keen debunker of myths.

"All I know," said Pif, "is that it's a very small town, and there ain't much there other than the odd beach bar, a few fishermen and some roosters. If you boys find a hospital in Pedrascada, I'll eat your hat. And those big blue panties of yours, kiddo."

"Jesus, this guy!" said Fabián. "*Me está mamando la vida.* Fuck off to somewhere else on the train, will you? Or, better still, get off it altogether."

"Listen, I'm sorry for spoiling your little macho lie about the whorehouse," said Pif. "I'm only trying to stop the two of you going on a wasted journey. But if you want me to leave you alone, that's cool. I'll see you later."

Pif picked up his pack and his stereo and edged off up the train to where a group of young Ecuadorians sat in a circle, getting drunk. Before long, he had introduced both himself and his ghetto blaster to the group, and hip-hop began pumping out across the roof. Fabián sat, staring thunderously after Pif. Casting around in search of something to divert his attention, I found myself looking into the eyes of an Indian boy of about nine years old. He wore a faded orange T-shirt and blue shorts and stood on a bank beside the train hawking cigarettes and fried banana chips to the passengers from a painted wooden tray slung round his neck. A small but vicious-looking crossbow was strapped across his back.

"Here, this kid's selling cigarettes," I said. "Why don't you just buy a packet of Lark and calm down?"

Fabián noticed the boy and called him over. He scampered up the ladder from the embankment and was soon on top of the carriage with us. Fabián spoke to him quickly.

"I didn't know you spoke any Quechua," I said.

"Not much, but enough," said Fabián over his shoulder. "You get a better deal from these kids if you do."

He and the boy carried on talking, even though the cigarette transaction was apparently over. A brief discussion took place. Fabián seemed to be trying to persuade the boy of something. I saw another note change hands.

"What else are you buying?" I said.

"A favor," he smirked.

The engines restarted, and the train edged its way down the slope. The drop now seemed even more vertiginous, as if the train were more likely to tip sideways off the tracks than make it down. Progress was slow, and the train had to keep stopping as points were switched and the direction was reversed.

"Now for the good bit," said Fabián under his breath when we had got about halfway down.

I thought he was referring to some part of the descent. Too late, I saw what he really meant: the cigarette boy knelt on a small hill, waiting for the chugging train, his crossbow ready at his shoulder. Pif was looking in the opposite direction when the boy fired. The bolt shot out of the crossbow and struck him near the top of his left thigh. I just had time to see the boy give a Pepsi punch of satisfaction in Fabián's direction, and Fabián's unobtrusive wave of thanks, before the boy was gone, disappearing over the brow of his grassy knoll.

"I never thought that kid would actually do it," said Fabián to me, when things had calmed down and it had been established that Pif's injury wasn't too bad. With periodic delays and reverses, we had almost reached the end of the descent.

"You hired that kid to shoot at Pif with his crossbow?" I said.

"Not so much hired. I just bet him ten dollars he couldn't shoot the stupid *yanquí* in the cap and paid him in advance.

Teach that idiot not to believe me. Fucking asshole. I was sick of him questioning everything I said."

I stared at him long and hard.

"Fabián," I said, eventually. "You aren't going to freak out if we get to Pedrascada and the clinic isn't there, are you? Remember what we said: this is mainly about the journey, isn't it?"

"Of course." He exhaled comfortably as he lay back down on the roof. "That Epifanio guy just pissed me off, that's all. It won't happen again."

"So, where did you really stay last night, then?" I said, trying to change the subject.

"Don't you fucking start as well," he said.

The drop in altitude gave me a savage pressure headache; clearly my head had been happy in the clouds. I kept opening and closing my jaw like a dog eating a toffee in an effort to release the pressure. Eventually I held my nose and blew: a whine, then a pop. I felt moisture on the inside of my ear.

Four hours into our journey, the Andes were behind us. Sweeping plantations of banana and sugar cane had replaced the grassy plains of the sierra and the wool and woodsmoke that scented the mountains had faded away behind the ripe, intoxicating reek of the tropics. The air grew more and more humid. It was as if someone were steadily turning up a dial to see when we might begin to crack, or singe. An early-morning start and a long journey are a disorienting combination, and suddenly, in this unfamiliar terrain, it felt like we were very far from home indeed—as if we had dropped from such a height that it would be impossible to get back up to where we had been without doing ourselves harm.

Pif had been subdued since his mysterious assault at the hands of the crossbow-wielding cigarette boy, and now he sat not far from us, smoking a joint. Fabián was alternately holding his plaster cast against his forehead for the coolness and swabbing his face again with his bottle of alcohol. I noticed him stealing the occasional glance at Pif and smiling inwardly at his own handiwork.

Exhaling, Pif offered me the joint.

"No thanks," I said.

"Not to try is not to know," he said, in an irritating singsong voice.

"I have tried it," I said. "I live here, remember?"

I'd smoked it a couple of times with Fabián, usually ending up green with nausea and coughing my guts up while Fabián giggled uncontrollably in a corner. But now, mingling with mango juice on the breeze, and with the sea not too far off, the smoke smelled sweet, pungent and right.

When the joint had been circulating for a few minutes, the mood on the train roof relaxed considerably. Fabián appeared particularly happy with the development and said, "I think I may be able to forgive this guy," a few minutes after it had crossed his path.

Pif now gazed stoically forward at the track being guzzled by the train as we proceeded. Every so often, he rubbed his thigh.

"Listen, man," said Fabián, leaning over. "I want to apologize to you for the crossbow thing."

Pif gaped at him.

"You made the cigarette kid do that to me?" he said.

"Yeah. I'm sorry."

Pif laughed silently, his shoulders bobbing up and down, then held his hands up in a mock-defensive position as he spoke. "Okay. You hired an assassin to get me. From now on, I'll believe anything you say."

"That's more like it," said Fabián, smiling serenely.

"You crazy fucking bastard," said Pif, shaking his head and laughing some more. "I would hate to be there when you get down to that beach and find out your clinic doesn't exist at all."

"I'll let that one pass," said Fabián. "But don't push your luck."

Our stop was a town called Bucay, which isn't on any maps. If you look for the place where the railway line stops on its way to Guayaquil, you'll find a town called General Elizalde, but nothing called Bucay. The thing is, though, in spite of whatever the illustrious general did to get a whole town named after him (albeit a somewhat mucky and unprepossessing one), everybody calls it Bucay. Because everyone calls it Bucay, Bucay is what it now *is*.

"Know who came from Bucay?" said Fabián, as the train drew in.

"Who came from Bucay, Fabián?" I said.

"Lorena Bobbit," said Fabián. "The dick chopper-offer. We should be careful here."

"Thanks for the tip," said Pif. "No pun intended."

The roads of Bucay were ochre-colored mud tracks. Prewar American pick-up trucks with improvised repairs jostled with rickety bicycles in the dirt. Political slogans crowed from every possible surface: on painted banners slung between the whitewashed flat-roofed buildings; in stencils spray-painted on to every wall. The declarations were defiant to the point of melodrama: *Ecuador fue, es, y será país amazónico* (Ecuador was, is, and shall be an Amazonian country); *Perú, Caín de Latinoamérica* (Peru, the Cain of Latin America). I had forgotten that the further south we traveled, the closer we were getting to Peru and, therefore, to the war. Soldiers leaned on every street corner in the town in combat fatigues and baseball caps, rifles slung casually over their left shoulders, pistols jutting from their belts.

"What is it with this war, anyway?" said Pif, his accent thickening a little now he was a bit stoned.

"You don't know?" said Fabián. "You're a fucking *Ecuadorian*, man!"

"I've been away. Humour me."

"Well," said Fabián, "even if you believe it is a real war—which it isn't—it's about roughly a third of the country that no one lives in apart from a few Indians. If you went and told them they were now Peruvian instead of Ecuadorian they wouldn't have a clue what you meant—that is, if you managed to get the sentence out without having your head cut off." Words spilled out of him with a kind of dreamy eloquence. Evidently, the weed had given him a taste for political rhetoric. "But there's another reason too," he went on. "Without a piece of the Amazon of our own we wouldn't feel right. We wouldn't feel South American. They want to take that away from us. Even you must feel that, don't you?"

"I guess," said Pif. "Kind of."

"Yeah, right—all to do with your Amazonian pride," I said. "And nothing whatsoever to do with all the oil in the disputed area." Sometimes living with a mother as earnest as mine had its uses.

"Well, I wouldn't know about that," said Fabián. "I prefer the Amazonian pride as a reason. We've never got on with Peru, anyway. We've been at each other's throats since Huáscar and Atahualpa."

"Always the poetic explanation."

"Fuck off."

When the train pulled in, Pif approached Fabián to say goodbye.

"No hard feelings. Here, take this. I'm flying down to Chile tomorrow and I can't take it with me," he said.

He handed Fabián a newspaper-wrapped packet of weed, clearly, to my mind, having seen the size of the military presence and thought the same as me about the wisdom of carrying drugs into this town. Fabián seemed to have overlooked this key fact.

"Thank you, man," he said, stuffing the package into the side of his rucksack. "Kind of you. Have fun in Chile. And sorry again for getting you shot at."

"Was it kind?" I said, when Pif had retreated, and we were ready to disembark. "Should we really be getting off this train with a load of dope in our bag?"

"The army won't care about that. It's the police you want to watch out for. Besides, we aren't tourists. They only bust people dressed like your friend back there," said Fabián. "And even then, only if you tip them off—which, by the way, I am half-tempted to do. I'd love to see the look on that *yanquí* bastard's face when he's being fist-fucked by the Bucay police."

"Lovely meeting new people, isn't it?" I said, as we clambered down from the train and into the chaos of the town.

———

It was now late afternoon. Fabián swaggered with his usual confidence as we made our way through the mud towards the bus station, but I got increasingly nervous. Every new soldier we passed seemed to look at me for longer than the last.

"Can't you at least take off that hat, if you don't want to look like a tourist?" I said.

Fabián carried on marching down the street, muttering something about how the last thing we should be seen to be doing was hesitating, even when selecting which bus to get on. Eventually, we boarded a lurid, collapsing vehicle, chosen by him apparently at random. Bucay and Pif were behind us.

It was just the kind of bus I had been looking forward to: a dashboard richly upholstered with crimson shag-pile; charms and talismans swinging from the rear-view mirror; live guinea pigs in a cage on the seat beside us. A total lack of suspension meant that we felt every contour of the road, and the only shock absorber in the entire vehicle appeared to be our driver's spring-mounted seat. He bounced gamely around on it, trying to stay upright. A winking cartoon Christ on a sticker above his head gave a reassuring thumbs-up gesture, and the speech bubble by his mouth proclaimed: *Relax: I'm riding with you.*

The sugar-cane plantations we passed through grew as high as the bus, so there was little to see from the windows. I dozed with my eyes half-open, still woozy from the dope on the train, watching the shards of a shattered beer bottle dance on the floor. The brown fragments leapt like earth-struck hailstones with every bump in the road; a graphic equalizer for the terrain.

Shortly after Fabián said to me that he reckoned we'd soon be approaching Pedrascada, the bus hit a huge pothole and everything within it flew into the air. My head collided with the ceiling. The driver wrestled control back from the road and slowed the bus right down. Then, without even checking behind him, he accelerated again as if nothing had happened. Two or three passengers shouted abuse forward at him:

"*Hijo de puta!* Why don't you learn how to drive, you fucking monkey?"

"What bad manners. We aren't cargo, you idiot."

Two seats in front of us, a large woman with blonde-tinted hair sculpted into a bun was rocking forward, clutching a bleeding hand. A piece of broken beer bottle had flown up into the air and cut the tip of one of her fingers.

"Madre de Dios," she repeated quietly, holding the finger in her left hand. When she released it briefly, I saw that the cut wasn't too deep, but it had cleanly removed one of her purple painted fingernails. Calmly, Fabián knelt down and removed his shoelace, then moved up the bus to sit beside the woman.

"May I, Señora?" he said.

The driver, observing the bleeding hand in his rear-view mirror, had started to slow the bus down again, but Fabián shouted forwards to him:

"Don't stop the bus; we'll deal with this. We'll be taking your name and employee number at the end of the journey. Now take it easy, okay?"

He leaned back towards the woman, hushing her as if she were an animal.

"Now then, Señora, no need to worry. We'll just tie this up to stop it bleeding and it will be fine."

He gave the woman his most charming, full in the face, green-eyed angel look as he was tying it, and she smiled as she held out her hand to him.

"There now, you see? The bleeding has stopped. And you'll only have nine of them to paint for a while, huh?"

Her tourniquet attached, the woman now laughed with Fabián.

"You sweet boy," she said to him. "Let me thank you for being so kind."

"I wouldn't dream of it," said Fabián, shooing away the purse she had drawn from her bag.

"But your shoelace—"

"Believe me, Señora, I can find myself another shoelace easily enough."

As he got up and stepped his way back up the bus, the remainder of the passengers burst into spontaneous applause. Fabián gave a modest wave and sat down beside me again.

"What's got into you?" I asked.

"No more delays," he said, watching the road ahead. "This journey has gone on long enough."

eleven

If you tried to translate the word "Pedrascada" into English, you'd come up with something like "Rock Storm." The name fitted the place. Colossal piles of igneous rock and sandstone book-ended the beach, taking turns to cast shadows over it at different times of day, like the elusive hands of twin sundials. And in view of all the local volcanic activity, the name wasn't so ridiculous an explanation for their existence. How else were the Galápagos formed? One day they weren't there, and the next, whole landmasses welled up out of the ocean: molten islands, boiling and slopping about on the surface until they set. In an environment where that was possible, imagining a storm of rocks wasn't too difficult. If you'd had the strength to overturn one of the huge boulders that studded the shoreline at each end, you might justifiably have expected to find a startled pre-Colombian skeleton underneath, primitive fishing rod stuck in hand since the moment a few civilizations ago when the meteor shower caught him unawares.

But for their matching natural towers, the opposing ends of the beach bore few similarities. At the south end, on your left as you faced the ocean, the sand curved away from the shore be-hind the rocks, hardening into a dirt track that became a rooster-pecked high street, along which Pedrascada the town slowly accumulated. Single-story, unfinished houses and bars became larger homes and shops along this road, culminating in the rough formality of the Plaza de la Independencia, where the town had evolved as far as it ever would: neat flowerbeds set among yellow dust and palm trees, street-lamps, a pharmacy and a post office that housed Pedrascada's only telephone.

Our bus had dropped us at the north end: the untamed, anarchic end. Apart from a scattering of beach bars topped with palm thatch, civilization here consisted of a crude com-plex of wooden cabins, set back from the shore amid scrub-land and leafless trees, behind a primitive wooden sign that read "Juan's." Up here, the beach ended abruptly where it met the northern rock pile, and the only way to get out and into the next bay was to pick your way around the base of the cliff face at low tide. No formal pathway existed, but the accumulated graffiti of countless pairs of lovers indicated that the route was well-used.

Beneath the surface of the water lay the coral shelf that gave the bay its celebrated long right break. It meant that the waves were big at Pedrascada, but could be treacherous if you surfed too near the north end. A small, red-painted shrine, like a car-toon dog kennel with a cross on top, sat in the cliff face, facing the bay—a memorial to a surfer who had misjudged things a few years previously and keelhauled himself on the reef. More than once, at night during our stay, I looked up and noticed that a candle had been lit there, although I didn't see how any-one could possibly have climbed the cliff.

Further up, behind the peaks and crags, stood a bright, incongruous metal dome to which there seemed to be no access. It caught the sun when the rest of the beach had been thrown into shadow, flaring like a daytime lighthouse. At different times in the hours after we first arrived, I was aware that each of us was staring up intently at this building, but neither of us mentioned it.

When the bus had pulled away, we dropped our bags and raced immediately towards the water. You have to, I reckon. If there's any life in you at all, the first thing you want to do when you see the sea after a long journey is run towards it and feel the salt on your lips, to punch a wave. We hit the surf, Fabián cursing his plaster cast and shouting at me for getting it wet.

"Know what we need now?" he said, when we emerged. He'd been keen to attack the weed again ever since we left the train. He took out the newspaper-wrapped parcel as we sat drying out on the rocks. Waves arrived with gentle slaps. The arches of my feet met with wet ridges of hard sand. It felt good after the heat and stench of the bus. Thoughtfully, Pif had given us a handful of cigarette papers to help us along. Fabián sat, his tongue out with concentration, wrestling with a paper he'd loosely sown with weed and the remains of a cigarette. His plaster cast didn't help.

"Fucking thing's screwing up all my hand movements," he said. "Good job I got laid last night. Jerking off with this thing is a nightmare."

"So now you *did* get laid last night?" I said. "Just so I know where we are . . ."

"Of course," he said, grinning. "She was called Ana; I told you."

"Of course you did. Forgive me."

Eventually, he had built something close to a joint. He licked its seam and folded carefully and ineptly.

"Are you sure it's supposed to look like that?"

"You think you can do better, be my guest. This baby's gonna do us fine. Don't you worry."

He took out a lighter, put the creation to his lips, and lit the end. The paper flared down its length on one side as if he'd lit a fuse, and half the contents dropped out on to the rock.

"Ha ha," said Fabián. "Don't worry, there's plenty more. Practice makes perfect. There, you see? This is working fine now." He puffed frantically, trying to get it going.

Enough remained for a few drags each. We sat with our backs to the rock, passing the joint between us and coughing. Then we rolled another, and eventually, we blundered our way into a pretty relaxed state. Fabián sat on the sand with his eyes closed and his back to the rocks. In the ferocious light of the setting sun, his face shone like a bronze. He spoke quietly.

"Up there. Behind us. Do you think that dome could be it?"

I kept my gaze on the water, where a perfect replica sun shone back at me. Networks of hissing foam fragmented on its surface.

"I don't know, Fabián."

"It could be, couldn't it? What do you think it would be like?"

"I don't know."

"I picture it with black and white tiles on the floor, like a checkerboard, and gleaming metal everywhere. Then there'd be signs on the walls to help the amnesiacs remember the basics. The obvious things they might have forgotten: *You have eaten lunch. The day is Tuesday. Sixto Durán Ballén is president. We are at war.*"

"Listen, about the clinic."

"Then the signs would get more and more specific for each person in their own rooms—which, obviously, would have to be signposted with photographs rather than names—and so you'd have notices saying things like, *you were found passed out on the beach near Salinas wearing a blue scarf,* or whatever . . ."

"Fabián. About the clinic."

"What about it?"

"I thought we agreed not to get too carried away about that. You realize it may not be here, don't you?"

"Hey, don't spoil it. The point is that it *might* be."

"But it might not be."

"That's right. But let's not find that out straight away. Let's not be sure of that until we have to be. Then it could still happen. Didn't you ever wait a few days after buying your lottery ticket before you checked the numbers, just to allow yourself to think you might have won something?"

"I don't play the lottery," I said.

We sat in silence for a while, listening to the suck and surge of the incoming tide.

"Fabián. You do know that the most likely explanation is that your mother died in that car, don't you?" I said. "Whatever you and I may say to each other."

He paused. "It's easy to believe that my father died. I picture him very vividly. What's more, we buried him. That helps.

With my mother it's different. I find it easier to believe . . . other things. Why else would I have seen her like that at the parade? It wasn't a memory. She was there. At that moment, for me, she was alive. What's wrong with that? It's a gap, isn't it? A gap that I can fill with whatever I want. Just like the inmates at the clinic."

"Which probably isn't there."

He scratched his head with a grimace, as if I had said something tasteless and he wanted to erase it from his memory.

"Whatever I may or may not know to be true," he said, "if there's anything—anything at all—that can make me feel that I'm investigating the possibility that she *didn't* die, then I'll do it. Can you see that? Can you see that even if this trip comes to nothing at all, it won't have been a waste of our time?"

"Yes. I see that. Let's stick to the idea that it *might* exist, though. Let's not try to plug the gap, because then we might be disappointed. Okay?"

I looked at him.

"Okay," he said.

"Do you promise?"

He said nothing.

"Do you *promise*?"

"Yes, yes. I promise. I'm not expecting you to understand. You don't know what it feels like. I feel it all the time."

Now his face was in shadow, with the roaring sun behind it. "I feel it like a pain in the blood."

I did not reply.

"Maybe they would stockpile memories at an Amnesia Clinic, like blood in a normal hospital," Fabián continued.

"Maybe even if we didn't find her, we might at least find some of the memories of her that I've lost."

I spoke hesitantly. "Just because you can't remember her as well as your father, it doesn't mean—"

"I'm not saying I don't remember anything. I do remember some things about her."

"Tell me."

He paused. "She loved peaches. She was always eating them. She always smelled of peach juice."

"That sounds—"

"Memory is a very strange thing," he interrupted. "You can create memories, you know. I could make you remember this moment for ever. All I have to do is mark it in some way, and you'll never forget it."

"We'll have to wait a while before you get a chance to prove that point."

"It's true, though." He sat up. "I could make this moment stick in your mind for ever, if I wanted to. I could make myself immortal in you."

"That'd be nice. Maybe we'd better not smoke any more weed for a while."

"I bet you," he said, "I bet you fifty dollars that I can make you remember this moment, in, say, ten years' time."

"Okay," I said. "I should think I'll have fifty dollars to spare in ten years. I hope so, anyway. But you'll have to remember this moment too, otherwise you won't be able to claim the money."

"I won't need to. You'll remember it. Is it a deal?"

"Yes, it's a deal."

"Give me your hand, then. We'll shake on it."

I held out my hand. Fabián grabbed my wrist, and with his

other hand he planted the lit end of the joint into my palm with his thumb.

"Cunt," I said, trying to pull it away. But he held it there, pressed into the flesh, fixing my gaze with a smirk on his lips until the coal had gone out. A welt bloomed in the center of my palm, bright red, flecked with ash. Fabián had another on the pad of his thumb, which he rubbed slowly against the first two fingers of his hand. I jumped up to plunge my hand into the water.

"Saltwater'll heal it quickly," he said, whisking his own hand round in a small rock pool. "But I guarantee you will remember this."

"Fuck you."

He was right, though. To this day, whenever I look at the palm of my hand, I see that moment. The mark is not much more than a pale little fleck, like a chickenpox scar, but it's there. To one side of it, there are two or three little fault lines that I like to think are part of Fabián's thumbprint, scorched into me for ever. Part of my DNA.

"You see?" he said, when the pain had started to fade and I'd sat down again. "It was an extreme way to make the point, but I could have done the same thing by *telling* you something memorable. Say if I told you that I had fucked your mum, and you believed it; you'd remember that. Words can be actions, too. The right sentence from me could have marked this moment in the same way."

"Except you didn't do it with a statement, did you? You marked the moment by burning my fucking hand off."

He relit the joint, which was now more crooked than ever, and puffed on it for a while.

"And the word was God," he said, making his lips into a

funnel for the emerging stream of smoke. "Do you think this is real weed? I don't feel any different at all."

I laughed so hard I fell off the rock.

We were about to get ourselves together and start looking for beds for the night, when a noise out to sea made us both look up: a muffled boom, like an explosion in the distance.

"What the fuck was that?" said Fabián.

"Perhaps it was something to do with the war," I said, getting up. "Maybe there's a naval battle going on." I scanned the horizon hopefully.

"Cool!" said Fabián. "Maybe we'll witness a famous sinking. Something historic."

Boom.

"Jesus, what is that? They must be using some pretty heavy weaponry."

"Could be mines going off."

"Could be torpedoes. Maybe the Peruvians are after one of our submarines."

"Do we have any submarines?"

"Dunno."

Boom.

"That's some battle."

"Yeah. Shit. This is serious."

"What the hell's going on out there?"

"Pelicans," said a voice.

We both swung round. An olive-skinned girl of about ten stood behind us. She wore a light summer dress in yellow and red, plastic-framed glasses that had broken and been repaired with Scotch tape.

"What?" I said.

"Pelicans," she said, again. She had a slight American accent when she spoke English, but I could tell it wasn't her first language. "It's brown pelicans, out to sea, dive-bombing for fish. They make that noise when they hit the water. Are you naked under that towel?"

Fabián clutched at his waist.

"No," he said.

"What do you mean, pelicans?" I said.

"What do you think I mean, pelicans?" said the girl.

"Pelicans?" said Fabián, pointing a finger. "Bullshit."

"It's rude to point. And my daddy says you shouldn't say 'shit' to strangers."

"I see. Where is he today?"

"Just over there. Those are our cabins. Are you going to come and stay with us?"

"I think we might," I said, picking up my bag. "What's your name?"

"Sol," she said, giving a cute little curtsy.

The girl led us away from the beach, between the guest cabins and towards a bar area under a thatched awning. In season this would presumably be packed with surfers, but now it was empty, save for a hippy with dirty, graying hair. He crouched near the bar at a charcoal brazier with his back to us, so low that his beard almost brushed the ground. He wore linen shorts and a white T-shirt cut off at the shoulders to reveal shoulders mottled with sunspots. From this angle, he might have been a hermit, crazed with hunger and solitude, waiting to devour some last resort of a morsel that had been unlucky enough to find its way on to his grill. As we got closer, we could see that, in fact, he was turning thin strips of beef on long wooden skewers. The flesh had curled in the heat, the cooked side blackened and hissing with juices and the raw side stretched over the curve, taut with bloody fibers. Hearing us approach, he looked up.

"Hey, baby," he said to the girl. "What you got for me?" Californian.

"Hi, Daddy," she said. "Customers."

"Want a room, fellas? Or some meat on a stick?"

"Both, please," said Fabián, dropping his rucksack heavily on the sand.

Sol's father introduced himself as Ray. He repeated our names several times after we had spoken them, as if the words were new to him and he was trying them out. He pronounced "Fabián" like "fable." Ray's appearance was daunting—his beard so overwhelmed his face that the rest of his features seemed to be peeking out timidly from behind it, and his teeth looked vicious for being framed with so much hair—but after we'd got used to his looks, Fabián and I quickly warmed to him.

Ray owned the cabins, but the business was known locally as "Juan's." Juan was a local fisherman who had decided to build beach huts for tourists when he retired in the late 1970s. Ray had been his first guest, staying before the majority of the cabins had even been finished (and when the town was still more fishing village than surfing resort). Ray had fallen in love both with Juan's cabins and with his nineteen-year-old daughter, and put in an offer on both of them. Ever since then, the cabins should technically have been called "Ray's," but Ray hadn't seen the point in changing the name. He liked the idea of continuing to honor his late father-in-law, and he didn't think it would necessarily be good for business to have a gringo's name over the door.

The guest cabins were clustered loosely around a central two-story building that served as the owner's house, and the main bar. One other shed housed a makeshift lavatory suspended over a sawdust pit and a shower fashioned from an old chain-flush cistern, with a bamboo drainage grille in the floor. The smells of charcoal smoke and lime juice clung to the whole area, and beneath the constant hum of suspended clouds of insects you could hear the trickle of an underground stream.

Normally, he assured us, Ray had plenty of paying customers, but for now we were his only guests. Although he was, in his own words, "a bum," he admitted to having plenty of inherited money with which to compensate for the fact that Juan's ran at a loss for most of the time. Like many Californians, he was a bum with a private income.

"Why would I *ever* want to go back to the States, man?" he proclaimed. "I have everything I need here. Can you think of a better job in the world than to show people how to have a good time?"

That evening, we built a bonfire on the beach and sat round it eating meat on sticks and drinking cold beer. I tried to imagine what it would be like to stay on this beach for twenty years, like Ray; to be so sure that this was the place for me that I would happily settle within the square mile. It seemed impossible to me. I couldn't envisage feeling strongly enough about any one place or person to want to bind myself to it indefinitely.

Ray's wife was called Cristina. She claimed never to have cut her hair, and it flowed abundantly from silvery roots right down to a dark, frayed little wisp somewhere below her hips. She wore loose-fitting clothes in indigo and pink, and her quiet confidence and comfortable, lived-in face were a reassuring counterpoint to her husband's more agitated demeanor. In spite of her generous build she moved gracefully; a wise gorilla to the manic monkey she had married.

Early in the evening, Sol fell asleep face down in the sand, at which her mother calmly scooped her up and took her off to bed. When she returned, Cristina instigated what was obviously a familiar ritual. There were large, flat stones on the beach, gathered round the fire. You waited until each stone was so hot you could only just bear to touch it, and then passed it round the fire, each person taking turns to absorb the heat. Meanwhile, Ray's main occupation was preparing more meat on sticks: soaking the strips in fresh lime juice before seasoning them and suspending them on a grill over the smoking fire. We alternately passed round the hot stones and the skewered strips, moonlit clouds towering above us like silvery nuclear explosions. I remember thinking that these charred, tangy mouthfuls, washed down with liter bottles of Pilsener and bulked out with handfuls of soggy rice from a pot by the fire, were the best thing I had ever tasted. My mouth loaded to bursting, I looked over at Fabián. Like me, he had been eating steadily for some time, but had now taken one of his leftover skewers and begun poking around inside his plaster cast with it.

"What's wrong?" I said.

"I lost something down the cast," he said. "Itches like crazy."

"What is it?"

"My Maradona '86 medal. I can't lose it. It's one of the only things my dad ever gave me."

The Maradona medal was a stained, bent object which Fabián kept on him at all times. He would flick it from finger to finger in idle moments, and it was the prop for many of his disappearing coin tricks and other sleight-of-hand gimmicks. Fabián had claimed to me early on that it was a genuine player's trophy from the 1986 World Cup, but that had turned out to be nonsense put about by his father when Fabián was young. It was nothing more than a freebie given out by a cereal company at the time, but I knew that it had attained for Fabián a kind of totemic power, and I guessed that the part about it being a gift from his father was true.

"You aren't going to lose anything up there," said Ray. "Wait till the cast comes off. Have a stone." Fabián threw the skewer into the fire and took the stone from Ray's outstretched hand.

"Now," said Ray. "What brings you boys here? Forgive me for saying so, but you're a little younger than my usual guests."

"Treasure hunting," I said, before Fabián had a chance to break his promise.

"First I've heard of any treasure hunting," said Fabián, amused at my desperate efforts to keep him off the subject of the clinic.

"You don't know the story?" said Ray. "Cristina, baby, tell them the story of Francis Drake."

"Only if they want to hear it."

"Course they want to, don't you guys?"

"Okay, but they probably know more about it than I do."

"Trust us: we don't know anything," said Fabián, burping mid-sentence.

"Nothing at all," I agreed, keeping quiet about what I knew. To have shown too much local knowledge would be as good as to declare to Fabián that I had manufactured the newspaper cutting.

"Okay then," said Cristina, gesturing out to sea as she spoke. "So, it's fifteen eighty-something, and out here, a great sea battle is in progress."

"Just like this afternoon," said Fabián, settling in.

"Shut up," I said. "Please carry on, Cristina."

"Your Englishman Drake has been chasing a Spanish galleon for months. His men are tired and hungry. They have been away from land for so long that they are living on seagulls, which they have taken to fattening up with the flesh of dogs for a few days before they cook them, to stop them from tasting too fishy."

"Cool," I said.

"Why not just eat the dogs?" said Fabián.

"No more interruptions," said Cristina. "In spite of this hardship, the men are not disheartened, because the prize in their sights is so magnificent and they have resolved to do anything to get at it. Drake is chasing a ship that Spanish sailors nicknamed the *Cacafuego* because it was so fierce in battle that it looked like it was shitting fire. After chasing it all the way up the coast from Chile to Peru to here, Drake finally captures it, and all of the treasure on board. It is a triumphant victory. He is out there, ready to take both of the ships back to Plymouth and his waiting queen, where he will receive a hero's welcome. Not only his own ship but the *Cacafuego* as well, and all of the silver in its belly."

"Nice work," said Fabián.

"Very nice," said Cristina. "Sadly, the Spanish have other ideas. Before the last of them are captured, they have enough time to scuttle the *Cacafuego*."

"What's that?" said Fabián.

"It's when you sink your own ship to stop it being captured," Ray explained. "Very noble behavior. Personally, I would just say, 'Take the ship, dude.' Not these guys."

"Do you mind?" said Cristina, laughing at Ray in spite of herself. "So, the *Cacafuego* is going down. But Drake vows not to lose one piece of Spanish silver. His men manage to rescue all the silver from the Spanish ship just before it sinks. Now, this, on top of what the *Golden Hind* already carries, creates a serious overload of treasure. One of the Spanish prisoners starts calling Drake's ship the *Cacaplata*, because it is now virtually shitting silver.

"It's actually a problem. The ship is now carrying so much treasure that Drake doesn't know what to do with it. Sailors are skimming silver coins off the side of the ship to watch them bounce on the water. Even the youngest little cabin boy—let's call him Hawkins, like in *Treasure Island*—even he is running around on deck with shining silver buttons in his jacket. The cook begins experimenting with it in the food. Silver is spilling over the sides with every lurch of the ocean. Do you get the picture?"

"We get the picture," said Fabián. "There's a lot of silver."

"There is a lot of silver," said Cristina. "People aren't even bothering to steal it off each other. There is so much of it around that it has lost all of its value. You see?"

"We see," said Fabián, getting impatient. "So what happened?"

"Drake calculates how much weight they need to lose to get back to England without sinking, and then he has to decide what to do with the rest of it. He sails into a tiny cove, near here, on an island called Cano—which we now know as the Isla de Plata. While the ship is taking on water and turtles for their journey home, Drake gets hold of a copper bowl and starts ladling up equal amounts of the treasure to his crew. And when he's done that, he throws seventy-two tons of it over the side, somewhere in the bay. He notes the spot so that, eventually, he can come back and claim it. But he never does. And it's still down there to this day."

Fabián had finished eating and now lay on his back with a hot stone on his belly, looking upwards in the direction of the Southern Cross. "Cool," he said. "Maybe we should go treasure hunting after all."

"Maybe we should," I agreed, keen to establish any new quest, however absurd.

"Ray'll take you tomorrow, won't you baby?" Cristina said.

"Okay. But first I think we should have a story from one of you two," said Ray. He pointed at Fabián. "I bet you've got a good one up your sleeve. Some highland folktale. I can see you've got the blood for it. Bet you can speak a bit of the *runasimi* too."

"No," said Fabián, sitting up. "My father spoke a little, but I don't." Ray's remarks had unsettled him. I don't think anyone had ever recognized his Indian blood before.

"*Runasimi*?" I asked.

"It's the word that Indians use to describe the language everybody else decided to call 'Quechua,'" said Cristina. "It means 'the language of real people.'"

Increasingly uncomfortable, Fabián claimed that he didn't know any folktales. Cristina told him he should make one up. She said that there were only a few rules you had to remember:

"First, start with guinea pigs, for dramatic effect. Either with 'All the *cuyes* in the house woke up at once' or with 'All the *cuyes* suddenly fell silent at once.' Second, make sure you stick in a symbolic animal or two somewhere. Third, draw your audience in at the end by addressing them personally and telling them you've got them a piece of cake from the wedding feast, or that your character still lives on, to this day."

Ray liked the sound of the challenge. "Tell you what," he said. "If you make up a good story for us, I'll take you out to the Isla de Plata in my boat tomorrow, all expenses paid, and we'll find some of Francis Drake's treasure."

I was lying on my back, balancing a hot stone between my knees and watching sparks from the fire fly away from me into the sky, so I couldn't see Fabián's reaction. But I knew that this incentive, as well as the challenge, would be too much for him to resist.

Okay. We'll call this story "The Boy Who Said Nothing" (said Fabián). The story goes that it was midnight in the village. It was a clear night, and the Southern Cross was twinkling away in the sky.

The boy knew nothing of this. He was in his bed and his mother was in the next room. His father was out night-fishing, and wasn't expected back until the morning. Suddenly all of the *cuyes* started making noise at once. They had been disturbed by something outside. The boy lit his candle and waited for the *cuyes* to settle down again.

He walked into the next room where his parents slept, and saw that his mother's bed was empty. He felt it, found that it was still warm, and assumed she had gone outside to piss, or to heat some chocolate for herself, as she sometimes did when his father was away for the night and she couldn't sleep.

He went outside. His mother lay on her back over a fallen tree. Her skirts were hitched up about her, her legs were spread and a great white bull was on top of her. Its hooves were planted squarely on his mother's shoulders, pinning her down, but she didn't seem to be struggling. Quite the opposite. Already, the boy knew that the sound of her cries would stay with him for the rest of his life.

The boy ran back to his room, pacified the *cuyes* and put himself back to bed. In the morning he told himself that what he had seen was a dream, and not the truth. He resolved to put it to the back of his mind. But the vision would return to him two months later.

He and his father were carrying sacks of barley to the market, and his father, unable to contain his happiness, told the boy that he was to have a baby brother or sister. The boy was old enough and tactful enough not to say anything about the bull, but for the next seven months, he woke in the night from atrocious nightmares about his mother being punctured from within by horns as she tried to birth the bull-baby.

And still the boy said nothing. On the night of the birth it was raining hard in the village. The priest came to the cottage. He told the boy he was getting in the way and asked him to leave for a while. The boy was only too happy to go. He was tormented by what might happen.

The boy ran through the fields, slipping in the mud as he

went, trying to escape the vision in his head. Whenever he tried to return to the hut, his mother's cries of pain would send him off again into the wet night.

The boy ran for hours, finally collapsing to sleep beneath a *quiñua* tree that kept the rain off him. When he woke up the next morning, he was covered with dried mud and leaves and the valley was shot through with the widest, most colorful rainbow the boy had ever seen. Everything he saw seemed filtered through it.

Taking this as a good sign, the boy made his way back to the cottage. The air was fresh and cold after the storm. The highland sun blinded him as he descended the mountain, and made his nose run. As he approached his home, he heard the sound of a crying baby and not the sound of a lowing calf, as he had dreaded. He started running, but the priest stopped him at the front door.

"Your mother is dead," he said. "But you have a baby brother. It's sad, but life will go on."

The boy saw that life would go on. But he saw at the same time that the morning, and the rainbow, were illusions—that the previous night would now never be over, and that a part of him would be stuck inside it, running up and down the mountainside in the rain, for ever.

Over the next year, the boy tried as hard as he could to love his brother, but he could not look at the child's face without seeing twisted bull-horns emerging like tree roots from his forehead. He began to fear that he might harm the child.

And so, to protect his family, he left home to work for a distant cousin, high in the mountains, where he could spend his days alone until he could stop living the same night over and over again. Even as he left, he knew that to outlive it would take longer than he had on this earth.

He's up there in the highlands still, even to this day. And if you are lucky you may see him up a hillside, eating grubs and insects and tracking a white bull that he knows he will never find, through the night, every night. That is the story of "The Boy Who Said Nothing."

The fire popped. Fabián stared into its glimmering heart as if nobody else were there, and then tilted his head with an embarrassed look. Ray opened another bottle of beer and passed it to him, along with a hot stone.

"Not a particularly feel-good story, is it?" said Ray.

Laughter rang out across the sand.

twelve

The next morning, I woke to the tickle of flies drinking sweat off my face. A spasm of revulsion brought down my mosquito net, which had obviously been ineffectual in any case. Half-awake, and shrouded in white gauze, I allowed panic to get the better of me and writhed for a minute or two like a suffocating fish before finally shedding the net. With shutters clamped across its windows, our cabin was airless and damp with sweat and bug spray. I swept the room a couple of times to make sure Fabián hadn't been present to witness my display, then pushed open the cabin door, stepping on to sand already scorched by the early morning sun. Recoiling from the glare, I made straight for the shower cubicle, where I stood flinching on the latticed bamboo floor and pulled the chain. Brackish, brown water sluiced over me. It felt good. I waited for the cistern to fill up, then flushed it a second time.

As I stumbled dripping towards the bar area, a prehistoric, animal cry broke the silence. I half-expected to round the corner and see Ray grappling with a brontosaurus he'd snared us for breakfast, hallooing a jaunty "good morning" as he swung from its neck. I couldn't see the animal in question as I put my head under the palm thatch, but I could tell that all was not normal. Fabián cowered on the far side of the bar with a chair before him, lion-tamer style, as Ray and Sol looked on in amusement.

"Good morning," I said.

"Anti, keep back," said Fabián. "Fucking thing'll take your finger off."

I expected a komodo dragon, or at least a giant iguana. As I walked in, I saw that the beast was in fact a parrot, albeit the largest one I had ever seen. Predominantly a glossy red, with a tail of bright greens and startling blues that extended at least two body lengths behind it, it staggered around between the tables, alternately shrieking and worrying at chair legs with a beak that did, to be fair to Fabián, look vicious.

Arkk, it squawked.

"Big parrot," I said.

"Technically, he's a scarlet macaw," said Ray. "Only he doesn't like people very much, thanks to our friends up there on the hill."

"The dome?" said Fabián, setting down his chair immediately. "We meant to ask you. What is that place?"

Ray spoke distractedly, keeping a patrician eye on the parrot.

"Matter of fact, we don't know. Whole boatloads of people go in and out of there, but we never see them, except out to sea sometimes. Place is completely closed off. My guess is that somebody very rich built it as a holiday home and hires it out."

"But you don't know that for sure," said Fabián.

"Why. You got a theory?"

I shot Fabián a warning glance. He stuck his tongue out at me.

"I guess it could be a club of some kind," Ray continued. "Maybe even a hotel. But if it is a hotel, it doesn't have a name. And it sure as hell doesn't take any passing trade."

"Why not?"

"Because the passing trade can't get to it. When they built it, about six years ago, they made a road on stilts to get the building materials up there, then destroyed it afterwards. Now the only access to the place is by boat. Or, if you prefer, you can use the helipad." He snorted. "Very fucking James Bond."

"Cool," said Fabián, enthralled.

"I used to climb that cliff quite a lot before, for the wildlife— there was a whole colony of rare sand lizards up there—and they just bulldozed right through it. Blew the top off and put down the foundations before we even knew it was happening. The environmentalists would go nuts if they found out, but I guess somebody got a backhander."

"Couldn't you stop them?"

"I went up there one day after they'd started building it to have a look, maybe talk to someone. Ran into the kind of people who don't negotiate, know what I mean? Didn't feel much like poking around up there again." He gestured at the parrot. "Anyway, one day, during the building works, I found this guy flapping around in the water at the bottom of the cliff, as good as drowned, with both his wings broken. God knows what they did to him—chopped a tree down with him still inside it, or something. Whatever it was, they screwed up his wings so much he can't fly. And now he lives down here with us, and we feed him so much that he can hardly walk. Don't we, buddy?"

Arkk.

"That's awful," I said. "No wonder he's pissed off."

"He's pretty harmless, but he does like chewing on my furniture. Just stay clear of the beak, and carry a few treats with you to keep him happy. You'll be fine."

I thought Fabián would be crestfallen to hear this refutation of his theories about the dome, but it didn't seem to have registered with him.

"What sort of treats?" he said. "I haven't got any spare flesh on me." Then, suddenly grabbing Sol, "But perhaps we can find a tasty morsel somewhere round here."

The girl squealed, then let out a peal of laughter as Fabián picked her up, put her under his arm and hauled her towards the parrot. The pair of them collapsed on to the floor, giggling. As they rocked about on the sand-covered planks, a worried look came over Fabián and his hand shot out behind Sol's head in case she came close to hitting it. The parrot gouged a piece out of a table leg, let out another screech of rage and shat on the floor.

Arkk.

"That's it, buddy," said Ray, soothingly. "You tell 'em."

Ray poured each of us a hair-raising dose of sweet coffee, then said, "We better hit the waves soon; this weather isn't going to hold. Coastguard says there'll be a storm this afternoon. It's the season for it: *El Niño*. Sorry guys, but I don't make the rules."

"We'll be ready in five minutes," said Fabián, getting to his feet.

"Are we really going treasure hunting?" said Sol to her father. Fabián had obviously been stoking her up.

"Sure, baby," said Ray. "But don't forget: *To travel hopefully is a better thing than to arrive.*"

"Okay, Daddy," said Sol, who was trying to fit a shell in her ear and not giving her father full attention.

"What?" said Fabián.

"Robert Louis Stevenson," said Ray. "Means that what you see on the journey is more important than the destination. Don't you guys read?"

"Whatever you say, dude," said Fabián. When we were out of Ray's sight, he mimed shooting himself through the temple with a revolver, and as we trudged back to our cabin, he muttered, "Fucking hippies. Imagine growing up with *that* as your father."

"You're in a good mood this morning," I observed.

He paused and looked around. "Yeah, I suppose I am. Must be getting away from home."

"I thought you'd be pissed off at what Ray said about the dome."

"Are you kidding? I thought it was fantastic. I love this place. I wish we could stay here for a week."

"How are we going to get away with that?"

"I don't know, but it's only Friday. We've got at least forty-eight hours until we have to think about getting home, so let's just enjoy ourselves."

There were four of us in Ray's wide-hulled, sturdy fishing boat. Ray stood to one side, piloting us at speed from the stern, his gray mane whipping about him in the wind like a cat-o'-nine-tails. I sat on a wooden bench opposite him, watching the water as we belted along. Fabián and Sol lay together on the prow, passing a pair of binoculars between them to scout for pelicans or whale tails. In spite of the hostility of their first meeting, Fabián and Sol had hit it off, and they had been fooling around together all morning. He'd even told me the previous night how much he'd have liked to have a little sister like her. I was pleased. Sol had provided an unexpected, uncomplicated distraction for Fabián, and it seemed to be making him happy.

The island rose slowly from the horizon like a dark loaf in an oven. Birds veered and swooped at its edges like parasites, as if the island were a breathing thing large enough to sustain life in exchange for grooming perks. We carved our way closer, through water that seemed to have changed color every time I looked down. Coffee-colored near the mainland, it had blurred to the gray of slate slabs as we gathered speed, and as we neared our destination, it now lightened even more. At one point I glimpsed a bloated, dead goldfish below the surface and thought of treasure. We approached a small harbor with a pier, where a boatload of tourists was disembarking, but Ray ignored this, gunned the motor and steered us round to the next cove, where there were only outcrops of black lava at which to land. He'd explained to us before we left that technically you were sup-posed to have a special permit to visit the island because it was a nature reserve. He'd also explained that he did not possess such a permit, and that our visit would therefore have to be fairly discreet.

The bay was bottle-glass green. Buds of coral grew within it, fed on by shoals of tiny fish. Ray brought us into what was obviously a favored mooring spot, where the boat would be hidden from the island by mighty lumps of pumice.

"I ought to have a smugglers' cave to show you here, but I don't," he said. "You'll just have to imagine one."

The boat tilted as I stepped off it. I imagined the weight of my one pace sending a ripple away over the surface of the ocean, perhaps momentarily unsettling a Japanese fisherman thousands of miles away. The rock felt rough underfoot, as if we had chanced upon an island of sandpaper. I looked down into the water as frequently as I could, hoping to discern, amid speeding fish and whorls of coral, the glint of Spanish silver.

Like its more celebrated cousins in the Galápagos, the island yielded little in the way of plant life, but it swarmed with animals: pairs of blue-footed boobies, stately giant iguanas, slow-motion flocks of brown pelicans, even an albatross we surprised nesting quietly behind a thorn bush. Ray proved to be quite an expert and excitedly pointed out to us the various endemic species as we walked around.

"But where's the fucking treasure?" Fabián whispered to me, as Ray enthused about a sea otter frolicking in the shallows.

Within the hour, we'd seen fine examples of lava gulls, oyster-catchers and frigate-birds, to say nothing of marine iguanas and lava lizards. Finally, Ray said, "If you want to see anything more, we'd have to get out to the Galápagos, which would mean chartering a slightly bigger boat. And breaking some much more serious laws. How about it, guys? Ready to head back?"

"What about this treasure?" said Fabián. "Where's it supposed to be?"

"Oh, that. Nobody knows, man. Could be in any one of these little coves. Wait. Do you know what that is? Vermillion flycatcher. Very rare."

"I think we'd really like to do some treasure hunting now."

Wet ropes of hair flapped on the back of Ray's vest as he turned away from the bird. "You're right. Let's go swimming before the storm breaks," he said. "Gonna be a big one." He led us to a bay of black sand and volcanic rubble, where the shallows extended far out to sea over large, egg-shaped boulders.

"Lots of good nooks and crannies round here where treasure might hide," said Ray. "I'll start over here, and you guys can fan out and cover the rest of the bay." He stepped out of his shorts, pulled off his vest and had soon become a collection of walnut-colored limbs forcing towards the horizon. Sol leapt into the water to follow him.

"This isn't right. We promised her a treasure hunt," said Fabián.

"She seems happy enough," I said.

"That's not the point. *I* promised her."

I sighed. "Okay. Look around you. If you were Francis Drake, where would you drop your treasure?"

"Don't patronize me."

"It isn't like you to be this crap at enjoying yourself. Come for a swim."

He held up his plaster cast in response.

"You could paddle," I offered.

"You go. Even I know that the treasure isn't going to be in a bay so shallow you couldn't even park a rubber dinghy. I'll stay here."

As I swam, I cast glances at the shoreline. Fabián sat, not even looking at the water, compulsively swabbing his face with alcohol. From a distance, it looked as though he were talking to himself. Ray gave up the pretense of the treasure hunt within minutes and began boosting his daughter into the air and catching her delighted little body as she hit the water.

"Weather's turning," he said when we got out. "We better grab a wave, or we'll be stuck here."

Clouds had begun to assemble overhead, forming a lid that pushed down tightly on the air below, like the palm of a hand on a jack-in-the-box. The temperature rose. The wildlife sped up: birds hurled themselves through the air; iguanas sloped off to safety.

"I'd like to take you further round the island, but we can't stay. The tourist boats will have taken off hours ago, and we should do the same," said Ray.

"We can't leave." Fabián was watching him intently. "I want to find some treasure. That was why we came here. You haven't delivered."

Ray laughed as he toweled himself off. "Listen, kid. Joking aside, there's no fucking treasure on this island. And if there were, we wouldn't find it. We have to go now before this storm arrives."

Fabián stood up. "This is bullshit. We came here for treasure."

"You're serious? You're not joking? I thought you were just doing this for the benefit of my daughter. You're fifteen years old."

"Daddy, can't we look for treasure just for a little while?" said Sol.

"Honey, we can look for it someplace else. We have to head back now or it'll be a rough crossing."

"Treasure," said Fabián. "I promised Sol we'd find treasure and we will."

Ray put an arm round Fabián's shoulder to take him aside, but Fabián threw it off.

"Treasure."

"Okay then. I'm a democratic sort of guy. Anti, you have the casting vote."

"Maybe we should come looking again tomorrow, if there's going to be a storm," I said. "Although the treasure was our objective, I suppose."

"Right. Now we have 'objectives,'" muttered Ray. "Okay. We'll go back to the boat and see what it's like round there. But I have final say. Fucking kids."

The waters in our bay frothed and chopped against the rocks. As we descended the track towards the shoreline and I scanned the water, I saw that even the fish had taken cover. Trees and bushes struggled against the wind, as if strait-jacketed and refusing to go quietly.

Ray began untying the boat from its moorings as soon as we were all on board. "I'm not about to risk my life and my daughter's for some kid who can't grow up," he said. "We leave now."

"Look." Fabián was looking over the side at the water's surface. "There's something there." For an instant, I thought I could see something metallic sparkling in the coral, but then a swell of angry tide wiped over it again. Fabián removed his T-shirt. "I'm just going to check what it is. It won't take long."

The boat reeled at this suggestion, and I was almost thrown off my feet. I felt sick just being on the water here in a harbor, without even contemplating the journey home. I grabbed hold of Sol, more to steady myself than protect her—her sea legs seemed to be fine.

Ray jolted the boat's motor into life, but Fabián was still staring into the water. Ray shouted at him over the engine noise and the wind: "You are not going in that water. With these currents you'll get grated up on the coral like fucking Parmesan. Forget it."

Fabián stood firm, riding each new wave as it hit the boat. "Don't be ridiculous. I'm not afraid of the sea. And there is treasure down there."

"You can't go in, anyway," I added. "Your cast."

Throughout this, Fabián had been rubbing his plaster cast against the metal side of the boat, as if scratching an itch. Now, he brought it crashing down on the side as hard as he could. As if cracking a troublesome egg, he raised and slammed it down again. Cracks appeared in the plaster, separating the signatures and quips of our classmates back in Quito. Then Fabián was pulling at the cast as if it were a kitchen glove, using the side of the boat for leverage, and finally it came free. He threw it in a wide arc over the sea, where it plopped and bobbed. Verena's felt pen heart bled red and violet into the water. His arm was paler than the rest of him and he rubbed it briskly, shedding flecks of dead skin on to the water like confetti. He stood, ready to dive.

"You aren't going in there," said Ray, darting across the boat to grab him.

"Treasure," said Fabián, winking at Sol. Then he was in, a harpoon through the froth, his body absorbed instantly.

"'I'm not afraid of the sea.' That kid has no respect," said Ray. "If he doesn't dissolve into a cloud of mincemeat within the next few minutes, we leave the second he gets back up here. Keep an eye on him."

Fabián was a good swimmer—as I said, he was good at anything that enabled him to show off—but I feared he might not come out of this well. Ray had turned his back to untie the final rope, and consequently didn't see what Sol and I saw. The shimmering shape made its way along the floor, black hair mushrooming in the current. It disappeared momentarily, thrown sideways by a surge, then made a lunge in the shallows before turning to push to the surface. The pale arm rose up, fist clenched in tight triumph, and burst out of the surf towards us as though propelled by a giant sea creature. Fabián's long limbs clattered against the side of the boat, which now rocked to battalions of incoming waves. As I helped him inside, I saw a thin scratch on his left leg, from which fine deltas of blood traced lines in his hair. Ray revved the engine and we were away.

"Happy now?" shouted Ray. "That was dangerous, man. Last time I do you a favor. What did you think you were going to find, anyway?"

"Treasure," said Fabián through heavy breaths, his back to the inside of the boat.

"Are you all right?" I said.

He ignored me and held out the still-clenched fist in front of Sol's face, which blossomed from concern, through disbelief, to amazement as he slowly opened it. Fabián wore an expression of joy unlike any I'd seen. The object in his hand was tarnished and bent out of shape, but was definitely and undeniably a silver coin.

We scudded from peak to peak towards the mainland, too roughly for conversation to be possible. I sat, holding on, next to Fabián, who stared back at the island with a glimmer of triumph in his eyes. Sol stood at her father's side, clutching his leg with one arm and turning the coin over and over in the other. After twenty minutes, we seemed to have left the storm behind us and Ray slowed the boat down, finally bringing it to a halt in calmer open waters. He glanced down at Sol's hand before picking his way back towards us.

"You've made her day," he said to Fabián. "So I guess I owe you an apology. Only thing I don't get is when you found the time to chuck it in. We were all watching you when you broke the cast."

"I can make anything disappear," said Fabián. "Ask Anti— he'll tell you. I finally got the coin out of the plaster when you were all swimming. Then all I had to do was get it in the water somewhere by the boat. And I wasn't going to leave it. It was one of the only things my father ever gave me."

"Are you sure you want her to have it? If it's anything to do with the World Cup it could be valuable."

"Nah—came free in a box of cereal. 'World Cup Heroes.' You should pass these things on. She should have it. I don't believe in it any more."

"There she blows!" shouted Sol from further up in the boat, still holding her treasure tightly up above her head.

Ray smiled at Fabián and said, "Well, thanks." Then he jumped back towards the wheel. "Which way, honey?"

Sol pointed and Ray snapped the throttle forwards, sending us forward at full pelt. Fabián and I stood up and scanned ahead to try and get first sight. After ten minutes, Ray killed the engine again and we were stationary, bobbing slightly. Apart from the slopping of water against the hull, I could hear nothing. A fine drizzle began to fall and a circle of mist encroached around us. Nobody spoke. Then I heard the noise: a deep-sea exhalation, followed by the spatter of water hitting the surface. Fabián and I looked at each other, then around. Still, the water within our white circle was calm. Everyone else was looking ahead, but I'd turned my head to the left, so I saw it first. A sea serpent. The Loch Ness Monster. A procession of great, ridged vertebrae shuttling out of the water, ten feet away, oblivious to us, making for some unfeasibly distant final destination. Then the noise again: the inflation of vast lungs beneath the sea, and the watery whoosh as the whale exhaled.

"Humpback," said Ray, quietly. "The best. We might get some spy-hopping."

We waited half a minute longer in silence, then the horizon burst. The whale threw itself almost entirely out of the water, not just spy-hopping but sky-larking, and came down with an explosion that sprayed the entire boat. It happened so quickly, yet was so exceptional, that the two moments, jump and landing, seemed to happen together. Spontaneously, we cheered.

I'd just come to terms with what had happened when Fabián spoke into my ear: "Don't look down." I looked down. Another whale moved underneath us, its gray, barnacled hide like the concrete of a submerged, post-apocalyptic tower block.

"If this one decides to have a jump . . ."

". . . then we'll be tossed into the air like a seal pup," said Fabián. "Awesome."

The whale continued under our hull, turning on to its back with slow indolence, and then slapped the surface of the water with a flipper once it had passed.

"He's waving at us," said Sol.

"Nah, they do that to stun the fish," said Ray. "It's called a fluke-slap. They can knock out whole shoals of herring doing it."

Fabián shot a mock-yawn in my direction.

The insistent rain no longer mattered. We waited, willing another jump, and then it came: a larger whale this time, putting on a full show, almost completely escaping the water, hanging suspended in the air for an instant then shattering the calm as it landed.

We watched as the whales headed north, swimming in formation, their tails rising and descending in unison. Presently, they were out of sight.

"You could follow them all the way to Colombia if you wanted," said Ray, "but I think that storm is still after us."

The silence in the boat was contented. Every time I closed my eyes the whale took wing again on my retina. I thought back to what Fabián had said about memory and wanted a physical mark to burn the occasion into place, so that I could be sure the experience would never leave me.

Ray was right about the storm. Though we had initially left it behind, it had now tracked us down with reinforcements. When I looked back in the direction we had come, the sea was rimmed with black edges, like mourning paper. A premature dusk had settled, and I began to shiver as the temperature changed down.

As we neared the mainland, we saw for the first time another craft in the water. Unperturbed by the rough weather, an enormous white pleasure-cruiser had rounded the arm of coastline at the north end of Pedrascada and was heading straight for us. Amber light blazed from its decks and colored lanterns strung between its twin masts swayed in the murk. The sharp lines and dark, tinted windows of the vessel felt like an affront to the romance of Ray's fishing boat, especially after our whale sighting.

"These guys better not get too close," said Ray, "or we'll be in trouble. That's a big boat."

His words worked like an incantation. Before they had even been uttered, it seemed, the ship was closing us down. I saw twin scimitars of violent froth panning out from its wake, easily big enough, even to my untutored eye, to capsize us. Ray threw the boat into full throttle in an effort to escape, but the contours of the rising waters swallowed every gasp of our straining motor in steady, regular bites. Trying to outrun the ship seemed only to be making things worse. We shouted and waved. Still the ship came. I heard the tinkle of cocktail jazz and saw a collection of men in blazers and women in smart dresses standing near the glass doors that led out on to one of the ship's many decks. I could discern their faces, hear every phrase of the music. I imagined I could hear the sound of crystal glasses chiming together as they made oblivious toasts. Ray gave three blasts on the claxon, which came out as pitiful toots but did attract attention from those on deck. A man in a bright blue blazer raised his glass in our direction, another doffed his hat, and their ship kept its course. It passed in front of us and Ray screamed at us to hold on as the wake approached. Ray tried to turn us into the waves so that we would cross them rather than be broadsided, but there was little he could do. For a split second we were suspended in the air, weightless, as if at the peak of a rollercoaster. I heard Sol cry out and saw Fabián clutching a rope with a confused look. Then we came crashing down. I hit my head hard on a boathook cloaked in seaweed and braced myself as a wall of water inundated us.

"We might have fucking drowned," fumed Ray later on. "Unbelievable. I'm going to make a formal complaint to the Port Authority."

The storm had arrived and was kicking in hard. Curtains of rain gushed from the palm thatch outside as Ray stood at the bar, chopping a red chili.

"I'll get this anger out of the way right now, then I'll make something that will make us all feel a whole lot better," he promised.

Making his way behind the bar, he picked up a whole pineapple and set it down on a table. He then took the handle of a sledgehammer that leaned against the back wall, hefted it over his head and brought the hammer down on the pineapple with a roar. Wood splinters and fruit chunks sprayed out around him as pineapple and table flew apart in unison. Sol giggled with delight.

"That's better," said Ray, returning to the bar to resume chopping the chili.

The parrot lumbered in to see what was going on and began picking about in the fragments of wood and pineapple. *Arkk.*

"I didn't see the name of the boat," I said.

"Doesn't matter," said Ray. "I know where it came from. Fifty bucks says it's someone staying up at the dome. I'm going to get them taken out of the water for good. Now, everybody relax—this will make everything all right." He had taken the finely diced slices of red chili and tipped them into a saucepan on the gas ring. Now he began to break large pieces of dark chocolate into the pan, stirring the mixture with a wooden spoon. "Hot chocolate, Maya-style," he said. "The perfect reward for successful treasure hunters—and an antidote to a near-shipwrecking."

We drank the chili-spiked chocolate as the rain throbbed overhead.

"Well," said Ray, when he'd drained his cup. "I'm going into town to telephone the Port Authority. I have no idea where my wife is. Can you guys man the bar for half an hour? If anyone comes, just give them a drink and tell them I'll be back. I can't imagine anyone will arrive in this weather, but you never know on a Friday night . . ."

"No problem," I said.

"Solita," said Fabián. "Wanna show me your treasure again?" The girl approached him, still clutching the coin. I doubt she would have let Fabián touch it at all if he hadn't been its discoverer, but she held it up dutifully, the light of admiration undimmed, as Fabián talked.

"You see, King Maradona was an Aztec warrior who fought bravely against the wicked conquistadores in the battle for South America. This coin must have been part of his treasure. You see where it says Mexico '86? That means it came from his kingdom in Mexico, and it must have been in, well, 1586."

"The battles with the conquistadores were later than that," said Sol. "We did it in our history class."

"You'll know better than me then," backtracked Fabián. "Go on, follow your dad."

She looked at him quizzically, then gave him the benefit of the doubt. Pocketing the coin, she ran out of the bar to follow her father to town. The parrot was now gnawing idly at Fabián's chair leg. He eyed it with caution.

"Pretty controversial reappraisal of the England–Argentina World Cup clash, that," I remarked.

"Shut up," said Fabián, good-naturedly. "You know, I'm beginning to see why people have children. They forget how to see things properly as they grow up—too much reality getting in the way—then they have kids so they can have a second chance. It's a personal failure."

"Does this mean you've given up on yourself?"

"Not me. No way."

"You must admit: what Ray said about the dome this morning does kind of rule out the possibility of it being the Amnesia Clinic."

"Who says? Ray doesn't seem to know what's up there any more than we do. All we know is that whoever is up there wants to keep himself to himself."

"But the boat . . . They looked a lot more like rich holiday-makers than hospital patients to me."

Fabián lit a cigarette and rocked backwards on his chair as he talked. His voice rose and fell like an instrument. He was riffing out loud, revealing the shortcomings of my imagination, showily dodging the obstacles put in his way by reality.

"Which brings me to my new theory," he said. "We know the clinic was going to be built here . . ."

"In theory."

"We don't yet know that the dome isn't it . . ."

"But it probably isn't."

"So the ship that almost ran us down could easily have been the good doctor taking some of his patients out on a trip."

"Fabián. We saw them. They weren't patients. They were having the time of their lives."

"Exactly. They were having the time of their lives, living for the present."

"So what's your point?"

"My point is, what if . . . what if, when you lost your memory, it was such a liberating experience that you *didn't want it back*? What if the people on that boat were having such a good time because, in the most incurable cases, making them enjoy the present is Doctor Menosmal's *only form of treatment*?!" He was delighted with his own improvisation. "That's brilliant."

"Okay, well done. But listen—"

"Think I'm giving up? No way. I'm not giving up yet." He lit a cigarette and exhaled a huge lungful of smoke. "Not for anyone."

He collapsed backwards on to the floor as his chair leg gave way under his weight, and under the parrot's insistent chewing.

"Including birds," he shouted, laughing in spite of himself. "You hear? Not for *anyone*."

Arkk.

"Hear that?" I said. "Someone's arriving outside."

thirteen

Sally Lightfoot's arrival changed everything. Alone, we might have got through our adventure without coming to any harm, but with her on the scene it was inevitable that things would go too far. She was like a horrid catalyst, energizing things, making every personality clash more heated and intense. Although we didn't know this at the time, we should have been suspicious from the beginning.

I mean, *I* should have been.

She must have been heavy-footed with her Chevrolet pickup, because we heard its roar over the rain, and stopped laughing, forgetting the fact that Fabián's chair had been eaten from beneath him by a parrot with a grudge. Fabián got to his feet clumsily and, when she came in, I stood up as well. In the self-important manner of boys to whom responsibility has been lent, we welcomed our visitor and imparted android-like the preset message: Ray's not here, he'll be back in a minute, can we get you a drink?

She threw us from the start.

"Is it here?"

At first, I put her in her early thirties. I found out later she was late twenties. She wore a familiar backpacker-style uniform: a blue bandanna that swept back cropped blonde hair, bulging combat trousers and no-nonsense brown boots. These, like the rest of her, were coated in a fine layer of dust in spite of the rain. Her skin was another contradiction: pale, though she looked like an outdoors person. An animal tooth dangled from a leather string around her neck, breaking up a bright red T-shirt roughly cut off at the arms.

"Is it here?" she repeated. Her accent was plausible in both Spanish and English, but tinged with something that I thought sounded Scandinavian. "*Está aquí?* Is it here? Can you two boys speak?"

"Um, Ray's not here. He's the owner. He'll be—"

"You'd know what I was talking about if it were here. It's not here. That's good."

Holding the bandanna in place, she pushed her hands on to her forehead as if to locate a thought. One fine lick of hair spilled forward. All of it would have been held back were it not for the fact that her wedding finger was neatly, charmingly severed at the middle joint. She screwed up her eyes into tight triangles that looked as if they'd been block-cut into her face and remained in this position for half a minute, her body quivering and coiled like a watch-spring. Then, the thought apparently located, the triangles flew apart again and her pale hands dropped to her sides.

"Good," she said. "That's good. It'll be here soon. That means I can stay, if I've got my tides right, which I can't guarantee. I bet you two don't know your tides. You don't look like proper beach bums to me. I'll have a beer and something to eat, please. And a bed."

"We don't work here," I said.

"But we can help," said Fabián. "A beer, you say. No problem. Allow me. Please: take a seat, if you can find one that hasn't been eaten by our parrot."

He went to the fridge behind the bar, pulled up a wet, glistening bottle of Pilsener and gave it to her, wiping the neck with a handful of his shirt.

"As for the food, I'm afraid that Raymond, our maître d', is busy at present negotiating with the Port Authority, but he'll be back shortly."

Sally Lightfoot took the bottle without looking at him, drank a long draught of beer, then wiped her mouth with the back of her hand.

"There's nothing to eat?" she said.

"My name is Fabián. This is Anti. We're guests here too. Much as we'd love to help you, we don't know where the food is. But perhaps you'd like a piece of me to chew on while we wait for Ray to get back?"

"I don't eat meat as a rule," she said. "But then I suppose you're only poultry, aren't you? No. I'll wait."

Fabián turned away awkwardly. He hadn't expected this feisty response.

"What's your name?" I said, hoping to steer things back on course.

"Sally Lightfoot."

Fabián snorted and plunged back in. "Are you a Red Indian?"

"Do I look like a Red Indian?" she said to me. "Your friend isn't very bright, is he? You must be the brains of the outfit."

Fabián, two-nil down, began tidying up the remains of his chair in a businesslike fashion. The rain scraped across the thatch above us like fingers.

"Interesting name," I ventured.

"It isn't real," she said. "But if you get on the right side of me I might tell you where I got it from."

The routine that followed seemed to be part grooming ritual, part safety check. She ran her hands up the length of her ankles, one leg after another, as far up as the trousers would allow. Then up her arms, the left hand starting at the right wrist, smoothing the freckled arm until her thumb rested in the armpit, and back. Finally, the right hand started at the left wrist, sliding to the left pit and back again, arriving and lingering where the third finger of her left hand came to its end. She caught me watching and closed her fingers over the stub, both concealing and caressing it.

"That's something else you don't get to find out about yet," she said.

Fabián, who had retreated to the corner with a beer, now cautiously advanced again and sat at the table with us. Brewed coffee and dried lime juice had sweetened in the wood of the cabin to a smell like brown sugar—a microclimate, trapped inside by water. This day would not be consumed in a blaze like the one before: it was drowning.

We sat in silence beneath murky rafters and half-broken lantern strings, amid the shattered timbers of chairs and tables, as water beat down on the sand outside.

"Ray should be back soon," I said, clearing my throat.

"Meanwhile, why don't we go and see if it's arrived," said Sally.

"What is it you're waiting *for*?" said Fabián.

"You'll see. Come with me." She stepped through the curtain of water and on to the beach.

Great steps of shoreline had been munched away in our absence and the water continued to pound in, gray as dishwater. Needle-sharp rain drilled from above, combining with the onslaught of the Pacific overbite to create a damage machinery of jaws and sewing machines. Sally seemed at home in the storm: whilst Fabián and I squinted against it, her face appeared to free itself up, relaxing into the weather.

"Can you see anything?" she said.

"What are we looking for?"

"The horizon should look different. The texture of it will change. Then you'll know."

Fabián looked as mystified as me. We followed awkwardly after her. Plenty of storm-tossed debris fretted the shore—nail-studded driftwood, a rusty oil drum, palm leaves, green coconuts—but none of it could be said to fit her description.

"Maybe the storm's holding it back," she mused. "Maybe I've got it wrong." She had taken off her boots and now trod the sand with a mixture of anxiety and anticipation. "It needs to be here, you know. I can't stay if it doesn't get here. Have either of you got any binoculars?" Streaks of rain dabbed away at the dust on her face.

The rain eased off a little. A thin gauze of mist drifted in.

"I need it to get here. Then I can relax."

"What *is* it?" said Fabián.

"It's my livelihood."

"Yes, but what *is* it?"

"Did you say the texture of the water had to change?" I said.

Between swells, fifty feet out to sea, the water seemed rougher than ever, almost jagged. A low, wide shape, floating mostly unseen beneath the surface, was washing up; alarmingly, it seemed to be moving.

A drip of water fell off her nose and Sally Lightfoot smiled.

"Here she is," she murmured.

Whatever it was seemed simultaneously to be trafficked and buffeted by the water, and not to obey its rules. Its ripples didn't make sense. The shape shifted in the mist even as it drew near. I became conscious of a sound, too: a squabbling, squawking noise of disagreement, emanating inexplicably from the object in time with the strange movements on its surface.

"I've been pursuing her for a week now. There'll be no money if I only get part of her. Okay, we can go back inside now. She'll still be here in the morning."

"Can you please tell us what that is?" said Fabián.

"Isn't it obvious? It's a dead whale."

"Oh."

Pause.

"Sally. If the whale is dead, then why is it making a noise?"

"Oh, that. Those are my helpers. They only get to work on it when it's very near the shore, when they know they're safe."

Pause.

She glanced at us and sighed in exasperation. Then she opened her arms to the rain, grinned broadly and shouted:

"Vultures!"

We stared dumbly out to sea.

"Come back inside and I'll explain."

We followed in silence, keen not to say the wrong thing in this world of new rules.

"I'll show you," she said, walking round the side of the bar towards the main roadside entrance to the cabins. She untied ropes and lifted a tarpaulin that covered the open back of her blue pick-up truck. The whale bones heaped beneath it gave off an oily, faintly rotten smell and were piled in chaotic clusters where they had been thrown. It was like peering into a desecrated mausoleum.

"See? These are what I've collected so far. I'm cutting her nose-to-tail, and it's a race against time. Her skull rides up front with me on the passenger seat and the rest of her is back here—apart from what's left in the blubber. She's only a baby, of course, or I'd need a much bigger truck."

"Bit muddled up," I said, trying to work out which bit went where.

"I'm sure someone at the museum will know how to put her back together," said Sally. "All I know is they sure as hell won't pay me unless I give them the complete package."

"Who won't?"

"Natural History Museum of Caracas. Flat fee of $5,000: One Complete Humpback Whale Skeleton. Tax free, no questions asked. They want it to put in their lobby. Been tracking her down the coast since she washed up dead halfway down Colombia last week. She washes out to sea every couple of days, then comes back in with the next tide. I watch her wash up, spend the day cutting what bones I can out of her—with a little help from my friends—then I let her go out again and head south." She drew the tarpaulin back over her hoard. "You think this Ray will be back yet? I'm starving."

She was already out on the beach by the time Fabián and I got up on Saturday morning. For some reason, Ray was unsure about the new arrival and aired his suspicions whilst frying eggs for us behind the bar. How can something so commonplace as breakfast have so much power? I can still taste the eggs Ray prepared for us that morning: the browned, crispy edges of the white; the velvety yolks, burst open by us over hunks of dark, heavy bread.

"All I want to know is, on what authority is she going round cutting up that animal?" he said, jerking the cast-iron pan around before him. "You know, if everybody went around dissecting every animal they came across . . . I don't like it. It doesn't seem right."

"Doesn't sound like you," I said. "Why shouldn't she do it, if it's there and it's already dead? Why shouldn't she make the money rather than let it sink into the sea?"

"I'll tell you why. Because it's disrespectful to the animal," said Ray, poking in my direction with his spatula. "You kids think you're smart, but you don't know everything."

Fabián was swabbing his face with alcohol—something he seemed to have been doing almost obsessively since we arrived. "I agree," he announced, dropping cotton wool freighted with grease into a shell ashtray. "I think it stinks, what she's doing."

He'd picked an odd time to evolve a conscience, but I ignored it. "What are we doing today?"

"I said I'd take Sol treasure hunting again," said Fabián, lighting a cigarette.

"How are you going to find any more 'treasure'?" I asked. "You only had one of those medallions to start with."

"Well, maybe today we'll find some real treasure, shit-stick. But I take it you'd rather stay here and bum-suck that weird woman."

"At least she's not underage," I said under my breath. I was terrified Ray might overhear, so it wasn't a very effective retort. I ended up saying it so quietly that I don't think Fabián heard it either, which in hindsight could only have been a good thing. He looked daggers at me anyway, so I drained my coffee and walked out on to the beach.

Sally Lightfoot knelt in lively morning surf and decaying whale blubber, sawing away with a large carving knife. Her bandanna rode high on her head and she wore a pair of blue rubber gloves that covered her right up to the armpits. As she worked, the vultures argued with each other across the contours of the flesh like truculent old men, their heads darting in and out from their ragged, brown bodies. Several even burrowed their heads all of the way into the whale so that their slender necks resembled the wrists of hidden, rummaging hands. Evidently the birds were entirely at ease by now with their strange human companion.

"Aren't they afraid of you?" I asked.

"Absolutely not," she said, without looking up or stopping to cut. A thin strip of blubber adhered to her cheek, which was coated in a thin film of sweat. Her hair had fallen forward over the bandanna again. "They're very pushy indeed. Doesn't bother me, though, so long as they don't get cocky and steal any of my bones. I'm getting to the end of her now, and the bones in the tail are much smaller, so I have to watch them a bit more."

She pushed back the hair with a curled left wrist and I noticed the sag in her glove at the point of the missing finger.

"It's getting to the point where I could cut the tail away from the rest of the body, then take it away myself to dissect in private and leave all this behind. But the truth is, I think I'd miss them working there alongside me. You probably think that's a bit weird, don't you? Ngah! Get out of there."

She had managed to cut away most of the flesh from a large bone towards the front of the whale's tail, but still it wouldn't come out. I stepped forward to help.

"No you don't. There's no room for brute force in this job. Be typical if I got this far only to have some eager little monster like you stepping in and snapping a vertebra. Besides, I'm doing this on my own. That prize is going to be all mine when I go to claim it, and that means I have to do all the work myself." I turned away to head back to the bar. She stopped cutting momentarily. "But that doesn't mean you can't stay and talk to me while I work."

I sat down in the sand next to her, trying to stay upwind of the sickly, decaying smell that emanated from the whale and simultaneously to stay as far away from the bickering vultures as I could. Fabián and Sol emerged together from the bar and walked away from us in the direction of the cliffs below the dome. They were tossing a ball between them, and Fabián was already smoking his first joint of the day. I hoped he wasn't going to do something stupid like trying to get Sol stoned, though as she was Ray's daughter she'd probably been toking since she could walk. *Let him be,* I thought. Something told me it was the best policy. I would talk to him later and make sure that everything was okay.

"Want to tell me why you're called Sally Lightfoot, then?" I said.

She leaned back, scowling, as the whale's body voided some new pocket of trapped odor.

"Well," she said. "It goes like this. When I got married, I was told that the reason why I was expected to take the name of my future husband was that this was the person in whom I could trust from now on. This was who I relied on. This man was my *life*," she grimaced, tearing away at a difficult strip of cartilage. "Could you please scratch my nose? Not there. Higher. Oh, yes. Great. Thanks. You can wipe that off your hand on to the back of my shirt if you want.

"Anyway, let's just say that after a year and a half of marriage I found out that all this reliability was a myth. One person is always a crutch for the other. And in my case it turned out that my man didn't just expect to lean on me, but to beat me up from time to time as well. Not what I had been led to expect, I can tell you. So, after we had . . . gone our separate ways, I decided that the next name I took would be one in which I really knew I could trust. The obvious thing might have been to take back my old name, but I didn't want that either. I decided to become someone new. Could you shoo away that vulture? Just take a swing at him with the spade if he won't go. Thanks.

"Anyway, I ended up working as a marine biologist out in the Galápagos. That's what I trained as. That's how I know how this lovely lady works, and how to chop her up. There I am one day, sitting on an island populated by no human beings at all, watching the turtles, minding my own business and playing with my wedding ring—just wondering whether or not to throw it into the sea there and then, but aware that I might soon be needing it for the money. And something in the movement of the metal attracts this crab. This *huge* crab. Two things you need to know about the Galápagos: one, the animals aren't afraid of people, because they've never known any predators; two, you get bigger versions of everything there, for the same reason."

"I know. I was there last year."

"In that case I'm surprised you've never heard the name Sally Lightfoot before. It's a kind of crab. Named after a famous dancer from the Caribbean. It only exists in the Galápagos. A stunning bright blue and crimson crab. One of the most beautiful things you ever saw. And it's the kind of crab that scuttled up and snipped at my wedding finger, just at the point when I was wondering what to do with myself. It cut about halfway down the finger, right down to the bone, then scuttled off again. It was like a sign."

"It only cut your finger *a bit*?" I said, waiting for the rest, picturing a bloodbath.

"Yes."

"So, what . . . ?"

"Well," said Sally, calmly, "I cut the rest off myself. I went back to my little boat, took a scalpel from my medical kit and finished the crab's job off for him. It was obvious to me that that was what I had to do. I'd never felt so good in all of my life. I sat on this black shelf of rock near my boat and cut straight through the middle joint, letting the finger and the ring tumble away into the water in front of me. The ring disappeared straight away, but the finger sank more slowly. I remember watching this smoky, rusty trail it left as it went down, and I just sat there, watching the fish crowd round and holding the place where it had been. At the time, it didn't even hurt. I bet it got eaten in seconds. And now there's a nice, clean little piece of bone of mine down there somewhere. Just . . . like . . . THIS one. Got it."

I stared intently at the edge of a pile of gray blubber, lapped at by the surf. I was certain that if I looked up, I wouldn't be able to take my eyes away from Sally's missing finger.

"The crab had made my decision for me. Taking that piece of me away, however painful, would make me stronger, even if it meant sacrificing a piece of myself. I called myself Sally Lightfoot after the crab. And now that is my name."

Sally Lightfoot tossed the bone she had just extricated into the red plastic bin beside her. She glanced at me before going back to work.

"You did ask," she said.

In the morning, I had watched as Fabián and Sol picked their way along the cliff base at the north end of the beach. I planned on keeping an eye on them to see how far they got, but at a certain point they disappeared from view. I stayed with Sally for most of the day, making a couple of trips to the bar to fetch a beer or some sandwiches, but she never moved from the carcass and barely looked up from her work during our conversations. She had resolved to finish the job before the whale left Pedrascada.

"This is almost a dangerous mania, you know," I said, slurping a beer. "If you aren't careful, you'll be washed back out to sea with her and the vultures will start picking away at you too. Zoologists will marvel at it: *the blubber of a whale, with the skeleton of a woman . . . remarkable . . . Have you ever seen any-thing like it, Jones?* And you'll be sent off on round-the-world tours to be looked at in museums alongside shrunken heads and frozen Inca princesses."

"Quite an imagination you've got there," she said, cutting away quietly.

"It's no joke. Without me here you'd be in serious danger."

As the day wore on, I'd been glancing towards the north end of the beach at regular intervals. Sea-spray spouted inter-mittently over the rocks. Above, the northern rock pile towered, and beyond it shone the occasional glint of light from the lurk-ing, malevolent dome. Of Fabián and Sol there was no sign. I was conscious of the tide, which would soon be coming in and sealing off their return pathway. But as afternoon became early evening, just when my niggling worries were building to gen-uine anxiety, two details of color appeared on the jutting head-land and became the moving figures of Fabián and Sol.

Leaving Sally at work, I picked up a fresh beer from the bar and walked up the beach to meet them as they climbed off the rocks. Bursts of their laughter filtered back to me between blasts of wind.

"Find any more treasure?" I said, passing Fabián the beer as he reached me.

"Most kind," said Fabián. "Not as yet."

"But we will," said Sol.

"We will," he confirmed. "You can't get lucky every day."

We ambled back to the cabins.

"But," said Fabián, "we did find something very interesting. Sol showed me this cave you can get to if you climb round the cliff base. Obviously you can only make it there when the tide's out, but when you do, it's awesome. It goes really far back into the rock. So far that we didn't even get to the end because it got too dark to see. But Sol says she thinks there might be a tunnel cut in there, with steps, that allows you to get all the way up to the dome."

"Really?"

"Yeah, really. Wouldn't it be cool to find some secret passageway up there, like a smuggler's cave or something?"

I spoke evenly. "After what Ray said, I'm not so sure it's a good idea to be trying to get up there."

"You do what you like. We're going back tomorrow with a torch, aren't we, Solita? It's up to you whether or not you join us."

"And what have you been doing over there all day?" I said.

"Usual cave-like activities. We caught this monster crab in a rock pool, and I wanted to cook it over a fire but Sol wouldn't let me, so we set it free again. Then we looked for treasure for a while. Told each other a few stories."

"Fabián told me all about how you beat up the muggers in Quito. The ones who attacked you with knives and water bombs," said Sol.

"Really?" I said. "I'm flattered. But don't go believing everything he tells you."

"I think Fabián is the best storyteller in the world," she announced. "One day he's going to put his stories in a book and be a famous writer."

"Is that right?" I said.

"Yes. I think it is," said Fabián, beaming. "It's my new plan. Good, huh?"

"Very good."

Sol peeled off towards the bar in search of her father, who had been busy preparing a grand "culinary experience" for us for most of the day. Fabián swigged his beer comfortably as we drew near our cabin.

"You know, that kid is incredible. I really do wish I had a little sister like her." He put a friendly hand on my shoulder. "What about you? Have you and your whale been having fun?"

He undid the padlock on our flimsy wooden door and we stepped inside the cabin.

"You're sure Ray doesn't mind your taking his daughter caving?" I said, picking up a towel to head for the shower hut.

"Come on, man, he's a hippie. Anyway, he and Cristina have been busy all day cooking up stuff for dinner tonight. Glad to have her off their hands. Free babysitter. And I told you—I like her."

I could have said anything at this point.

"What?" he said. "What's this silence bullshit?"

All I had to do was say *something*.

"You think there's something dirty about this, don't you?" said Fabián, lowering his voice. "Jesus Christ. She's only ten. I would never . . ."

Finally I found my tongue. "No, of course you wouldn't. I know. Hey, I'll go and wash this whale blubber off myself, then how about we get really, really drunk?"

"You're fucking sick," he said.

I sighed and closed the door.

Sally Lightfoot had told Ray from the moment she arrived that she wouldn't eat red meat, and Ray had decided to rise to this challenge by cooking a feast of fish for us that evening. He'd disappeared in his boat straight after breakfast. Whether he'd been fishing himself or just motored round the point to visit the fishmonger's in town, he'd reappeared with a splendid haul: shrimps, crabs, two types of fish I'd never seen or heard of and one, like a huge goldfish, that I had seen—floating dead just beneath the water's surface as we sped past it the day before. Ray assured me that the two weren't one and the same animal.

Since his return, he'd been at work, marinating the white fish and shrimps in lime juice and coriander to make a huge ceviche, and burying the goldfish with handfuls of herbs under a heap of hot coals on the beach. For her part, Cristina had been baking and the area round the cabins was alive with smells: the citrus tang of the ceviche, the homely waft of fresh bread. The two clashed intoxicatingly and also served the useful function of masking the lingering odor of rotting whale blubber. Ray and Sally had discussed the matter of the whale, which, as the evening drew on, was gradually reclaimed by the sea. They concluded that it would wash back up the following day, just further south, towards the town. The roasting pit on the beach, which evolved into our communal bonfire as the evening drew in, also helped to combat the smell, as well as scaring away the few hopeful vultures that lingered.

But other dangers were circling. Fabián had been laying into the beer since his return from the cave and had already graduated to rum by the time we were ready to eat. I decided again that the best thing to do would be to stay out of his way and hope he would cool down, so I installed myself beside Sally Lightfoot on one side of the bonfire, leaving him, Sol and Cristina on the other.

Ray had just gone to the bar to fetch the ceviche when Fabián lit himself a Lark with the glowing end of a piece of driftwood and turned towards Sally as he exhaled.

"So. Happy with your animal?" he said.

"Very," said Sally Lightfoot. "Just one more day's work and I'll be done. The whole skeleton."

"I didn't mean that animal. I meant your new pet there."

I knew better than to respond to this.

"No aggression round my fire, guys," said Ray. He brought over a huge white dish, crouched down and ladled the mixture inside it into bowls. We fell silent as everyone gave in to the ceviche and to Cristina's warm, doughy bread. The combination of lime juice and coriander, so fresh and sharp it made you shudder, seeped in and saturated us just as it had the fish. The goldfish, when it had been disinterred from the coals, was charred, smoky and succulent. Sol made her own contribution by popping corn in a saucepan over the fire.

"That was truly spectacular, Ray," I said, licking my bowl. I lay down with my head in Sally Lightfoot's lap, watching the movements of her firelit chin from beneath as she ate. I hadn't asked permission, but it seemed like the natural thing to do. She'd changed into a sarong, and the material felt warm to the touch and soft under my neck, though the thigh beneath it was tensed firm.

"Do you think that the whale died of natural causes?" asked Ray, who had clearly retained his suspicions.

When she spoke, I felt faint reverberations shimmer through her body. "Obviously, there are lots of ways they can die, most of them perfectly natural, but I've seen no sign of disease on her. When I found her, there was a strange puncture wound to her head that I'm almost certain was responsible."

Fabián, who was devouring his food messily on the other side of the fire, looked up. "A puncture wound?"

"Yes. She could have just swum into something, I suppose, but it was weird. Perfectly round. As if someone or something had meant to do it to her. And a fisherman I spoke to up the coast said he'd never seen anything like it."

"Is that right?" said Fabián. He loved a mystery. His mind was already at work, embroidering some far-fetched explanation.

"There'd be no way to prove it, of course. And what about you? How was your day?"

"Sol and I have been exploring," said Fabián.

Sally smiled. "Exploring, eh? Sweet."

Fabián's tone sharpened. "What do you mean, 'sweet'?"

"Sorry," she said with a look of mock-solemnity. "Tell me. Where were you exploring?"

He spoke distantly and mechanically. "We went to a cave round the side of the headland. We think there might be a way to get through the rocks and up to the dome on the hill."

Sally turned to Ray. "I've been meaning to ask: what is that place?"

"It's a hide-out for a James Bond villain," said Ray, stripping flesh from a piece of fish carcass with his fingers. "He's called Saratoga, and he's got two belly buttons. A master criminal."

A smile wriggled across Sol's face in the firelight.

"We have a different theory, don't we, Fabián?" I said, sitting up.

"Do we? I'm not so sure we do." He looked at me darkly.

I have since tried to tell myself that I broke the agreement because I thought it might help him, that I thought he'd be pleased when I did it, that it would give his fantasies a chance to breathe in the open air. This is, of course, bullshit. I was showing off.

"We reckon the dome is an Amnesia Clinic," I said. "A place for people who have lost their memory. It's run by an eccentric billionaire named Victor Menosmal, and everyone up there has to go through the day not knowing who they really are. Tell them, Fabián."

"No."

"Go on, tell them."

"Don't do this." He looked at me as if he were ready to kill me. I began to regret what I'd said, but it was too late. Sally's interest was piqued.

"That's beautiful," she said. "A hospital full of people inventing their own lives. Maybe that's why you can't get up there. Maybe they don't want to be discovered. Maybe," she said, gesturing with a fork, "maybe they don't want their memories back at all. I'm not sure I would."

"It was a stupid idea," snarled Fabián. "Of Anti's. A fucking stupid childish idea."

"Fabián—"

"Shut up," he hissed. "How could you do this?"

He became conscious that Sol didn't like the anger in his voice and was looking at him with a new, scared look. His tone softened immediately and he gave her a reassuring smile. It reminded me what a good actor he was. Whatever his real mood, he could always reach for a mask that concealed it if he so chose. Now his voice changed as well. He spoke grandly, expansively:

"What I think is that the dome is home to the gathering of a secret society of ultra-powerful people. They meet regularly to direct world events in secret, trawl occasionally for sunken treasure and consume endangered species. The boat that nearly ran us down yesterday is theirs, and it's called . . . Let's say it's called the Anti-Ark. It was responsible for the death—by harpoon—of Sally's whale, and it travels the seas round the Galápagos, picking up animals two by two so they can be cooked and eaten at great big feasts."

He grabbed hold of Sol and pretended to munch down on her arm. She let out one of her infectious giggles. Cristina, who had been observing the proceedings with a benevolent eye, remembered her daughter and said, "And now I think it's time we put this particular little animal to bed."

She got to her feet and held out a hand for Sol, who yawned automatically and disappeared with her to the house.

"I like your theory very much," said Sally to Fabián. She was trying to patch things up with him, but under the circumstances she could only sound condescending. "You've got a powerful imagination."

He glowered. "Just a question of making the best of the available information. Something my so-called friend over there knows fuck-all about."

I said nothing.

"What's the matter? Cat got your tongue? Can't think of anything to say?"

Still I said nothing. I'd seen him like this before.

"My God, you're pathetic. Pathetic, wheezing little English boy."

Ray stepped in. He said that he wouldn't have this kind of

conflict round his fire, and that he'd kick us both out for good if we didn't change the subject.

"Fine," said Fabián. "Let's change the subject. Let's talk about the dome. I want to get up there and take a look. I'm sick of all these gaps. I want to know once and for all what it is. Now how do we do it?"

"I don't know, man," said Ray. "You might be right about this cave, I suppose, but I seriously doubt it. Or we can try and get there by boat, just motoring round to their jetty. But why bother? It's just some high-design holiday home, all plate-glass and concrete. Let it go. I'm sure the version in your head is better."

"Well I'm fucking sick of the version in my head," said Fabián, letting his temper fly now that Sol had gone. "I want a little more certainty. I'm going up there tomorrow to find out once and for all what it is. And then I'm going home."

He stormed off into the darkness, leaving a loud silence in his wake.

His departure somehow freed me into conversation. After a pause, I turned to Sally and said, "Ray likes to reward good stories. Why don't you tell him the story of your finger?" Thinking I'd gone too far, I hastily added, "Not if you don't want to, of course."

"Shouldn't you go after Fabián?" she said.

I explained that I thought it was better to leave him to cool off for the moment. Then I feared I'd broken a confidence with my request, and that her story had been meant just for me, so I reiterated that she should only tell it if she felt like it. Eventually, she told it anyway—a more detailed version this time, which included revelations about her marriage that made me properly guilty about having dragged it out of her. Apparently, her husband had not only hit her but threatened her on several occasions with a kitchen knife. I didn't lie back on her leg, thinking it might be an imposition now, but reclined with a warm stone nearby so I could still get the same "chin's eye" view. During the telling of the story it made her seem vulnerable, exposed. While she was speaking, I noticed that Fabián had quietly crept back to the shadows on the opposite side of the bonfire.

Ray loved the story, particularly the stuff about the crab. "Far out," he said. "Sally, take this stone. You want some more goldfish?"

I wanted to know whether Fabián had heard it all, and what he thought. He respected a good story more than anything in the world and I imagined it would make him warm to her. Since his return, he had sat silently in the darkness, but now his voice came ringing across the fire like a sniper's bullet.

"Isn't it lucky that species of crab was called Sally Lightfoot and not Dung Hopper, or Fist Fuck?"

He gave a coarse chuckle. "I call that a very nice coincidence. What a crock of shit." He got to his feet, kicking sand on to the fire in the process. I looked nervously to see how Sally was reacting but could tell nothing from the angle I had.

"Okay, then," said Fabián. "Here's another story. And listen hard to this one, because there's something special about it." He picked up a stone from the ground and threw it into the center of the fire, instantly demolishing the bright core as if it were a set of skittles.

"This story, motherfuckers, is *true.*"

fourteen

You might have heard an earlier version of this one (said Fabián). Let's see now. What shall we call it? How about "The *Real* Story of the Boy Who Said Nothing"? Are you ready? Then we'll begin.

One night, when the boy was almost nine years old—not that much younger than little Sol, who's now all cozily tucked up in her bed—he woke up in the middle of the night. The air-conditioning had broken down and the apartment felt very humid. The boy didn't feel well: his throat was parched and ragged, and the maid, whose name was Anita, not that it fucking matters, had cleared away the jug of water that the boy usually kept by the bed, so he decided to go to the kitchen and get himself a drink. He was afraid of getting ill. His parents had promised to take him walking in the highlands the following weekend and he really, really wanted to go.

Yawning, he padded along the main corridor of the apartment, past his parents' room. He heard the tell-tale little snuffling sounds his mother made when she was very deeply asleep, and smiled to himself, wondering how the hell his father put up with it every night.

As he walked into the kitchen, picturing a huge, cool glass of *naranjilla* or *maracuya,* he noticed that someone had left the light on in the maid's long, narrow pantry area to the side. The temperature in the room seemed to be leaping up by a degree with every step he took and his back was running with sweat, but he thought he'd better turn the light off anyway, so he started walking towards the door. And then the pantry light turned itself off.

The boy was alone in the kitchen, with only the yellowy light from outdoors and the long shadows this cast on the cork-tiled floor to show him the way. His first thought was that a burglar must have got into the house, heard him approaching and turned off the light. He remembered what his father had always told him: "If you hear anything in the night, Fabi, you come to me first. We'll get the gun and go get 'em together. Can't take any chances!" But the boy didn't want to look stupid. He knew that light-bulbs sometimes just blew up when they were finished, and that was probably what had happened here.

As he crept towards the door there was an explosion outside and, for a split second, white light flooded the kitchen. The boy stood, transfixed. It felt like his heart was trying to punch its way though his ribs. Then he realized some kid had just let off a firecracker in the street outside, and the boy told himself to grow up and stop being so afraid of everything. He opened the pantry door and put his head inside.

Three seconds later he closed it again. He left the kitchen in silence and made his way back along the corridor, once again hearing the muted snorts and stops in his mother's breathing as he went. He had gone back into his room, lain down and pulled the covers back over himself before he realized that he had forgotten even to get himself the drink.

He lay, thinking over what he had seen in the pantry. He told himself that with the afterglow of the firecracker still dancing on his retina he couldn't be sure of the identity of the eyes he'd seen in the corner. But though they had been half-closed in fear and surprise, he knew they could only have belonged to Anita the maid. Who else could it have been? He recognized the frilly sleeve of her blouse where her hand clutched the back of the man she hid behind.

And the back itself? Who could that have been? Whose trousers were they, tugged clumsily down that hairy pair of legs? It could have been anyone, theoretically—one bare arse is much the same as any other, and this one might have belonged to any boyfriend Anita had sneaked back into the apartment after her evening off. On the other hand, the boy knew only one person in the world who wore such a fucking stupid red and white neckerchief.

All the boy's worries about not getting ill were in vain. The next morning, he felt as if his throat had been slashed at by razors and he had a high fever. His mother told him he wouldn't be going to school and kissed him on the forehead. The kiss was the most refreshing thing the boy could remember feeling, and he lay as still as he could after his mother left the room, on sheets greasy with sweat, in the hope that the cooling imprint of her lips would stay on his forehead for ever.

No I do not want a fucking hot stone.

He didn't go to school that week but stayed home, where

his mother fed him soups and juices. He particularly asked *her* to bring him these things, instead of Anita. On the one occasion Anita did have the nerve to show her face in the boy's room, he spat at her as she laid down the bowl of soup. She did not return. He expected a visit from his father at any time, but she obviously hadn't had the nerve to tell his father about having seen the boy in the pantry.

The boy couldn't decide what the best thing for him to do would be. For the moment, he resolved to keep the information back, thinking vaguely to himself that it might one day come in useful. By the weekend, he felt better and had begun to forget about what he had seen, though he knew well enough that it had happened. He told his mother that he was fine to go on the hiking trip as planned. "Let's ask your Papi," she said.

His father walked in, red and white neckerchief at his throat as if he wanted to taunt the boy. The boy could feel sweat forming on his forehead; his fever had broken out again in the short time it took for his father to get across the room.

"I don't think he's quite ready to take on the sierra, do you?" said his father, feeling the boy's forehead. "Come next time, Fabi. You must be tough to attack a whole mountain. Why not go and stay with your Uncle Suarez this weekend, and we'll pick you up on Sunday."

When they had gone, the boy writhed in his bed, clutching and ripping at the sheet beneath him. It wasn't the matter of Anita and his father that made him so angry. Rather, it was that his father had denied him a trip to the mountains and taken his mother away from him for a whole weekend. He decided there and then that when they returned on Sunday, he would tell his mother what he had seen in the pantry. The boy and his mother would leave Papi to his whore of a maid and go and live somewhere else. Although his mother would be upset, it was better that she should know.

They left the boy at his uncle's house and drove off into the foothills. And they never came back.

Never came back.

Car flew off the road, and pheeeeeeuuuuuuw . . . poof.

All gone.

No chance to tell anyone anything now. What use was the knowledge if nobody cared to hear it? What would the information be now but a story? What *value* did the truth have?

And later on, throughout one certain funeral and one uncertain, but very likely, memorial service, in an empty church coated with plundered Inca gold, the nine-year-old boy gazed upwards through clouds of incense at the multicolored, crying statue of the Virgin, trying desperately to hold back his own tears, and he realized that if he had spoken out and told the story he would have stopped his parents going recklessly off into the mountains without him. If he hadn't kept quiet, his mother—and his father for that matter—would still be there with him now.

And there you have "The *Real* Story of the Boy Who Said Nothing."

"So you see," said Fabián, waving a stick in the general direction of the bonfire, "that there is a difference between real pain and imagined pain. Some of yours may be genuine. But if there's one thing I know how to do, it's to tell when someone's talking themselves up."

He pointed at Sally. "So your husband used to knock you around. Big fucking deal. I killed my mother. Which would you rather live with?"

Before she had a chance to answer, the gloom beyond the fire had absorbed him as he stomped off towards the cabins.

I had hoped we might linger together by the fire for a while, but Sally went to bed shortly afterwards. She kissed me once on my forehead and muttered something about how we were still only kids and had a hell of a lot to learn. Then she swept her legs from under me, so that my head dropped abruptly on to the sand.

"Goodnight," she said. "Boy."

Ray had gone too. I lay on the beach with my arms starfished around me and the memory of Sally Lightfoot's kiss delicately evaporating on my forehead. I imagined that I could feel the curve of the earth beneath my hands, that gravity and the axis of the planet were tangible, fathomable qualities, and for a second, I almost believed myself. I'd drunk enough, but forced more beer down myself to justify staying away from Fabián for a bit longer.

When I got to the cabin, I thought I would knock on the door before going in, even though I didn't have to since it belonged to both of us. But before I'd even raised my hand to knock, his voice punched out from inside.

"Don't even think of sleeping in here. Fuck off and sleep with that mutilated bitch if you're such good friends."

I decided to go back out and sleep by the fire. I could stoke it up for warmth, and was easily drunk enough to pass out there. But as I walked back towards the beach, I saw that her door was open and a candle flickered inside, casting a flighty sphere of light on the walls.

I lay down on the foam mattress next to her, as quietly as I could. Soundlessly, she threw her blanket sideways over me, and I ducked my head inside and curled up against her back, inhaling deeply the smells of wool, sweat and salt.

fifteen

"Swim?" I said after breakfast, in a spirit of reconciliation.

We'd resolved disagreements in this way before. Any falling-out over a girl or a disputed version of events, however serious, could be swiftly drowned in the Sporting Club's deep blue rooftop pool. It was one of a few locations (Suarez's house being another) where we could slip into predetermined modes of behavior, disregarding the tedium of details, and get back to the more fun, more abstract business of being kids. But reconciliation seemed to have become an increasingly complicated business since the earthquake on the day of the Easter parade—and not just because Fabián's arm had been stopping him swimming.

"No thanks," he said.

He sat at the bar, dabbing at his face and arms with alcohol-soaked cotton wool. The practice had become a habit whose prolonged effects would have horrified Eulalia: it no longer merely sluiced out grease from his pores, but had begun to remove layers of skin. The nooks on either side of his nose had reddened brightly, and the surface of his right arm, shocked by sudden exposure to some unexpectedly harsh new elements, looked positively raw. It had added a new, haggard dimension to his face, giving him the air of a punch-drunk boxer or a malarial explorer.

"Come on. What about a bit of negative buoyancy in the sea? You haven't even been swimming properly since you took the cast off."

Without meaning to, I had managed to adopt the tone of an irritatingly jovial parent, and I knew even as I spoke that I would be punished for it. Sure enough, he shot me his most withering look—eyebrows raised in condescension, the lids crumpled like paper round his glowing green eyes—the look he always gave me when I thought something was still cool but he had decided to grow out of it. I held my temper.

"Why not? What else are you going to do?" I asked.

"You realize it's Sunday today?" he said. "If we're not back by tomorrow then certain people are going to start freaking out. Or had you forgotten that?"

I'd lost track of the time we'd been away. But now it was I who wanted to stay put a little longer.

"All the more reason to seize the day. Come swimming now and we'll talk about it later. If we leave tonight, or tomorrow morning, then we can still get back by the time school ends to-morrow, and we'll only get busted for missing one day."

"That will never work. Anyway, I don't want to swim. My arm hurts. I don't think the bone had a chance to set properly before I broke the cast off."

"I don't think all this alcohol-rubbing can be helping," I said. "Your *skin*'s coming off."

"Stop worrying about me. I'm fine. I'm sorry about last night. But at least now you know the truth." His hand shook as he drank from a glass of water. I noticed fibers of cotton wool clinging to his arm, smoothed in the direction he'd been swabbing, with the grain of his thin dark hairs. "Now you know why it bothers me so much."

"Yes. Now I know." I sat down beside him. "Why haven't you told me about it properly before? What really happened, I mean."

"If you want the truth, it's because I've never really thought about it. If you stop to think about what happened, the problem is that there really isn't anything to think about. We know nothing other than that the car went off the road. What else is there? Where do you direct your 'if only'? Who do you get angry with? The government, for not building safer roads? Nature, for causing landslides? The car company, for not making something that sticks better to a mountain?"

He went over to the fridge behind the bar and hoisted out a Pilsener. He'd barely swallowed his breakfast, but I held my tongue.

"No . . . The only person I could find to blame was me. And I couldn't even tell anyone. I had no brother or sister to confide in. And Suarez would fuck anything with a heartbeat, so I doubt it would have enraged him much to know that Papi was cheating on his sister with the maid. He'd have expected it, almost."

He poured beer into a tall glass, took a mouthful of froth and wiped his mouth. He smiled. "What's more, you don't exactly *want* to remember the fact that one of the last times you ever saw your father alive he was buried to the hilt in another woman with your mother asleep in the next room. See what I mean?"

I nodded.

"And then a really strange thing started happening. My imagination began filling in the gaps left by what I didn't know, or couldn't remember. I found myself thinking, *well, why were they driving so recklessly? Was it to get away from something? Or to get somewhere? To a hospital, maybe?* Suarez had taken me to this bullfight, and told me how dangerous it was if anyone got hurt up in the highlands because of the distance to the nearest hospital."

He lit a Lark and rotated it slowly with his fingertips. The filter made a soft crunching noise as the nook of charcoal granules in its center collapsed.

"...I mean, we know nothing about what went on up there. We never will. Anything at all could have happened. And I'm fucked if I'm going to stick to the obvious explanation.

"So I told myself other versions. And it helped. I found myself avoiding thinking about what had happened before they went. If I avoided the fact that I knew he was fucking Anita, then that made it better. What if I had told my mother he was fucking the maid? Well, that's one thing. But better still, what if he hadn't been fucking the maid at all? What if Mami and Papi had been a happy couple in love? What if he'd even been dying, and she'd been rushing to save him? And because we never found her body—because of that, especially—what if she was still alive somewhere? You can see how it happened. The possibilities spread around me like a creeper, and soon they took over everything. I see that bullfight far more clearly than I see what really happened. Just as I see the Amnesia Clinic."

He exhaled a thin line of smoke and looked me in the eye for the first time.

"I see every single detail."

"Doesn't it feel good to have finally told someone the truth?" I said. "Think about what Sally said about cutting away a part of yourself to become stronger."

"Oh yes. Good old Sally. Let me tell you something: if coming here has helped, which I think it has, and forced me to live in the real world a little more, which it might have done, then it has nothing whatever to do with your whale-woman, okay?"

"Okay, okay," I said.

"If anyone is to be thanked it's Sol. She's shown me how to have fun again. When I'm playing those stupid, childish games with her, I don't feel it any more."

"But you can't play those games for ever," I said.

"You're quite right. You can't. Just look at this arm." He had taken out his bottle of cane alcohol again. "I've got rid of all the dead skin on the surface, and now I'm getting down to the bloody insides. It may hurt, but it's real. It's fucking *real,* man. And that is why today, I am going to go to that cave with torches and find the tunnel that goes through the rock up to the dome. No more uncertainty. No more speculation."

"Why not come over and at least see the last bit of the whale being cut up before you go?"

"What is it with you and that whale? No. I'm going to stay here and get unspeakably stoned. Then Sol and I are going back to the cave. You go."

"You're sure?"

"Yes. Go. You have your fun. Whatever floats your boat.

Good luck to you." He stared into the beer glass as cigarette smoke clouded round his words:

"If you don't go right now, I'll hurt you."

I got up and left the bar.

She let me help her this time. But I experienced no feeling of triumph at finally removing the last fragment of bone from the body of the dead whale. Although the two of us worked hard at it so as to beat the tide, and although the carcass was now so far south that it would certainly not wash back up at Pedrascada the following day, only Sally Lightfoot was genuinely elated by finishing. I cast repeated glances back at the bar, and across at the north end rocks, for any sign of Fabián and his "little sister."

The whale's remains lay like a great gray sock on the beach, fully exposed now to the mercies of the vultures. Sally took her bucket of bones and dragged the end of the tail away with her.

"This bit's more difficult," she said. "Lots of small bones and cartilage. I think I might just keep it for now and go and boil it up somewhere later to get at all the insides. Well done." She ruffled my hair with fishy wet hands. "Thanks for being my assistant. I think we should celebrate."

When she'd dumped the final pieces of whale in the back of her truck, she met me back in the bar, where Ray was at work reassembling some of the furniture that had been broken by recent events.

"Where can a girl take a bath round here?" said Sally.

"Only got the shower back there, sorry," said Ray through a mouthful of nails.

"I'm not standing under that crappy trickle of brown water," said Sally. "I've finished my work and I want a proper bath."

"You want some real fresh water, I'd recommend the waterfall," said Ray. "Listen. Hear that? That's the underground stream. On the other side of the road it flows over ground. All you have to do is follow the stream through the plantation on the other side of the road, past the leafless trees. You'll find a waterfall back there. It's not much, but it's fresh."

The fairy-tale instructions were too tempting for me not to accompany her.

We walked out of the roadside entrance to the cabins and back on to the road. A chaotic bus rattled past, a burst of salsa music escaping from its windows. I thought how it might have been the same one that had dropped us off three days and a million years before. Presently, we were making our way across a scrubby field behind the road. Crickets droned and bunches of cactus thrived, but I could see no fresh water.

"Stream's probably still underground here," she said, striding on ahead.

She was right. We soon came upon a stream of water passing into a concrete irrigation pipe in the ground and began following it, away from the beach, along a narrow dirt path. The vegetation beside the water grew more lush and green as we followed it. Threads of green weed waved in the current, like hair. Pink water-hyacinth accessories bloomed.

"Please don't take Fabián too seriously," I said between wheezing breaths, trotting along behind her and wishing we'd brought some water to drink on the walk. "I'm sure he didn't mean to hurt you last night. He mostly only ever shouts at himself."

"Don't worry. It takes more than a little shouting to upset me," she said over her shoulder. "I'm not going to bear him a grudge."

This struck me as odd, because it hadn't occurred to me that she might bear him a grudge.

It wasn't a large waterfall—not much more than a clatter of flimsy spray on to some rocks—but the pool that had collected beneath it was deep, and easily wide enough for swimming. Gingerly, I put a foot in and felt proper cold for the first time in days. The darkness of the water was shot through with silvery fish which flashed intermittently against the greens and grays of moss and stone beneath. Sally stepped out of her shorts, shrugged off her T-shirt and stepped in, shivering with pleasure. I watched a wave of goose-bumps ripple across the pale skin of her mole-peppered back, which drew my eye to other features of her body: a patch of red skin under a twisted bra strap; her tiny waist encircled by the water; her thighs beneath the surface, falling away into the dark. She jumped forward into a breast-stroke, nodded her head under and scrubbed at her hair manically, whooping as her head resurfaced.

"What are you waiting for?" On her back now, kicking away from me across the small pool. I unbuttoned my shirt slowly, slipped off my shoes and stepped forward. Tendrils of weed embraced my right foot. A second step took my left into sucking gray mud. I trod carefully, my arms waving beside me in a balancing motion. The cold soaked into my shorts as I moved in deeper. Fish brushed against my legs, almost at waist height. I flinched involuntarily.

"Oh, come on. The fish won't hurt you. Jump in."

Obediently I fell forward, ducked under the water and

pushed myself towards her, emerging near her with my hair swept back from my face. I had taken a mouthful of water, intending to spit it at her as I came up, but as I twisted upright to find my feet between the fish on the rocks beneath, her legs clutched my waist, pulling me in and grasping me. She retreated slowly into a small but deep bay on the opposite side of the pool, bringing me with her. I bounced awkwardly on the floor so as not to tip forward. The fish were concentrated and agitated here, as if in anticipation of a feeding frenzy. As if Sally Lightfoot had power over water creatures.

"Boy," she said, her hooded, triangular eyes on mine.

I watched her pupils dilate as her legs shrank and tightened around me. The friction between the two thin pieces of material between our legs had become a hot new world. Without consciously deciding to, I arched my back, jutting towards her, and her mouth opened a little. Certain she had me now, her legs relaxed around mine, her feet tracing lazy lines up and down the backs of my legs.

"Boy," she repeated. "Did you know the Indians call waterfalls 'the sperm of the mountains'?"

My reply, if I had formulated one, was cut off when she brought her slippery lips to mine. Her tongue tasted of wet apples. Her fingers sank into the water, pulling my shorts down at the front, and with her other hand she popped the stub of her ring finger into my mouth, tracing the outline of my lips in saliva. Then she moved the hand around the back of my neck, clutching me there, holding my gaze.

"Shall we feed the fish?" she said, turning with her right hand on me, pulling slowly and steadily, her eyes on mine, until, looking away from her, I came in gossamer tendrils that spiraled downwards in the water. Sure enough, a rising fish scooped it up, taking every last blob. One last bit must have clung lazily to the end, because a fish swam up and kissed me for it. I continued to look away into the water, ashamed to look her in the eye as she withdrew her hand.

"How's that for primordial soup?" she said.

"Don't you ever regret chopping off your finger?" I said, as we walked back. I could think of nothing else to say to her.

"You are what happens to you. And it's one of the best things that ever happened to me. Even if I regretted it, it would still be me." She stopped walking. "You're nothing but a patch-work, you know. A patchwork of what's happened to you. I just added a little piece to yours. And now you have a real story to tell your silly little friend."

She smiled, popped a cold kiss on my cheek and looked away again. "By the way, I'll be leaving as soon as we get back, and you will never see me again."

sixteen

The thought that she might leave before we did hadn't occurred to me. I had envisioned an altogether different scenario: a teary farewell as Fabián and I stepped on to a bus and rattled off into the sunset, followed by a last-ditch realization on the part of Sally Lightfoot that she needed me. She would chase after the bus for a while, but it would be too late. Then, a few weeks later, I would be emerging from the school gates, sporting unawares with a group of slender, attractive, female classmates, and something would make me stop and look up. She would be standing motionless on the other side of the street, wearing a desperately hopeful smile, and would break into a run as she approached, etc., etc.

Not, "You will never see me again."

When we got back I made straight for our cabin to determine in private how to react to the news. Kicking open the door with suitable melodrama, I threw myself on the foam mattress, bringing down my mosquito net again in the process. I lay in the dark and shouted into my pillow once or twice before the sickly concentration of marijuana and cane alcohol in the air became apparent. I lifted my head, looked over and saw him.

"Jesus. What happened to you?" I said.

Fabián lay sideways on his bed with his back slouched against the cabin wall and his legs tangled in front of him where they had fallen. I unbolted the wooden shutter and opened the window. He flinched at the light. Although he was pale and sweating from booze or dope or both, there was something else. His plastic bottle of cane alcohol was almost empty and his arm, which before had merely been scaly, now glistened in the half-light, wet and red. Thin seams of blood sprang at the corners of his lips and he'd streaked his forearms with dried skin through rubbing messily at the holes.

"Did you fuck her, then?" Speaking opened the cracks in his lips up even more.

"Fabián, Jesus . . ."

"Did you fuck her? I'm not jealous, I'm just interested. You did, right?"

"What have you done to yourself?"

"Just a bit pissed, that's all. Cleaning. Nothing to worry about. So tell me, did you? Probably didn't have the balls, as usual. Should have been you playing with the kid and me getting the girl; still, bet she regrets it now."

A white bowl of roasted, salted maize sat in his lap, and he tossed a few pieces of it into his mouth before reaching down beside him to a bottle of *aguardiente*. Not only was he rubbing it all over his face, he was drinking it as well.

"What's happened here? Why are you behaving like some Vietnam veteran?"

He sat up straighter on the bed, then collapsed to the exact position he had been in before. The jerkiness of the movement put me in mind of an old-fashioned wooden puppet.

"Been a bit of an accident," he said. "It's okay though. Sol hurt herself, but she's okay, I think. *Madre de Dios,* this arm hurts."

Through the window, I saw Ray striding towards our cabin. Ray never strode, and I had never seen him looking so purposeful: something was wrong.

"I think we may have to go soon."

"What's happened?"

"May have to go quite soon."

Ray looked in at the window.

"Mind if I talk to you?" he said to Fabián.

"I'm sorry, Ray. It was an accident," said Fabián, getting clumsily to his feet and stumbling in the process. "Is she okay?"

"She's a bit upset, man. And she has a cut on her leg."

"Let me talk to her." Fabián careered towards the door and outside on to the sand, spraying roasted maize before him. The bowl landed with a clatter on the wooden floor. Ray held Fabián by the elbow, half holding him up, half stopping him in his tracks.

"I don't think that's such a good idea, kid. She doesn't want to see you."

"It was an accident, for God's sake. I would never hurt her."

Ray steered Fabián firmly backwards into the cabin and stood in the doorway as he lurched back to his bed and sat down.

"Do you want to tell me what happened?"

"I told you: it was an accident. We were up at the cave, trying to follow the path further back into the cliff, and she fell backwards. I tried to catch her, Ray, I promise. It wasn't my fault. Next thing I know, she's screaming and running away from me all the way back here."

"She—Jesus, this is awkward—she says you pushed her on purpose. She says you hurt her."

"I only meant to try to stop her falling. I swear. I would never hurt your daughter, Ray. Who do you think I am?"

"Okay, listen." Ray stepped into the cabin and sat down next to Fabián on the bed. His hair swung forward on either side of his face, like curtains. "It's your word against hers, but don't worry: I know she can be a bit of a fantasist. I just think it's probably for the best if you stay away from her for the rest of your stay, okay?"

"But it wasn't my fault."

"I'm sure it wasn't, kid."

"I—"

"Please do what I ask and I won't get mad. I know you guys are leaving tomorrow anyway, so let's just forget about it and enjoy the last day. But don't go near my daughter again. God, I hate confrontation. Can we forget about this now? I've got furniture to mend."

"It's forgotten," I said, closing the door behind him. I watched through the window hatch as he loped back towards the bar.

"Is there anything you want to tell me?" I said, turning to face the bed.

Fabián was crying in slow, soft sobs, like a wounded animal.

"I couldn't see the pathway," he whispered.

"What do you mean?"

"We took torches, but I couldn't see any pathway into the

rock. We got really far back. We even disturbed a load of bats who went flying out over our heads like something from a horror movie. Then we reached so far back in the cave that we couldn't even see the daylight coming in behind us. I was sure it carried on, but the walls were getting narrower and narrower around us, and Sol started to freak out. Said she wanted to go home."

"What did you do?"

"It made me so angry," he said, through a mouthful of tears and mucus. "I got so angry thinking that there might not be a way through. So I guess I might have lashed out at her. In the dark. But I didn't mean to hurt her, I swear. It was just so frustrating. You have to believe me, Anti. I've got to go and see her, to say sorry. I'll explain it to her. Then we can go back again tomorrow, with better torches or something."

He straightened his legs again and half got to his feet. I don't often surprise myself. My cowardice can generally be relied upon in any given situation. But what I did next was a surprise to us both. I planted a palm on Fabián's chest as he got to his feet and shoved him back on to the bed.

"I think it might be for the best if you stay here and sober up for a while," I said. "And I think both of us ought to stop with all this shit about the cave, and that stupid dome."

I left the cabin before I had the time to lose my nerve.

On my way to the bar, I heard the soothing sound of Cristina's voice coming from the direction of the shower cubicle. The door was ajar and, as I passed, I saw her crouched inside, delicately applying a piece of cotton wool to her daughter's leg. Cristina must have brought Sol in here to wash dirt from the cut before she dressed it, and although the girl now stood stoically beneath the still-dripping shower head, it was obvious from the jerky rhythm of her breathing that she had only recently stopped crying.

I put my head inside the door. The smell of antiseptic filled the cubicle.

"Is everything all right?" I said.

"Everything's fine," said Cristina. "Solita had a little fall, but she's going to be fine now, aren't you?"

The girl nodded automatically before wincing at the touch of the cotton wool.

"That's my brave little girl," said Cristina.

"Fabián says he's very sorry. And I'm sure he didn't mean to hurt you," I said.

"We know that, don't we?" said Cristina softly, still dabbing at the leg. "We know it was a mistake."

"It wasn't!" shouted Sol without warning, pushing her mother's hand away as she did so. "It wasn't a mistake! I'm not stupid. I told you. He pushed me! He meant to do it."

"Now stay calm, honey, please. I told you, you can't be sure of that. Now just keep still while I do this and then we'll go and make you a banana milkshake, okay?"

Sol nodded, pacified by the prospect of the milkshake, but I could see that she was still trembling with anger at the injustice she felt she'd suffered.

"She'll be fine," said Cristina to me, over her shoulder. "I'm sure it was an accident. Tell Fabián not to worry about it. Honestly."

But there was less warmth in her voice than usual.

When I got to the bar, I found Sally Lightfoot in the middle of paying her bill to Ray. She had taken a wad of notes from her shoe and was peeling each one off carefully, counting it down on to a table as Ray read out the invoice:

"So that's two nights' full board and lodging, plus—how many beers do you think you drank? That all? Okay. So that will make 15,000 sucres. Then again, you did tell an excellent story. Call it 12,000."

It was heartbreaking to watch her leave. I tried to think of anything I could do to stall her, any pretext at all. But nothing came to my mind, and so I watched dumbly as each of my weakly-imagined futures dwindled away in front of me.

Sally's wad of money had apparently come to an end, and what had seemed like an impressive quantity when it came out of the shoe had dwindled to a paltry-looking sum. The cash fluttered on the table in the breeze.

"I keep the rest of my money in the glove box of the truck," she explained. "Safe-keeping. Back in a minute."

Ray and I sat, gazing out through the palm thatch at the in-coming tide. Two pelicans flapped past on the horizon.

"Ray, I want to apologize . . ." I began.

"Forget about it, man. It's in the past now. Just make sure your crazy friend stays away from my daughter until you leave. It was stupid of me to let a total stranger take her out for the day, and I'm sure that . . . Wait a minute." He narrowed his eyes and pointed north. "What the *hell* is he doing now?"

Fabián had escaped unseen round the side of the cabins and run off up the beach. Now he stood on the short outcrop of rocks at the north end. Standing Christ-like, his arms extended, he was facing out to sea, but he clearly very much intended to be visible. And then, as if we'd unwittingly fired a starting pistol simply by laying eyes on him, he began clambering away from us, across the boulders at the base of the cliff that led round to his cave, his unbuttoned shirt bulging behind him in the wind.

"He better not be thinking of going across there while the tide's coming in," said Ray, "because I guarantee you that this time he will kill himself."

"I'll go after him," I said, getting up.

"No. You haven't got time. You'll get caught too. I'll go fetch the boat and we can go round and pick him u— . . . Bitch! Fucking bitch!"

The Chevrolet pick-up outside had roared into life, and we heard a spray of gravel as Sally Lightfoot and her whale skeleton reversed at speed on to the main road.

"Sorry, kid. More important things to deal with," said Ray, leaping behind the bar to collect his car keys. "But I advise you to stop Fabián getting any further round that headland if the two of you intend to walk each other to school again." Cursing, he sped out of the bar towards the spot where his old Lada was parked.

He hasn't got a chance, I thought, almost smiling to myself at the thought of Sally Lightfoot and her light-footed departure. Automatically, I began following Ray out towards the road. Then I remembered Fabián and turned back to face the beach. His blue shirt traveled slowly but steadily across the rocks, filling with the breeze like a sail. Even at this distance I could see how close he was walking to the froth of incoming waves. I felt a concentrated fury swell inside me, all of it directed intensely at that retreating scrap of color.

Fuck you, I thought. *Fuck you, and your cave, and your stories, and your Amnesia Clinic.* I wavered for a moment, then turned away from the beach and began running in the direction of the road.

My resolve didn't last much longer than ten paces. I changed direction without even slowing down and broke from a half-run into a sprint across the hard, wet sand, trying to convert both the anger and the fear that I felt into the energy I needed to get to him.

By the time I reached the rocks, the air in my lungs had already turned to pain, stabbing sharply with every pace. He knew this would happen. He was doing it to me deliberately. Wheezing heavily, I placed one foot on to the rocks and began picking my way across. The sandstone contours felt coarse under my thin soles. I looked ahead to Fabián. Already, sea-spray spouted between the two of us. I had to move fast. Apart from the physical advantage that Fabián had, he'd also covered this ground four times over the past two days and knew it far better than I did. My chest swelled up inside my ribcage. I fought rising panic as the pain increased, trying to kid my bucking lungs into relaxing and loosening themselves up. If I panicked, I would have a full-on asthma attack—which was probably exactly what Fabián wanted.

I tried to breathe as slowly and deeply as I could, timing my paces from rock to rock with each breath. Simply moving forwards without slipping sideways into the sea or being blown around by the wind required so much concentration that I became absorbed by the process and, in this way, managed to calm myself down. I advanced for some minutes, fixing my gaze on the ground, and when I did look up, I saw that he wasn't far ahead of me and that he had stopped. I slowed down even more so that I wouldn't be a hacking mess when I finally got to him. Waves broke over the rocks beside me, splashing the bare, open tops of my feet with cold water. I glanced up at the red shrine on top of the cliff, which was close enough now that I could see the areas where its paint had peeled to reveal the grain of the wood, toughened by salt-breeze. I saw fresh flowers attached to the shrine and wondered again how the hell anybody had got up there.

"Come back, you idiot," I shouted.

He stood firm and turned his head out to sea, as if to say that he wouldn't speak to me until I reached him. But even as he did so, a powerful gush of water shot upwards like a geyser through a gap in the rocks to his left, and he stepped away in surprise. As I drew nearer, I saw that small waves were already snapping at his heels. We'd both have to climb to escape them. He must have had the same thought as me, because he placed his hands on the cliff face and began climbing it just as I arrived where he'd been standing.

"Please stop. This is dangerous. You'll kill yourself," I said. It didn't necessarily have to be such a hazardous situation, but what did that matter to Fabián, who was such a danger to himself?

"Scary out here, isn't it?" he shouted, laughing down at me.

Relinquishing his grip, he slid easily back down the slope and extended his arms as he landed, pretending to waver, with a mock-scared look in my direction. This had the desired effect of showing me precisely how good his balance really was.

Exhaustion flooded my legs, making them shake for real. Fabián grabbed a large piece of sandstone.

"Fabián, just talk to me . . ."

"Worried about me, are you? Eh? *Hijo de puta.*"

He put his hand down on the rock shelf in front of him and, keeping his eyes on me, he heaved the rock down on his arm at the point where it had broken.

His scream turned to laughter. "See what I can do to myself? What the fuck do you think you can do to me if I can do that to myself?"

He threw the rock against the wall. Chips of sandstone flew off to the sides.

"Please," I said. "Please stop. Let's go back and talk about this. I'll do anything. Please."

"No. We stay here. Anyway, look—the tide's already coming up. Where are you going to go?"

He was right. White spray detonated where only minutes before I had been walking. The angle of the horizon seemed to have changed as the tide leaned forward into its momentum. We were marooned on the ever-decreasing sliver of yellow rock.

"Don't worry your little head. All we have to do is get up to the cave. The tide does fill it up a bit, but it goes far enough back into the rock that we'll be safe."

I stood, breathing heavily, looking at him.

"What's the matter?" he said. "Don't you believe me?"

"I don't think it's safe."

"So you don't believe me."

"Yes. Yes, I believe you."

"Come on then. You never know," he said, turning his back on me as he faced the rock to look for his handhold. "When we get up there, you never know what we might find. I told you, this cave goes right back into the rock. There's still a chance we could get up there. There's still a chance we could find it."

He crouched down, ready to spring upwards at the rock face to climb away from the water level and towards the cave mouth. Lightly, I touched him on the elbow, conscious of how I could hurt him if I wanted by touching his bad arm.

"Find what?" I said.

He didn't turn round. "You know damn well what. The Amnesia Clinic."

"I thought we agreed not to—"

"Fuck you and your agreements. I'm going up there to find it. You never know. That clinic might be up there. My mother might be up there. We have to at least try. Wouldn't you rather know for sure?"

"I DO know for sure," I shouted. "And so do you." This time I grabbed the bad arm. He spun round quickly with the pain.

"And why is that?" he said. The hatred in his eyes shocked me.

I took a breath before speaking. But I had to say it.

"Because I made it up," I said. "I faked that newspaper article to make you feel better. I made the whole idea of the clinic up, and you know that I did. And you *know* it isn't real, don't you?"

He said nothing. His face contorted again into that expression of disgust, as if I had said something in bad taste, and his voice quavered as if he were trying to shake away my words.

"Shut up. Shut up."

"You know that," I repeated.

"Of *course* I know!" he screamed, eyeballing me and pushing at my chest. "Idiot."

He was crying again and he shook me once more as he

spoke, more quietly this time: "But that doesn't mean it won't be there."

"What do you mean?"

He sighed. "You never understood it at all, did you?"

"Obviously not," I said.

He grabbed me by the front again and my lungs clenched inside me. He drilled each word into me, calmly, methodically, channeling his fury: "It's good. I should be happy that you made me tell the truth. Are you happy now? You cunt. You fed me a bad lie. That's what you did, bringing me here. You told me something you could never back up. Fucking clinics. Dr Menosmal. You're a fucking bad liar."

I was panicking, and I spoke quickly. "Don't tell me you believed it. Don't you tell me you believed it, because I know you're not that stupid. It was only meant to help you. To show you that I believed you."

"This never had anything to do with me at all. You pretended we were coming here to make me feel better, but it was only ever for you. Some fucking sightseeing tour before you go home to your new school. You make me sick. You're nothing but a fucking tourist." He spat at me, and it flew over my shoulder and down towards the rising, slopping sea. I reasoned that I had to find some way of calming him down. I decided that I ought to be the one who stopped us going to the cave once and for all. Somebody had to end this Amnesia Clinic stuff, and I was the one who had started it. So, quite placidly, I stepped forward and slapped him in the face.

Some sounds travel well through time. Some barely make it through intact at all. I remember the feel of the slap as if it were five minutes ago—the soft stubble of his cheek on my palm surprised me—but I have no memory of the sound. Other sounds from that day—the crack of skull on submerged rock, for example—are much clearer.

"You're going to regret that, you little shit."

I realized that he was making me very angry. "What did you do to Sol?" I said, screaming now myself. "Did you touch her? Is that what this is about?" And then there were no more words, and there was no more composure. He grabbed me and tried to throw me backwards against the rocks, but I managed to escape his grip and I leapt away from him, scrambling upwards and around the headland towards the cave mouth.

My palms slipped on rocks dampened by the sea-spray as I climbed. I told myself to concentrate on getting away, to move as quickly as I could, upwards, to reach the cave. At that moment, I felt his hand round my ankle, cold, like a steel manacle, and I began to slip on the rocks.

"Let go!" I shouted. "You'll kill us both."

He gripped my ankle even more firmly and I felt my chest begin to tighten again. I struggled against it, trying to climb higher, but he had both strength and gravity on his side, even with one wounded arm.

In my panic, I raised my foot and drove my heel downwards. Both of us lost our footing and slipped as one towards the water. My arms flailed around me, looking for a new handhold, and my legs bicycled in the air around his head. I managed to place my foot again but, as I looked down, I saw his hands reaching once more for my legs. This time, however, his broken arm was so weakened that he couldn't grip me with any force. My kick must have scored a direct hit.

I know now that when he reached for me the second time it was for support, and not to drag me down, but in that instant I thought differently: I assumed he was trying to grab me, to do me harm. So I kicked out again, at his head this time.

The last I saw of his face was a disbelieving look as his arms reached out around him for something to hold on to. There was a vivid flash of blue as he fell backwards and his shirt caught the wind. I heard a dense, sickening whack as his head struck the rocks beneath us, so loud as to be audible even over the suck and wash of the sea. Then, losing my handhold again, I slid down the cliff face. I tried to find a footing where we had been standing before, but my feet were quickly swept from under me by the pawing of chilling waves. I fell sideways, and a fist of salt water punched down my throat.

I remember a lurch of nausea and a feeling of desperate, breathless panic as I thought about the need to escape the water, to get Fabián out, at all costs.

And then there is nothing but darkness.

seventeen

My mind had hijacked the scene of the dream from a newspaper article I once read. It was about some poor soul who, attempting to kill himself at a station, ended up stuck between the train and the platform with his legs twisted round and round like a corkscrew beneath the trunk of his body. His wife and children were brought to the platform edge to say their goodbyes in the certain knowledge that he would be dead the moment anybody tried to move the train. The image had always affected me: a person so damaged that the movement of any component part of his environment would spell death, in a situation where remaining static was out of the question. In my dream, I found myself pinned to the platform of a high-altitude railway station in the same way, except that it was not a train that kept me there but a vast, dead whale, its barnacled skin ripping into mine as I struggled to get out. When I looked down, I noticed that the platform had changed into a giant version of Sally Lightfoot's back, as, with great whale-sized snores, and facing away from me, she slept.

———

I woke to find myself lying in a metal-framed bed in a green hospital ward. Trying to sit up, I found that I could not move, as if I were strapped in, and yet I could see no restraints. My tongue felt furry and was coated in the metallic taste of blood. Ancient plumbing bubbled and clanked, and the overwhelming smell was of formaldehyde.

Looking ahead, I saw neon signs flashing on the wall at the end of my bed. *Your name is Anti. You were found in a cave in Pedrascada. You killed your best friend.* I could not turn my head but swiveled my eyes to another wall, where a new sign flashed up that read: *Only joking. Everything's fine really. Ha ha ha.* Returning my eyes to the front, I found a man standing at the foot of my bed. He wore a white boiler-suit and small, round glasses with thick rims and had a moustache so tiny it might have been penciled on. He carried a stainless-steel clipboard.

"My name is Menosmal," he said in a clipped, precise tone. "I believe you have been looking for me. Although," he added hopefully, "you may not remember."

"You look like someone I know," I said.

"It must be your imagination," said Menosmal. "You don't know anybody, so far as I'm aware. Otherwise you wouldn't be here." But even as he said it I became aware that with a slightly thicker moustache, and without the glasses, he would have looked, in the face at least, just like Suarez. I tried again to sit up, but my body would still not respond.

"I know you can't be Dr Menosmal," I said, "because he doesn't exist. I made him up."

Menosmal made a tick on his clipboard. "Interesting. You are seeing things you have invented. This is perfectly consistent with the behavior of my amnesiacs. And it means that you are in exactly the right place. Now, I think you should rest awhile and see if anything comes to you. In some cases, my patients remember after only a few hours. Although I fear," he went on, "that this has become increasingly rare lately, as our amenities have improved. It's almost as if some patients decide upon arrival that they rather like to be here, liberated of their memories . . ." He winked. "More and more frequently, I find myself having to address delusions about their pasts that I know my patients have concocted within hours of being admitted here at the clinic."

"Is that right?" I said.

"Take this poor boy." He gestured towards the bed adjacent to mine with his pen. Looking over, I saw that the boy in question was Fabián. His broken arm, which was still streaked with fragments of his own dead skin, flapped as he waved at me, and I noticed that blood continued to trickle from the sides of his lips and nose as he smiled. He wore a green backless surgical gown. "He washed up here yesterday, remembering nothing," said the doctor. "Nothing at all. Didn't even know his own name. And now, he and this other woman have suddenly decided that they're mother and son."

Fabián had been joined by a slender, dark-haired woman in her mid-forties. She had the same striking green eyes as Fabián, and when she got up and walked over to the bed to shake my hand, she smelled of fresh peaches.

"Of course, it's ridiculous," said the doctor in a low voice when she had left my bed and returned to sit at the foot of Fabián's. "She's one of my oldest patients. Been here almost since I started up. She's never said anything about a son to me before. It's just what she wants to believe."

Straining my eyes to look at the bed to my right, I saw that the woman had now begun stroking Fabián's hair with one hand and swabbing his face with alcohol-soaked cotton wool with the other. He was smiling up at her.

"I must admit, however," said Menosmal, "that it is a delusion that both patients share. One of the more powerful I've seen. She is also quite convinced that she is his mother." At this, Fabián and his putative mother both waved in my direction as if they were posing for a cheesy holiday snap, then tilted their heads at each other, smiling continuously. "Still, if it makes them happy, I suppose they might as well believe it until the real truth comes along."

"You're an unconventional doctor, aren't you?" I said.

"You're an unconventional patient," said Menosmal. "I've treated some extraordinary cases in my time, but nobody has ever claimed to have *invented* me before now. That's really something."

We both laughed.

"Can you explain something to me?" I asked.

"I'll try."

"Why am I unable to move? It's because I'm still asleep, isn't it?"

He looked around, nervous all of a sudden.

"Admit it," I said.

Briskly, he slotted his pen back in his top pocket and began whistling. "Must be going," he said.

"Ha," I said. "Got you. I knew I'd made you up."

"Clever boy," said Menosmal, snapping his fingers and turning into a blue-footed booby.

I closed my eyes.

———

When I opened them tentatively some time later, an intense yellow light burst in, so I closed them again straight away, electing to concentrate this time on potentially relevant sounds. I could hear the near-silent hum of efficient air-conditioning, the faint rustle of newspaper pages, a peppering of high heels on hard floor. I shifted on cold, clean, cotton sheets, and found that, although the rest of my body was now fine, I still could not move my right arm. I felt the residue of terrible pain in my elbow and the promise of more to come.

"He's awake. Did you see? He moved." The voice came from the direction of the heels. My mother.

The newspaper was lowered with a scrunch.

"Make sure you don't wake him up." My father.

"He's been out for two days. We need to get to the bottom of this."

Two days? What had I been doing for two days? Perhaps events had been repeating themselves in my head. I kept my eyes closed to try and fix what had happened with more clarity, knowing that when I opened them there would be no time to think. Confused memories began to seep back, and I felt the beginnings of a kind of mischievous happiness at what we had dared to do. I wanted to see Fabián as soon as possible, to make my peace with him and to begin the exquisite process of preparing a version of our adventures worthy of public dissemination. But before the pride, there would have to be contrition: I must avert my eyes sorrowfully, mutter profound apologies, offer reparation. However much I might want to feign sleep until my parents went away, they weren't going anywhere anytime soon. So I took a deep breath, ready for the onslaught of questions (*What did you think you were doing? How could you lie to us? What were you and Fabián fighting about?*) and opened my eyes.

The buttery yellow light blazed though Venetian blinds on to a gray linoleum floor and off-white walls. A battered TV clung on to a metal arm that dipped out from a corner opposite the bed. My father sat beneath it on an aluminum chair, his jacket crumpled, the newspaper open in his lap. My mother stood on the opposite side of the room in a powder-blue suit, staring distractedly through a reinforced glass porthole in the wooden door. She spun expertly on a stiletto as my movements registered.

"Anti," she said, and stepped towards the bed. "Anti."

"Where am I?"

"You're in hospital in Guayaquil," said Dad. "Don't you remember? You were talking nineteen to the dozen when we arrived—though not much of it made sense. Who's Sally?"

"Slow down," said my mother. "We can get to that."

I lifted myself further up the pillows with some difficulty.

"You're a lucky guy, you know," said my father, folding his newspaper and standing up. "You weren't that far from the war zone. It's flared up again down in the *Cordillera del Cóndor*. Fifteen killed this week. Some of the wounded have even been brought to this hospital." He pointed at the paper in his hand for my benefit. "Though not over here in the expensive side, obviously," he chuckled.

"For God's sake." My mother pushed him to one side. "Anti, how are you feeling?"

My father adopted a more concerned expression and took up a different position on the opposite side of the bed from my mother.

"Listen, before you both start," I said, alternating between the two of them, "let me just say that I'm sorry. I'm sure you're both terribly angry, but if you just let me explain *why* we did it, then . . ."

"We're not angry," said my mother, in a soft tone. She swept back the hair from my forehead with a fragrant hand. Something was wrong. "We're not angry, Anti. But there's some very bad news."

This, then, was not another dream.

His body was flung repeatedly against the base of the cliff as the tide came in and eventually found face down in the water, his foot snagging on the rocks directly beneath the red memorial hut to the unfortunate surfer. Not the sort of detail I was meant to discover, I'm sure, but somehow I did. I have since imagined that there might be another little shrine up there now for Fabián, and that whoever it was leaving out fresh flowers and lit candles for the surfer might now do the same for him. I hope I'm right.

I left the country without even attending his funeral, so I never got to experience the pomp of an Ecuadorian send-off, but I had no difficulty imagining it. Fabián had furnished me on many occasions with such detailed and lurid descriptions of funerals that I felt I knew what it would have been like without having to go: women in black caught up in epic weeping fits; solemn processions; possibly even the traditional white coffin afforded to those who are considered to be too young in the eyes of the church to have committed any sin. All I have is my imagined version. I never got to stand there amid the incense smoke and the incensed relatives and look up at all the "plundered Inca gold," as he'd called it, or see him buried, or cremated, or whatever it was they did to him. It wasn't . . . required of me.

But, as I have found, the more abruptly someone disappears from your life, the more vividly they live on in your head. It turned out that I didn't really need to say goodbye, because Fabián has been within me ever since, tempered and channeled by regret, but living there still and showing little inclination to leave.

I tell myself to try to let him go, that many people form intense friendships in adolescence that end abruptly and are never resumed, that this one just ended more definitively. And that only makes it worse, because one of the most difficult things to live with is the knowledge that we probably wouldn't have remained friends, had he lived. We were heading in different directions: me to school and life in England, Fabián to whatever Suarez and he came up with out there—most likely involving college in the States and some lucrative profession or other. We'd have corresponded for a few years, maybe seen each other once or twice, but it would have gone no further than that. Our friendship would have dried up into dusty static images, and that would have been fine, because he wouldn't be here now, in my head, had he lived. He'd be out there telling someone improbable stories, had he lived. I would barely remember him, had he lived. But I do remember him. His smile is fixed perfectly in my memory, like the grin of a new recruit in a sepia photograph. And I am left with three words that will tap away at my skull for ever, like a toffee hammer: had he lived.

I hate him for that.

———

As my parents and I left the hospital, we had to pass through the main casualty ward, the corridors of which were lined with soldiers wounded in a jungle ambush by the Peruvians, laid out, awaiting treatment. I met and returned the patience in their eyes. I walked stoically between them, looking calmly at each one in turn as if I were their Field-Marshal, inspecting the bandages around their various flesh wounds that were filling slowly with thick, arterial blood and even bestowing on one or two of them an approving or reassuring smile. My parents walked ahead of me, anxious to leave the building as quickly as possible, but I took my time. One of the soldiers, who could only have been a few years older than me, shot me a wink, then held his wounded hand up to his face. The bullet that had struck him had gone straight through his palm, and through a little red tunnel in the flesh I saw the glistening pupil of his eye, heavily dilated from painkillers, on the other side.

I remember the bright sunshine of the car park outside the hospital and the breathtaking heat of the car as I sat in it for the first time. I remember the silence as we pulled on to the blinding highway. For the early part of the journey, I tried to keep my eyes open and watch the scenery outside. But this didn't last: in the eye of every roadside mule or bored bus passenger, even in the expression of a nun speeding along in a beaten-up old Cadillac, I saw him—as if, by the power of guilt, Fabián had insinuated himself into every living thing in my path.

I remember next to nothing about the rest of the journey north. I know that under no circumstances could it ever have been as exciting as Fabián's and my journey south had been. My parents were possessed of an efficiency in the world, a mastery of adult tools that came into its own at times of crisis. In their hands, the great voyage upon which we had embarked a few days earlier was reduced to nothing more than a few hours in an air-conditioned people-carrier. I kept my eyes shut for as much of the rest of the journey as I could, in order to preserve the version in my head, and avoid all of those recriminatory eyes.

Within a week, I had left the country, never to return. At my mother's instruction, I was removed from the country as promptly as possible, like an airlifted hostage. The decision that I would not attend Fabián's funeral was also made for me. In view of what had happened, I was to be left out of the decision-making business for a while. And that suited me just fine. I wanted decisions to be made on my behalf for the rest of my life.

According to my parents, it was likely that the authorities would record a verdict of accidental death. But in spite of this, one more thing was to be asked of me when we got back to Quito. At his own personal request, and in the company of my mother and father, I was required to go to his house and explain to Suarez how his nephew had died.

eighteen

A meeting between Suarez and my parents, with Suarez's house as the venue: it would have been a surreal clash of cultures even without the colossal fact of Fabián's death. With it, dangling away above us all like a puppeteer's hand, the visit was unbearable. From the moment the security gates parted to admit the three of us in my father's people-carrier, I felt a rising sense of panic, a sense that wrong things were being allowed to happen. This wasn't the way it was meant to be: these gates were a portal to pleasure, through which one was ferried, crying with laughter, in the back of a bullet-proof Mercedes. That day, it felt more like being led to an execution. My unease continued to build even with the appearance of a friendly face: Eulalia opened the door clad in black mourning dress, and gave only a muted greeting before she showed us into the library. No cooking smells enticed from the kitchen. No music blasted from the jukebox. No dogs cascaded down the stairs to greet us. The accumulated effects were that even before Suarez set foot in the room, I felt hot and uncomfortable, as if the guilt were somehow scalding me, and that by the time he came in, I was positively poaching in it.

As we waited, my parents attempted with false nonchalance to familiarize themselves with Suarez's habitat. My mother stalked up and down the bookshelves with an affectedly knitted brow; my father stood over the jukebox with his hands on his hips. I felt affronted on Suarez's behalf by their presence, and in particular by their crude appraisal of a place so familiar to, and treasured by, me. I fought an urge to run from the library, through Byron's exotic flowerbeds and away down the Pan-Americana, kicking the red mud from my shoes as I sprinted away to the south.

"What an awful encyclopedia," said my mother to no one in particular, pulling a volume from the shelf. "It looks as if it were written for a child."

"It is my experience that the books we prize as children can be our most formative influences," said a voice from the doorway.

The authority and confidence carried by that familiar accent provoked in me an automatic surge of anticipation, an incongruous burst of joy and excitement. In spite of the circumstances, and in the certain knowledge that no great story could possibly be on its way, my imagination salivated at the prospect all the same, like an idiotic Pavlovian dog.

But the man who followed the sound into the room was a reduced, desiccated version of the Suarez I knew. His voice bore the same sting, but the man . . . It was as if one of his beloved Shuar Indians had cursed him, performed some *ayahuasca*-fueled rite intended to drive away his soul and rip out his inner strength. His shoulders were slumped loosely inside his jacket, his hair seemed grayer and thinner, and he had removed his moustache, which gave his face a naked, defenseless appearance. Suddenly, he was an old man.

I realized that I, knowing everyone in the room, was expected to take the initiative with the introductions. It was the first time I had ever introduced my parents to anyone by name. The formality felt preposterous. With a courtly bow, as if he wanted to compound the absurdity, Suarez kissed my mother on the hand. She shot my father a sideways glance.

Eulalia set down a white dish of fat green olives, with a second, smaller compartment within it for the stones. She also brought in an opened bottle of red wine and some glasses on a tray. When Suarez raised the bottle over my glass I shook my head and asked for juice. I caught a distant flare of the old mischief in his eye, and even a twitch in the corner of his mouth, before he turned his head away from me. When he uttered the word "juice" to Eulalia it was with a trace of mockery which only I could possibly have discerned. As for the olives, their smell has induced nausea in me ever since.

Some preliminary small-talk ensued as drinks were distributed and chairs assigned. My parents offered their condolences to Suarez, and said how much they had enjoyed Fabián's company when he'd come to stay with us at weekends. Suarez reciprocated with a few choice compliments about me. He said I had been "a delight and an inspiration" to have around. I was beginning to think that the conversation would proceed for ever at this brutally ponderous pace until, finally, when the four of us were settled round the table—that same table which had seen so much enchantment in the past, and at which, mere days before, Fabián and I had been merrily necking shots of tequila—there was silence. Suarez put down his glass and wiped his lips, though they hadn't yet touched the wine.

"Thank you all for agreeing to come here," he said. "Let me start by saying to you, Anti, that I know this loss will be every bit as painful to you as it will be to me. I know what close friends you and Fabián were. I want to say also that I hope you won't feel at any stage that you are being blamed for what has happened. I know what a headstrong boy my nephew could be, and I am fully prepared for the fact that this terrible accident is likely to have come about as a result of his own hot-headed nature."

Suarez lifted his wineglass again before continuing. The liquid inside it caught the light from a lamp above his head, acting like a ruby filter. I thought of the too-red blood of Hammer horror films.

"And so, Anti, you needn't withhold anything when you tell us what happened. There's no question at all in my mind of pressing charges against anybody, or of taking the thing to trial."

The remark operated on my confidence precisely as Suarez had intended it to: on the surface, as a reassuring tonic; in reality, as a powerful corrosive. The idea that anybody might want or even be in a position to press charges had never occurred to me. I picked up the glass of *naranjilla* in front of me to give my hands something to do, and hoped that the fear and surprise I felt were not written all over my face.

"But we do need to know what happened," said Suarez. "Whatever it was, whatever you both did, you have to tell us. And you have to tell us *everything*. Do you understand?"

I cleared my throat, but said nothing.

"Come on. Don't be nervous," said my mother. "Sr Suarez is being exceptionally understanding."

I was tongue-tied. In an unthinkable situation, I was facing two people—Suarez and my mother—to whom I would offer opposing versions of what I'd had for breakfast, let alone what had happened in Pedrascada. Still more unsettling was that Suarez, with his mention of charges and trials, had made it clear that I couldn't necessarily rely on him to be on my side.

"Why not start by telling us why you decided to go to this place . . . Pedrascada?" my mother suggested.

Suarez agreed. "Yes. What happened?" he said. "What made you both lie to me in that way?"

"To *all* of us," my mother reminded him.

"Quite," said Suarez.

"I'm sorry, Suarez," I said. "We—"

"Anti, I told you. There will be no recrimination today. That will be the last time you apologize. Just tell us the truth."

I sipped my drink but could hardly swallow. The liquid trickled slowly over the back of my throat. The sensation made me want to retch.

"I suppose the truth is that we just wanted some sort of adventure. I knew that I was leaving the country soon, and Fabián and I had always said that one day we'd get out of the city and explore some of the country together. I guess you could say that I just wanted something . . . *big* to happen before I went. Something a bit less safe. So Fabián and I decided to go away for the weekend. On a sort of farewell expedition."

Suarez nodded at me in a way that suggested full understanding. I glanced at my parents. My father radiated goodwill and sympathy, while my mother wore her most terrifying look of full concentration. Any second now, I expected her to get out a notepad.

"That's not all," I continued. "Something was wrong with Fabián. He was more agitated about his parents than I'd ever seen him. I thought it would be good for him to get away and stop thinking about them for a while. He'd started telling me stuff about them that couldn't *possibly* be true. About how he'd seen a vision of his mother at the Easter parade, and how his father had been killed in a bullfight, and how his mother wasn't dead, she was wandering around in the mountains with amnesia. Crazy stuff. I didn't know what to do about it."

"I see," said Suarez, frowning.

I turned to him. "I should have told you. That night when we got drunk, I should have told you all of it then. I'm sorry."

"I told you: no apologies."

"You got drunk?" said my mother. "When was this?"

Suarez ignored her. "You didn't want to give him away. I understand." Then he said to my parents, "I don't expect Anti ever told you of the circumstances surrounding the deaths of my sister and her husband—Fabián's mother and father."

My parents confirmed that I had not.

"It's understandable. I believe Anti only found out the truth himself comparatively recently. What happened was a very unfortunate car accident, around six years ago now. Their car came off the road high in the cordillera, and neither of them survived."

My mother made suitably sympathetic remarks.

"Anti and I had a revealing chat a few weeks ago, during which it emerged that Fabián believed that his mother might be alive somewhere because her body was never recovered from the wreckage. And now it seems that he had been concocting glamorous stories for some time to explain her disappearance—to fill in the gaps left by what we knew. How very sad."

"I'm sorry," I added, in an ineffectual, distant voice.

Suarez took no notice. "For some reason I have never been able to fathom, I think that Fabián blamed himself for the loss of his parents. It seems these stories were his way of avoiding the truth."

"You knew about this?" said my mother, turning her gaze on me. "You knew how deluded he was, and you told no one?"

"He was my friend."

My father was thinking. "That's all very well. But it doesn't explain why you chose that place in particular. It's miles away. You could have gone on your adventure anywhere, much nearer to Quito."

My father. The one person in the room I thought I could rely on. Disappointing.

"It's a good question. Why Pedrascada in particular?" said Suarez.

"Yes, why?" my mother asked.

The ridiculous thing is that, at this point, I could have looked up at the bookshelf, pointed out the encyclopedia, shown them the entry in it relating to Pedrascada and told them that's where I got the idea. And it wouldn't even have been a lie. But I wasn't thinking straight at all. I was at a crossroads, but I hadn't seen it coming: I was too busy looking behind me. When I should have been considering which road to take with maximum care, I shot blindly through the junction, panicking, desperate to save my skin and get away. I condemned myself without giving it a moment's thought.

"We went to look for the Amnesia Clinic," I mumbled.

My father sat bolt upright. "What?"

It tumbled out of me. "Fabián and I had found this newspaper clipping, all about a clinic in Pedrascada where people who had lost their memory could stay and be treated until they remembered stuff."

My father gulped at his wine. "What are you talking about, Anti?"

"It was a stupid idea, I know. But that's why we went there."

"I see," said Suarez. "And this was the latest explanation Fabián had latched on to to explain where his mother might be? Is that right?"

"That's why you went to Pedrascada? To look for the Amnesia Clinic?" said my father. He was desperately trying to establish some sort of communication with me without giving too much away. But I was very far from being reachable. "Come on, mate. That can't be right."

Suarez suddenly appeared very interested in what my father had to say. "You've heard of it?" he said. "You have heard of this . . . Amnesia Clinic?"

My father set his glass down on the table awkwardly. I felt sorry for him. He wanted so badly to stay on my side, but the circumstances were making it very difficult.

"Anti and I talked hypothetically about the idea once," he said. "That's all. It was just something we made up. I doubt anywhere like it really exists."

"As do I," said Suarez. "And yet Anti appears to be telling us that it was to get to this . . . hypothetical place that he and Fabián decided to go to Pedrascada."

"It's a preposterous idea, of course," said my mother. "You're going to have to do better than that, Anti."

I saw a window and leapt for it. I was panicking.

"I know it's crazy. It was just another one of Fabián's lunatic ideas to try and keep his mother alive. He decided that Pedrascada was where it would be, this clinic. And I didn't know how to tell him it wasn't. That was stupid. I know that now."

Suarez was staring at me with an ominous, mocking expression as my words tailed off. I stared at him, mystified. If it hadn't been out of the question, I would have said he was *enjoying* himself.

He sat comfortably back in his chair, letting me stew for a while in my lies. Then he took out his chunky gold lighter and lit a Dunhill International. He sucked in a great blue mouthful of smoke and then turned the packet in my direction with a raised eyebrow.

"Cigarette, Anti? No? Okay then." He exhaled through pursed lips, then blew a thick, perfect smoke-ring, gazing at the ancient disco-lighting on the wall behind my mother's head. Then he said, "Speaking as a doctor, I am fascinated by this idea of a treatment center entirely dedicated to amnesiacs."

He laid his cigarette in the ashtray. I watched as his hand hovered momentarily over the white dish on the table before selecting and picking up a plump green olive. He threw it to the back of his mouth and munched down on it with the right-hand side of his face, chewing it with relish before palming the stone discreetly and dropping it into the relevant compartment in front of him. He was looking straight at me as he swallowed.

"The thing is," I spluttered, "it was just a stupid—"

He raised a hand to shut me up. It was the faintest of gestures, but he might as well have struck me across the face. His mouth squirmed sardonically as he went through the final, laborious stages of consuming the olive. He picked up his cigarette again and took another long, slow drag. The silence felt like the hush over a bullring before the *coup de grâce*. And then he struck.

"It may surprise you to know that, as a matter of fact, I *have* heard of your Amnesia Clinic."

My stomach lurched. The black and white squares of Suarez's checkerboard library floor swam and multiplied before me, and I feared I might soon be following Fabián's example in emptying my guts all over them.

"I was looking around in Fabián's room yesterday, trying to work out how to start clearing it out—such a heartbreaking task—when I happened upon a newspaper clipping that my nephew had left tucked into the front of my road atlas, which was for some reason hidden under his bed."

He reached into an inside pocket of his tweed jacket, took out the cutting, unfolded it and smoothed it down on the table in front of him.

The air swarmed with unspoken forces. Silent, breathless panic from me, and speechless confusion from my parents. From Suarez, a barely concealed, burning triumph, bordering on mania.

"It's a curious piece. And one of the first things that struck me as odd about it was the date. It purports to have been printed on the 29th of February 1989. Now, I am an old man. My memory may be failing. But unless I am very much mistaken,

29 February 1989 is a date that never existed. 1989 was not a leap year." He swallowed a mouthful of wine and smiled. "Would anyone like an olive? They are very good."

My mother cast desperately around the room for help. "Does *anyone* know what this man is talking about?" The question wasn't directed at anyone in particular, but at a point in space somewhere just above the jukebox. If she'd clocked the ashen look on my face she might have found her answer.

Now Suarez was looking directly at me. "Don't you think it strange that a medical institution featured in a nationwide newspaper only seven years ago should have disappeared without a trace, with no record of its ever having existed? Funny. Almost as if the clinic itself had developed amnesia. As if so many amnesiacs had passed through its walls that they had somehow infected the building itself with their condition." He laughed at his own joke. Unfeasibly, he suddenly seemed to be the happiest person in the room.

"There is a second article here in the clipping," he continued, "which is even more extraordinary. Imagine how flabbergasted I was to come across it. This article, if you can believe it, reports a version of events surrounding the deaths of my sister and brother-in-law that we know for a fact that Fabián *made up*."

"Okay, listen—" I began.

"I suppose it is possible that another couple were unfortunate enough to come off the same road only a few weeks after Fabián's parents. It is *even* possible that Fabián saw this article and decided to extrapolate from it the version of events involving the bullfight."

I sat mutely, staring into space. He couldn't be stopped.

"But those sound to me like some very remote possibilities. No. It's almost as if someone—a very well-meaning person, no doubt—someone who knew Fabián, and the pain he was in, had taken it upon himself to create a reassuring piece of documentary evidence, to soothe Fabián . . . to make him believe his version of events was real and drive him not closer to consolation but further away from reality."

Now everyone in the room was looking at me.

"Don't you think, Anti, that it's time you told us *exactly* what happened?" said Suarez.

"Anti," said my mother. "You didn't—"

"He did. Didn't you?" Suarez held up a hand before I could speak. "I know, I know. You thought you were helping him."

"Blank newsprint," muttered my father. "I *thought* that was a weird school project."

"He didn't really believe it!" I shouted. "I know he didn't."

Suarez sat chewing another olive, watching me. Then he leaned forward and pointed at me as he spoke.

"We had an agreement. I trusted you. I asked you to tell me if you thought things were out of hand, and you promised to do so."

I spoke without thinking. I said that what I had done had been for the right reasons, that Fabián had known it was a joke, that Suarez of all people should know that. My protests were met with silence.

"Let me prove it to you," I blustered. "Let me tell you what happened when we were in Pedrascada."

"That is a story that I am most anxious to hear," said Suarez. "The story of how my nephew came to be found lying face down, dead in the sea."

I tried to collect my thoughts whilst maintaining an out-
wardly contrite expression. I reasoned that to appear suitably
devastated at the exposure of my initial deception would make
any further, more serious untruths seem impossible.

"Can you all promise me something?" I said. "Please promise not to say anything until I've told the whole story."

The three of them nodded assent.

I cleared my throat to speak, glanced up above the jukebox
and saw the shadow on the wall, feathered with beer-spray, that
remained from where Fabián had thrown his Pilsener bottle in
frustration only a fortnight previously. I heard his voice, mocking as ever: *What would the unimaginative person say had happened here?*

"There was this dome," I said. "At the beach. This metal
dome, on a hill."

nineteen

"We were captivated by it from the moment we arrived, because it seemed so out of place. The town was nothing more than a muddy fishing port with a few surf bars and tourist hostels tacked on, but this place looked as if it had come from the future: all gleaming metal, hidden tantalizingly away from us behind the tower of rock on the hill. What's more, Ray, the American hippy who owned the cabins where we were staying, told us there was no road going up to it, no access to it at all other than by boat or helicopter. Other stuff, too: how the builders who'd constructed it had broken his parrot's wings, and how he'd been chucked out by security guards when he tried to go and discover what was up there. Then, on our way back from a visit to the Isla de Plata, Ray's boat got swamped when this great big pleasure-cruiser that was moored at the dome sailed too close to us. From that point on, Fabián and I got obsessed with the idea of getting up there and taking our revenge. Eventually, we decided to go on an expedition to find out once and for all.

"Ray's daughter, Sol, had shown us a pathway round the base of the cliffs that you could only access at low tide. She'd told us there was a cave round there with steps carved into the rock that led up to the dome. A sort of secret entrance. She was only ten, so I wasn't sure what to make of what she said, but Fabián believed her from the start, and on the second or third day, whenever it was that Fabián . . . that he had his accident, we climbed round the headland to try and get to the cave.

"My worry was that it wasn't safe. It was getting late in the afternoon when we set off, and water was already starting to wash over the rocks of the pathway. We might easily get trapped if the tide came back in before we returned. But Fabián insisted. He'd . . . we'd both been drinking, and he was adamant. We argued a bit on the beach and he said he would go alone, even if I didn't go with him, and stormed off. You know what he was like when he got cross. I followed him.

"After chasing him for some time, clambering from rock to rock, I looked ahead and saw that he'd disappeared from view. Sure enough, when I got round the next crag, I saw him waving from the mouth of a cave just above me, his blue shirt ballooning behind him in the wind. I asked him to wait and then hauled myself up there, losing my breath, slipping and scraping my chest on the wet stone, but by the time I got to the spot he'd been standing on, he'd already charged off into the darkness.

"When I got to my feet, I looked down and saw a half-eaten blue and red crab, dried-out and overturned on a piece of sandstone. It proved to me that the tide came up that high, and that what we were doing wasn't safe. I shouted ahead into the darkness, calling Fabián an idiot, telling him he'd get us both killed. But he just shouted back at me: 'Don't be so unimaginative.' The sound of his voice seemed to be getting further and further away. Either the cave acoustics were playing tricks on me, or somehow he was advancing very quickly.

"I shouted that I couldn't see a thing and asked how he was getting so far so quickly. He told me to use the steps. I said I couldn't see any. He said, 'Just because you can't see them, doesn't mean they aren't there.' My silence must have told him all he needed to know, because then I remember him shouting, 'I *told* you there were steps. Why does nobody ever believe me?'

"I hated admitting it, but he was right. As natural light began to seep in from above, it because obvious that we were climbing a set of man-made steps: they were roughly, unevenly cut into the stone, but quite definitely real. The light glistened off the moisture on the carved-out cave walls more and more as I climbed."

"Hold on a minute," said my mother.

"What?" I said, furious with her for breaking my concentration.

"This story is getting too poetic for my liking. Get to the point."

I sighed. "I'm telling you what happened. You promised not to interrupt."

Suarez cut in. "Let's hear him out. We promised him that."

"Thank you," I said, not daring to look at my mother for fear that I'd lose my nerve.

"By the time I reached the top of the steps I was short of breath and starting to wheeze. But the state of my lungs became irrelevant when I saw what was waiting for us at the top of the cliff.

Fabián must have been gob-smacked as well, because he was just standing there taking in the view: a formal garden of rose beds and box hedges that was a million miles away from the disorganized cluster of sheds where we'd been staying, and had been hidden from view by the looming rock formation we'd just emerged from. It felt like I was smelling cut grass and water sprinklers for the first time in my life, especially after the dank, fishy smell of the cave.

"An avenue to our left led down to the jetty where the pleasure-cruiser lurked—the one that had nearly run us over before. It was sharp, and tapered. It didn't sit right in the water. It seemed . . . too man-made. Like an upside-down steam iron or something. I hadn't liked it when it nearly drowned us, and I liked it even less now. Fabián was all for going down there right away to examine it, but I held him back, pointing to our right, up the hill—towards the dome.

"It was the first time we'd seen it up close. I'd never seen a building like it: a circle of concrete pillars with sheets of curved, tinted plate-glass in between; on top, the shining silver roof, reflecting evening sunbeams. As we slowly advanced towards it, I saw that in spite of its clean, uniform appearance from the beach, the roof was made of a mish-mash of hammered sheets of metal, riveted together. And although Ray had told us it was only six years old, the building had aged badly: water from overflowing drainpipes had stained the concrete walls in brown and green; an angular modern statue was rusting in a corner; the fishponds were clogged with weeds and algae. In one of them I saw a fat, golden fish floating dead under a lily."

———

"This is getting stupid." My mother had been suppressing another interjection for some time. I'd noticed this, and as a result had been addressing myself mainly to Suarez and my father, which had only fired her up even more. "Enough scene-setting. When are you going to get to the point?"

"You said you'd let me speak."

"This is very serious, Anti. We're here to find out how someone *died.*"

To my relief, Suarez interjected again. "As I said before, we agreed to hear him out. Please—no more interruptions."

"He's *my* son."

"And he's telling us of what became of *my* nephew, so if you respect my wishes at all, Madam, then let him speak. You're welcome to leave the room if you don't want to listen to what he has to say."

I could tell that she was tempted to take up this suggestion, to show her contempt for the credulity I was enjoying, but she couldn't bear to miss out on any part of the proceedings either.

"As you wish," she said, through tight lips.

This show of support from Suarez gave me strength, and I carried on, resolved to continue my story with as much loitering as I could. I wanted to test myself—and everyone else in the room.

"As we got nearer the dome, we could hear music playing—jazz, over a tinny PA system. Also, the buzz of people talking. As if there were a large drinks party going on somewhere. We walked through a set of automatic glass doors into an air-conditioned lobby that might have been part of a hotel, except that it was deserted and there were no signs, apart from one of those black plastic boards you stick white letters on to advertise conferences and things. The letters in this one had been arranged to read: NOT TO TRY IS NOT TO KNOW. There was no one sitting behind the desk, so we decided to head for the sound of the party.

"The noise came from behind a large set of wooden doors at the end of the lobby. Our shoes squeaked on the slate floor as we approached them. We stood outside the room for a moment, trying to listen in, but we couldn't make out anything except for the incoherent babble of the party. I was about to suggest that we retreat, maybe go back down to the boat and snoop around there, when, with no warning at all, Fabián threw open the doors and walked in.

"It was a spectacular room, painted in white. Crescent-shaped picture windows gave on to lush gardens and the Pacific sunset outside. About thirty people stood around, talking excitedly. All sorts of weird-looking people. All different. From the doors I glimpsed a few of them: a woman in an indigo dress who had the longest hair I'd ever seen; a guy in a dark suit with a red and white neckerchief knotted at his throat; a younger girl, about our age, with three earrings in one ear and tinted blonde hair. One old woman was happily standing around chatting in a pair of pink slippers, while others were really dressed up for the occasion, with ceremonial swords on their belts and spurs at their ankles. Curved tables laid with blue cloths lined the walls of the room, and these were heaving with food of every description: dishes, tureens, platters, trays, all piled high and steaming. The room was full of weird, exotic cooking smells, none of which I could quite place.

"I expected Fabián's dramatic entrance to cause people to stop speaking and look round, like in films when you enter the Wild West saloon and everything goes quiet, but everybody just carried on talking, so we went in, letting the doors close behind us.

"We got about halfway across the room before we were noticed. A red-faced man with a moustache, who must have been in charge, had a word with one of the waiters, who then came over and asked if he could help us in that way that means 'you shouldn't be here.' The waiter escorted us outside again, into the lobby, and asked us again whether he could help us.

"Fabián went into this whole explanation about how we'd been shipwrecked off the coast and had washed up nearby. It was a good try, but I could see the waiter wasn't convinced. He was smirking throughout and eventually he interrupted. He thanked Fabián for his story and said that we needn't worry, we weren't going to get into trouble, because he only worked there. So we told the waiter the truth and made friends with him. Soon the three of us were having a cigarette together in the garden outside.

"The waiter's name was Epifanio. He was originally from Guayaquil, but had been to university in the States. He was working as a waiter to make money to pay for his fees. He said that the job paid very well but was quite unusual.

"I . . . I don't know if what he said was true, or whether it was just some story he made up. But this is what he told us. He said not to breathe a word of it to anyone, but that the group of people we'd seen in the room was a kind of club who went around having these . . . banquets. They traveled around in the boat, all over the world, eating endangered species. He said that they even had a name for the boat: the Anti-Ark. Because it went around collecting the animals two by two, then cooking them. Taking them *out* of existence instead of saving them.

"He talked and talked about the club, telling us every last detail: how they had a special harpoon device on their boat that they used for whaling; how they fed up blue-footed boobies with dog meat before killing them so they didn't taste fishy; how they made soup to an old recipe from giant Galápagos turtles; how they ate everything from dove's hearts to iguana brains to badger ham; how today's special menu featured scarlet macaw and a rare crab called a Sally Lightfoot.

"As he talked, I saw that Fabián was getting more and more agitated. He kept interjecting while the waiter was speaking, swearing and cursing. And eventually he said, 'We have to do something about this.' I said I didn't know what we could do about it other than tell Ray when we got back to the beach. But Fabián was in a crazy mood. He said that this was our opportunity for doing something heroic. He said that we could salvage our trip, that it wouldn't have been for nothing. He said . . . he said he was going to go down to the jetty and scuttle the Anti-Ark.

"Before I knew what was happening, he'd run off down the garden. The waiter told me that Fabián would get into serious trouble if he tried to get on the boat, because it was heavily guarded, so I chased after him. From the garden, by the archway in the rock that led back down to the cave, I saw him leap on to the boat and get tackled by one of the security guards. He was huge, much bigger than Fabián, and he grabbed him and threw him . . . he threw him over the side of the boat. That must have been when he hit his head. That's when he ended up in the water.

"I tried to run down to the jetty to help him, but I should never have started running again. I hadn't recovered from my last asthma attack. I stood in the archway, trying to get my breath back, but I think I must have blacked out for a second and fallen down the steps. That's how I ended up back in the cave.

"That's how it happened. So you see it was nothing to do with the Amnesia Clinic. Fabián wasn't deluded. He just died trying to do something right. Do you see?

"Do you see?"

twenty

Any answer to my question that might have been forth-coming was cut off abruptly by a loud, flat crack as my mother slapped me across the face. She used her left hand, and her wedding ring struck hard against my cheekbone.

"That's for being stupid enough to think you could tell such an idiotic story," she said in a low voice, as if anybody around the table could fail to overhear. Then, to Suarez, "I am sorry. I had no idea that Anti would be so impudent."

The precise details of the next few minutes are lost to me, but my mother dominated the conversation. I remember the expressions "breathtaking disrespect," and "incredibly naive." As she spoke, I fidgeted silently, looking towards Suarez for help, but none seemed forthcoming. He sucked on his cigarette slowly, deliberately—as if commenting on my mother's ongoing harangue by behaving as calmly as he could. Finally I found my voice. But my chest was tight with nerves and asthma, and I spoke so quietly that it was almost a whisper.

"Sometimes it doesn't hurt to let people believe what they want to believe."

"What?" said my mother. "What did you say?"

I looked imploringly at Suarez. "That's what you said to me. Sitting here."

This agitated my mother even more. "Anti, whatever conversation you may or may not have had, there is simply no excuse . . ."

I tuned out again as best I could. All my attention was focused on Suarez. As my mother worried at me like an agitated, pecking bird, a change seemed to come over him. The guttering flame of support that I sought in his eyes seemed to draw new strength from my pleading look and shortness of breath. Finally, he exhaled deeply and spoke while my mother was still in full flow.

"Just a moment."

My mother stopped in mid-sentence. Her head whirled round to face him.

"Your embarrassment is endearing, Madam," he said, with a wan smile. "And it is considerate of you to give your son this public dressing-down for my benefit, however unnecessary. In fact, I found Anti's story quite stimulating and interesting. As well as the reception it received."

I'd seen the look on his face somewhere before. It took me a few seconds to realize where: it was an echo of that same expression of distaste I'd twice seen on Fabián's face in Pedrascada, when he had seemed to want to shake my timid, imaginative shortcomings out of his head.

My mother paused. "I'm staggered," she said, "that you see

fit to praise Anti's outrageous flight of fancy like that. I thought we were here to get to the truth."

"We'll get there one way or another. However, I would be lying if I said I didn't enjoy listening to what Anti gave us."

"What he said was ridiculous," my mother protested. "Banquets. Secret societies. Scuttling ships. Nobody could possibly believe it."

"My dear woman, even if I agreed with you about that, which I do not, I should tell you that I gave up long ago the unfortunate habit of believing the mere plausible."

He allowed himself a brief smile—a distant flare of his old self, ignited by the negotiations—and then it was gone.

"I'm afraid that only confirms my suspicions about you, and your elastic view of the truth. I've been wondering for some time, given the bizarre things my son says after staying at this house for the weekend, whether it was wise to allow him to continue. Now I see that my fears were entirely justified." She slammed her wineglass down, but it glanced off the edge of the table, splashing wine on the top of her hand. She patted it off swiftly with a napkin.

Suarez turned his full attention on her slowly, dangerously. "As I trust my opening remarks made clear, I had hoped to avoid apportioning blame during the course of this discussion. It would be terrible if we were to make an occasion of great personal tragedy—specifically to me, if you don't mind my saying—any more painful by getting into an unpleasant cycle of recrimination. Let us not forget that these events were precipitated principally by your son. Please—let me finish. I see now that I bear some of the responsibility for what has happened. It's true that I encouraged Anti, up to a point, to indulge

Fabián's delusions, so long as they remained harmless. And I stand by my advice," he added, before my mother had a chance to interject. "In spite of the way Anti chose to interpret it."

"You're as mad as each other," said my mother. "What about the *facts*?"

Suarez gave her what must have been an infuriatingly dismissive shrug of the shoulders and reached again for the olives.

In her desperation, she turned to my father and said, "*You're* very quiet."

"I'm thinking," he replied.

Suarez seemed to enjoy this minute exchange more than anything he'd heard all evening. I could have sworn he tried to suppress a grin.

"Sure you won't have a glass of wine, Anti?" He seemed perkier than ever.

I shook my head sorrowfully, but inside I felt triumphant. Somehow, he was back on my side. The relief was astounding. My breathing had never been clearer. I could feel my chest relaxing and filling with oxygen in spite of the nauseating, adult atmosphere in the room, of wine, and tobacco, and olives. But it wasn't over.

Suarez's face slackened again into seriousness. "Unfortunately, Anti, your mother is right. We haven't quite finished. Much as I enjoyed your story, we both know that a story is all it is."

I swallowed.

"Perhaps you don't realize, but I went to Pedrascada myself while you were in hospital. You look surprised. Do you think I wouldn't want to see the place where my nephew died? And, as it happens, I know exactly what your mysterious dome is. Do you want me to tell you? It's a holiday home, owned by a man who led this country two or three presidents ago. In his retirement, he is cultivating a long-held passion for astronomy. There's no more mystery to it than that. Now, while he wasn't the most incorruptible politician we've ever had, I seriously doubt that endangered-species banquets such as the one you describe are his cup of tea. As I recall, his environmental track-record was one of the few laudable aspects of his tenure. Nor, before you suggest it, do I think he has gone into the business of curing memory loss in his retirement. As far as I can remember from his days in office, having a selective memory served him rather well."

He allowed himself a chuckle at his own joke, then met my eye again. "I am touched by your story, Anti. I applaud it. But now we need the mundane version, if you don't mind."

"Really?"

"It's nothing but a formality. A boring one, I know, but quite necessary. Whatever it is you have to tell me, however banal, I need to hear it. From tonight, you may remember what happened in Pedrascada however you please. With my blessing. Add to it all you like. That is your prerogative. But first, if you please, the facts."

His voice suddenly hardened. "Now."

This time, I spoke very quietly, very quickly, looking at nobody. I was not interrupted.

"We'd always told each other stuff that wasn't true. It was our thing. I thought we both knew when things had gone too far, and when to stop. But down at Pedrascada things went over the top. Fabián was telling more and more stories that couldn't possibly be true. And I . . . I suppose I got a bit competitive.

"It started on the journey. The night before we picked up the mountain train. He disappeared for the whole night and left me on my own in this weird little town in the middle of nowhere. All mist and mountains. In this hostel, run by some crazy old woman who kept these screeching, scratching, shitting birds everywhere. It scared the *hell* out of me. I barely slept all night. I was ready to turn around and come home on my own.

"And when he finally turned up the next morning, he didn't even apologize. He just told me this bullshit story about a brothel, about how he'd got laid then got into trouble with the pimp for not paying his bill. I was furious with him. And determined to get him back.

"Then, on the train down to the coast, we got talking to this guy—a traveler—and for some reason he gave us all his weed."

Hesitantly, I looked at my mother. She shifted in her seat at this revelation, and one eyebrow shot up, but she retained what composure she had left and didn't interrupt.

"I suppose he was just being generous. Anyway, Fabián was delighted, and he threw himself into smoking it for the rest of the journey. I guess it was some sort of release for him. But he wasn't being himself at all.

"In Pedrascada, Fabián had a sort of . . . regression to childhood, I guess is how I'd describe it. He took to playing games all day with Sol, Ray's daughter. He called her his little sister. It was quite odd, but on the other hand, he was the happiest I'd seen him for ages so I didn't worry about it too much.

"Then, on our second day, this woman, a Danish marine biologist, turned up in Pedrascada and took a cabin at the same place as us. We both liked the look of her immediately. Plus, she seemed . . . mysterious. Enigmatic.

"She was following a dead whale down the coast. It washed up every night, then went out to sea again, and she was cutting out its skeleton for a museum. It had become a sort of quest for her.

"Fabián and I tried really hard to make friends with her, but she was cold and standoffish. She got cagey when we asked her anything about her life, and didn't seem to want to get to know us at all. So while she was kneeling in the water, cutting up this whale all day, Fabián and I sat around watching her, and just for fun, we sort of . . . *made up* her past. We even gave her a new name. We called her Sally Lightfoot, after those crabs you get in the Galápagos.

"Finally, on her second night, she relaxed a bit and told us some genuine facts about her past. She'd had a rough time. Somehow, she had managed to marry this horrible guy who beat her up all the time. And when she filed for divorce, he got so mad that he cut off her wedding finger with a carving knife. He said if she wasn't going to stay married to him then he'd see to it that she could never put on a wedding ring ever again.

"I know. Awful. She was obviously very messed up by it, and I felt guilty that we'd been so nosy as to get the truth out of her. But Fabián reacted in a strange way. I guess he saw her story as some sort of challenge—like she was in danger of putting him in the shade or something. In response, he told everyone round the fire the true story about the weekend his parents died. I think it was the first time he'd ever spoken about it properly."

"And what was this truth?" said Suarez, quietly.

I paused. "He said that he felt responsible for his parents' deaths. That he knew his father was having an affair with their maid, that he'd seen them together in the maid's pantry, and that if he'd told his mother the truth about it then his parents might not have gone off hiking together that weekend. He believed he'd killed her. Or made her disappear."

I looked up. My father was uncomfortably transferring an olive stone from one hand to the other. My mother looked concerned, no longer angry in the slightest. And—something I never thought I would see—Suarez was crying.

"Anti, please continue," he said, blinking and shedding a half-tear that had been left behind. It plopped on to the table with no equivocation.

I hesitated.

"I'm fine. Please carry on."

"Fabián thought that I was somehow taking Sally's side against him. He got so furious with me he wouldn't even let me sleep in our cabin, so I spent the night on the beach. When I woke up the next morning, Sally had already left. Without even saying goodbye. But Fabián was too busy playing his stupid treasure-hunting games with Sol to have even noticed. I decided to disappear for a while, so I went for a walk in the town. It was a peculiar place—the street was knee-deep in mud because it had been raining a lot, and there was nobody around but fishermen and roosters—but eventually I found a bar and went in for a beer. I met a surfer there who was staying in the town, and he offered me something to smoke. I don't know what was in it, but it made me feel hideously ill, so I decided to get away from the town, but I didn't want to go back to the cabins.

"Then I remembered something Ray had told me about an underground stream that ran under his cabins and away to a waterfall, so, looking for something new to do, I thought I'd go and find it. I was determined to show Fabián that I was capable of finding a good time on my own.

"It was disgusting. The place where the water landed was nothing more than a cesspool, all bugs and shit and algae. The 'waterfall' was nothing but a trickle of water coming out of a concrete pipe. From the smell, I thought that either it was a sewage outflow from the town or that an animal had died in it and was decomposing into the water. In my stoned state, I tried to go for a swim anyway, but the stench made me vomit.

"As I walked back to our cabin with flies buzzing round my stinking face, I got more and more furious with Fabián. Our entire trip seemed to have been spent sitting on this stupid beach, getting wasted. I also thought that Fabián had scared Sally Lightfoot away by being so aggressive, which made me realize how sick I was of the fact that every story had to revolve around him. What's more, he'd abandoned me again for a ten-year-old girl, leaving me alone for the day, playing in sewage. I got more and more angry the more I thought about it.

"I found him in a terrible state. Yet again, he'd been drinking. He'd also got into this obsessive habit of cleaning his face with pure alcohol, and looked awful. To make matters worse, he'd had a falling-out with Sol. It was nothing serious—she'd just slipped in a rock pool when they'd been out looking for crabs—but I managed to build it into the attack on him that I unleashed when I got back to the cabin. I accused him of betraying me by hanging out so much with Sol. I was so angry, I didn't know what I was saying. I even accused him of trying to . . . molest her.

"And then I told him that I'd been with Sally. I told him that we'd been alone all day, screwing under a beautiful waterfall. It was nonsense, of course, but I wanted to get him back for what he'd done to me. He was in a vulnerable state and I knew he'd believe me. That's what got him so angry. That's how it started.

"We said a lot of stupid things to each other, but I think it was mainly to do with what we had done, running away: it was beginning to catch up with us. It didn't seem like a game any more. It . . . it involved talking about the Amnesia Clinic, too, and him screaming at me that I'd never meant to help him when I made the newspaper cutting. That our journey had all been for my benefit, not his. Then he ran off round the cliff base to try and get up to the dome.

"He'd been to the cave before, so he knew there wasn't a danger of getting caught by the tide if you got there in time, but I didn't know that, so I followed him, because I thought he might get into trouble.

"When I reached him, I was almost having an asthma attack—I just wanted to stop, get my breath back and talk. But he was very angry. We ended up having a fight out there, on the rocks, pushing each other around and screaming. Somehow, we both ended up in the water and hit our heads. I managed to get out and climb up to the cave. But I couldn't see him anywhere. Then I must have passed out.

"You wanted the truth. Well, there it is."

———

My father dropped his olive stone in the dish with a clink. My mother gazed down at the floor with a grim expression.

Suarez stared at me, then exhaled slowly. I tried to get some signal from him, some indication that he was still on my side. But the twinkle in his eye had been snuffed out once and for all.

"So," he said, eventually. "Just so we're clear about this: you took it upon yourself to wind Fabián up, who was in a fragile enough state as things stood, so you could get him back for some harmless boyish story."

"I have to agree, Anti," said my mother, quietly. "It sounds like very irresponsible behavior to me. Even *malicious*."

"But it shows you—it *proves* to you—that it wasn't because he believed the article. The Amnesia Clinic had nothing to do with it. He was just crazy as hell anyway!"

"Thanks to you," Suarez said coldly, "we will never know the truth of that. One thing is certain: I will never forgive myself for not discussing the matter of Fabián and his parents more with him. Look where it has got me." He shook his head. "Félix Morales screwing the maid. I should have known that pissy little mountain boy couldn't keep his hands off his own kind."

My mother didn't like the sound of this. "Hang on. There's no excuse for—"

"And what do you know?" he snapped. There was a new edge to Suarez's voice. An unfamiliar spite that made me feel sick.

"Plenty, as it happens," said my mother, "when it comes to intolerance in this country. But, under the circumstances, I will bite my tongue."

Suarez laughed in a particularly scornful, dirty way. "Please,

Señora, don't hold back your views on my account. I think you'll find I am strong enough to take them."

I told my mother to shut up and let me handle it. The last thing we needed was for the conversation to degenerate into one of her social crusades. Then I turned back to Suarez.

I talked for a while. It involved any excuse—conflicting excuses: *I didn't think Fabián would take it so seriously. It was to make him feel better. You said real life can be disappointing. You said that sometimes it doesn't hurt to let people believe what they want to believe. You said grief asks different questions of us all. You, and your stupid, pithy aphorisms for everything. It's you. It's your fault, not mine.*

Heroically, my mother leapt to my defense. "Quite right. Whose influence was it that made the two boys decide to run away in the first place?" she demanded. "From what I can gather, you not only encouraged but positively *fueled* the 'headstrong' nature of your nephew, as you described it, and I don't imagine that my son would ever have made the decision to play truant and travel halfway across the country without your encouragement."

"Even a man who stands accused of having 'an elastic view of the truth' can see that this is bullshit," said Suarez. "This has nothing to do with me, or with Fabián. This is to do with your son."

The malicious energy that lit his eyes combined with his gaunt appearance to transform his expression. He turned on me like a snarling, slobbering pit-bull.

"You are parasitic. A cuckoo."

I started.

He pointed at me, marking each word with sickening precision. "And like the cuckoo, laying its eggs in a weaker bird's nest, you are nothing more than a vandal."

"Weaker? How could *Fabián* be the weaker one?" I pleaded.

"You are perpetually scared. You are a coward. That makes you capable of anything. As far as I am concerned, you as good as killed him."

"Enough." I had never heard my father's voice so firm. I thought someone new had walked into the room. "He's only a boy."

"He's man enough," Suarez snapped.

Suarez stood up. He strode to the doorway and then, with almost absurd melodrama, he spat on the floor.

"Leave," he said. "You're no fucking storyteller."

The three of us sat dumbly, shocked into paralysis.

"Leave," he repeated, shaking with rage. "Before I set Byron on all three of you."

"Suarez. Please." I was determined not to cry, but it was too late. My cheeks were streaked already, and I could feel the tears trickling into the back of my mouth. I tried to find more words but I had no breath left to speak. All I could do was wheeze.

My mother strode smartly out of the room without giving Suarez another look, while my father helped me up. At the door, Suarez said, "One more thing before you go, Anti. I wouldn't be so sure Fabián was lying about that brothel, if I were you. There is something of a predilection for whoring in my family. As, indeed, there is for storytelling." His inability to control himself was heart-rending. "Fabián's world was fantastic because it *needed* to be. What's your excuse?"

———

And so the front door of Suarez's house closed on me for the last time. As we left, I heard my mother muttering, "What a horrible man." The sound was distant, drowned, irrelevant. The unreality of it all felt like pins and needles in my face. Byron's exotic rose beds and cacti, the whitewashed walls of the house, the red earth by the driveway, our stupid, practical car— I expected all of it to dissolve away at any minute and leave me alone. I realized that I hadn't even said goodbye to Byron and Eulalia but, at that point, I could not have cared less.

In fact, the strongest feeling I had was one of regret. Not for anything I had done in Pedrascada, or even what I'd just said in the library. I regretted the fact that I had embarrassed Suarez and made him drop his mask in such an ungainly way. With that single loss of composure, the last of the bright illusions that had sustained my life in Ecuador had expired.

My mother offered what solace she could. "Anti, you know you aren't the person he's really angry with, don't you?"

She started to say something else as I climbed into the car, then saw the expression on my face and stopped. It was too late for any more conversation. We drove home in silence, down a deserted motorway eerily lit by pale street-lamps. When we passed through the Old Town, its whitewashed fronts and empty, cobbled streets lent it the ghostly quality of a deserted stage set. I resented all of the colorful people who would have been bustling round the place during the daytime for being absent now, on my last journey through, when I needed them the most.

twenty·one

The following afternoon, I stood at the airport saying goodbye to my father, still unable to believe that someone in a shiny suit was not going to appear from behind a screen, escorting a grinning Fabián and telling me the whole thing was a joke. My parents would stay on for a few weeks more to finish what business they had left in Ecuador, and I would be met at Heathrow at the end of my flight by an uncle I barely remembered, to be looked after until their return. I wanted to ask my father whether there was any way I could stay on for Fabián's funeral the following day, but I had left it too late. My suitcase was checked in and my connection to Caracas would leave in an hour.

"This arrived for you this morning," said my father. "From Suarez. Delivered by that enormous chauffeur of his. Apparently it was something of Fabián's he wanted you to have."

I took from him a heavy, square parcel, covered in brown paper and wrapped tightly in masking tape.

"Bye, mate," said my father, giving me a hug. "Call us as

soon as you get to the other end. And try not to think too much about all this for a while, if you can."

"I'll try," I said.

We hadn't discussed the crime I'd committed in manufacturing the newspaper article, or my father's small degree of complicity in it. But, I reasoned, there would be plenty of time to talk about that later. Fabián's death was a topic of conversation that would be around for a very long time.

I walked through passport control with the package in one hand and my hand-luggage in the other, pausing to give my father a brief wave at the door. I just caught him wiping his eyes before he turned around to leave the airport building.

A customs official dressed in light brown with a huge pistol strapped to his belt stood behind a long table by the X-ray machines. I saw his eyes light up at the sight of me, the approaching gringo, with the suspicious brown paper parcel.

"What's in the package, my boy?" he asked. His breath smelled awful: stale coffee and cheap, black tobacco on a bed of halitosis.

"I'm not sure," I said, "it's a gift."

"Come on, son, you know the rules. If you didn't pack it yourself, we can't allow you to take it on the plane without looking at it."

"Of course," I said, putting the package and my duffel bag down on the table.

The customs official took a knife from his pocket and slashed open the package down one side. He bunched a hand on either side of the opening he had created and ripped it apart crudely. The parcel had been well wrapped, but it yielded to his ham-fisted persistence and tore open to reveal an object wrapped in old newspaper. The customs man, who had by now been joined by a colleague no less mean-looking but several pounds fatter, pulled some of this to one side. I saw a shock of straight, black hair and smelled a familiar preservative smell. Of pickles and hospitals.

"You know what this is?" asked the customs man.

"I'm not sure, but I have a feeling that it might be a *tsantza*," I said. "A Shuar shrunken head."

The man's eyes widened. "Is that right? If it is, you'll have to pay a heavy tax to take it out of here, you know that? And I'll need to see your export license."

I sighed. Leaving wasn't going to be such an easy business after all. Already, in my head, I had begun to calculate how long it would take my father to retrieve his car and drive back home so that I could call him and tell him to come straight back to the airport to pick me up. On the plus side, it meant that I would definitely be around the next day to attend the funeral. Surely they wouldn't deny me access if I was still in the country?

The customs man took the head, lifting it up by the hair, and yanked it free of the packaging. Its dried-up face popped through the aperture in the parcel in a grotesque caricature of childbirth.

The customs official held it up crudely, allowing the head to spiral slightly beneath his outstretched hand, and peered at those ineptly sewn-up eyelids. He smirked and then burst out laughing, then brought it right up to the face of his colleague in a bid to scare him.

"Okay, kid," he said, smiling and dropping it back on top of the mound of brown paper, tape and newsprint, where it landed with a thud. "Very nice. On your way, now. Take your *tsantza* and get out of here."

"You mean I don't need an export license?" I asked.

"You would need an export license," said the customs man, "if what you had there was anything resembling a genuine shrunken head. What you have there is a piece of molded pigskin. I hope that whoever gave it to you didn't pay too much for it. Enjoy your flight."

He and his friend smirked for a while longer as I tried to rewrap the parcel, and presently they laid eyes on their next victim. I made my way through to the departure gate.

Even as I waited for the plane, I could feel my memories beginning to solidify and coalesce into picture postcards. Already, different occasions had begun to blur into one another and the things that had happened were beginning to transform at the edges into the things I felt should have happened. The simple act of going through customs had brought on the early stages of my amnesia.

As the plane taxied out, preparing itself for the strain of getting off the valley floor and escaping that basin in the mountains, I looked out at the New Town, trying to identify which was our apartment block and to spot the balcony where I had spent so many afternoons with my father, happily devising improbable explanations for the noises that floated up from below. Already, life in Quito seemed vague as Ecuador started to become My Ecuador, the one I would tell people about when I got home. I tried to embark in my head on the process of working Fabián's and my experiences up into a good story, then I stopped and reminded myself that thoughts like that, this early, were wrong. Besides, I had lost my audience.

The gift of the head might have been Suarez's idea of a pardon, or it might not. He didn't enclose a note. Certainly, I felt no forgiveness. The *tsantza* should have been Fabián's, and now it was mine, and I felt nothing but the cold clutch of its curse around my neck.

Once we were in the air, in a suffocating environment of bad coffee and tired air-filters, I shifted my gaze from the head in my lap to look sideways through the window as we picked our way out of the Andes. Seeing the volcanoes from up there felt wrong. The plane flew so close to some of them that you could almost look right down into the intimacy of their craters, blow-holes and all. It didn't feel right. It didn't seem to me to be a view I had earned. When you were down there, anywhere in the city, they could surprise you. They had the power. That was how things were supposed to be. Whether you were climbing into your jeep to play tennis in suburbia or buying a single lottery ticket from the blind man in a dusty Old Town square, it could happen to you. When you least expected it, you would look round and they would be there: blobs of ice-cream peak, flickering behind the apartment blocks on the highway or peering down at you through the belfries of churches. Then, sometimes, if you were in the right place, a full dose: round the corner you would come, minding the task in hand, and BANG, the volcano would shoulder its way through the city and take you square on, letting the distances and scale differences involved unfurl in your mind until you were snow-blind, mountain-struck, breathless with insignificance. Up there, from that tired old Airbus, you could see it all. I didn't want to see it all.

———

I have never been back to Quito in real life, although I have replayed the approach many times in my head. It's a thrilling ride. You come in low, banking over green, terraced agriculture and russet foothills, and, incredibly, absurdly, there is a city, spread out like shattered dice fragments in a valley of baize, waiting to be rediscovered. Waiting for some other punter to step up to the table and try his or her luck. Technically the plane is descending, but it always feels as if an extra spurt of height might be required to heave it over the lip of the basin and drop it into the valley. And this hurdle over the mountains can't help but seem random, as if the pilot has altered your itinerary at the last minute in order to explore some chance gateway he's never seen before. The captain always misses a trick here. He just goes into the same, tired old routine of seatbelts and extinguished cigarettes. Just once, I want him to deliver a voice-over that tallies with the sheer implausibility of what I am seeing through my window:

Señoras y señores, this is your captain speaking. We will shortly be arriving at our final destination, so would you please now put your seat backs in the upright position and—Jesus Christ! What's that? A city in the clouds! Quick—let's take a detour!

It never happens like that. But I live in hope.

author's note

While most of the locations in this novel exist, some are purely imaginary, and readers shouldn't necessarily expect to find them on maps.

Cristina's guidelines on how to tell a good Quechua folk tale derive largely from my reading of Johnny Payne's *She-Calf and Other Quechua Folk Tales* (University of New Mexico Press, 2000). Any inaccuracies or elaborations are my own.

Special thanks to Clare Alexander, Samantha Francis, James Gurbutt, Enda McCarthy, Tina Pohlman, and Rose Grimond.